TALE OF A TOOTH

ALLIE ROGERS

Legend Press
Independent Book Publisher

Legend Press Ltd, 107–111 Fleet Street, London, EC4A 2AB
info@legend-paperbooks.co.uk | www.legendpress.co.uk

Print ISBN 978-1-7871985-2-4
Ebook ISBN 978-1-7871985-1-7
Set in Times. Printed by Opolgraf
Cover design by Anna Morrison | www.annamorrison.com

Allie Rogers was born and raised in Brighton. After studying sociology at Leeds University, she completed a Master's in Information Management to qualify as a librarian and has worked in university libraries for the last twenty years. Her short fiction has been published in several magazines and anthologies, including *Bare Fiction*, the *Salt Anthology of New Writing* and the ground-breaking *Queer in Brighton*. Her first novel, *Little Gold*, was published by Legend Press in May 2017.

Follow Allie on Twitter
@Alliewhowrites

For all the Meemaws in the hardest times

CHAPTER ONE

Meemaw was yellowy-orange this morning. When I waked up she was sitted by the big window and her dressing gown pulled tight round. Her head in the outside for having a rolly.

Morning, sleepyhead.

Smoke was turns and dances round Meemaw. A smile. Bluey smoke but in it a bright Meemaw of yellowy-orange and a sunshine day.

Last of rolly gone Meemaw squashed it out. Throwed it away. Closed the big window thump.

If everything's quick this morning then we can go to the library after. Sound good?

I did a nod of yes.

Does Spiney want some Rice Krispies of his own today?

When Meemaw's yellowy-orange it is good things. I spooned my krispies and Spiney had his in the egg cup.

Meemaw at the end of the Cretaceous era when it was the mass extinction was it a meteor came from space?

Well that's what it says in some of the books, isn't it?

I did another nod.

On a Meemaw grey day she closes up her ears and I have to say it over over. Sometimes on a grey day is no answers at all.

Phone Meemaw?

Go on then, just while I do this bit of washing-up and put the bed away. Then we've got to get going. The appointment's half nine.

Today is the twenty second so still lots of data not like on the fifteenth when you're nearly at the end. Once I saw a sign in a shop in town. On one day a Thursday. Sign said all you can eat data. But Meemaw telled it was very too expensive.

You can't eat data, can you, Danny? Not when you actually need beans or bread or something.

On YouTube I watched *Walking with Dinosaurs*. It is from when Meemaw was fourteen. Very old. It was one of two allosaurs come by a river. They devour a Stegosaur. They are the best predator of the Jurassic. I am going to get one when I'm five from the internet I am sure.

I watched in my softy sweatshirt that is a blue cave inside. Inside with Spiney. Inside there is just us glowy phone screen and smell of me and rightness.

Teeth, Dan!

I didn't hear of Meemaw. The mighty stegosaur fallen.

Danny!

Meemaw's hand on my shoulder meaned now.

Teeth is minty and Meemaw beside me. Meemaw says do mind counting of a hundred and brush all over. But at sixty two I needed a poo all suddenly. Poo comes when it likes no arguments Danny. I spitted.

Meemaw! Poo!

Today the poo was a hard and painful stool. I heared a lady say of it on a advert. Meemaw telled it was poo that's hurty and a big push.

A hard and painful stool Meemaw!

I said in a push voice. My feet dingle dangling. Meemaw laughed but it wasn't a joke it wasn't a joke.

Oh, sunshine!

The poo was such a angry growl and push. But still not comed. In my mind I maked it gone away.

Gone Meemaw no poo today.

Meemaw went to fast words.

Danny! We'll end up at the doctors again with this. You need to relax and let it come.

No!

I tried getting down.

Danny, Danny, love, get back on the toilet.

Meemaw catched me up and sitted me back on the toilet.

Noooooo…

A snap of tummy hurting.

Meemaw went softer droopy down. Her hair dangled. Not so yellowy orange. Not so bright like before.

Just relax, poppet, and wait, can you? Can you relax? I'll read you a story.

I sitted on the toilet and Meemaw readed me a whole story from Magic Hare book. Then poo came sudden and sneaky on me. Mighty poo maked a splash and wetted my bot. Bot was sore and sorry of it when Meemaw wiped.

There we are, all done! Do you feel better?

I didn't say.

Right, right, come on, wash your hands, under here! Danny! Danny, concentrate! Wash your hands, we need to get going.

Spiney was wanting another story of Magic Hare.

No!

Meemaw pulling and fast I hate. Bad of Meemaw the pulling.

Magic Hare!

We haven't got time now. We'll be late for that bloody appointment. Come ON!

That poo had maked us late and then it was all to rush. Rush of coats and shoes and down the steps.

On the bus Meemaw went all the way to brown. Brown as the enemy poo. Then darker darker because all the time was gone away and now we were really very late.

At Asda a old man getted on. He had a bandage on his leg. All dark and blood bits. His leg gone scaly. A reptile of the modern day. He smelled very silverblack and wrong for a person.

I holded my nose. Meemaw pulled my hand down.

Danny!

Meemaw's teeth closed. Closed of biting. A fierce velociraptor.

I wasn't talking to Meemaw then. I counted people who getted on at Asda and there was eleven. Smelly man was worst and best a black man who had big red headphones. Shiny as Chupa Chups.

Like your dino, bro!

He meaned it to me even though I'm not bro. That was a nice man and his headphones shiny and like your dino bro. But all the time by Asda Meemaw went whispery.

Christ's sake! Oh, for Christ's sake come on...

Looking at her phone because the poo had maked us late maked us really rather late.

But Meemaw had pulled. I didn't care of it the lateness.

By the roundabout the button already pressed. Light saying wait. The red man on on. I feeled Meemaw's hand sticky. I didn't want to hold. I pulled then.

Be patient, Danny! Please, love, just try to be patient and stand still.

Things were wrong. All was wrong the air gone nasty of car exhausting and too glarey splash on the windscreens.

We went across the road. A lady was too close. Her bag was a leopard's fur. Perfume smell I hate.

Just cool it, love. Come on, Danny. You can do it.

I closed my eyes. Keeped them closed all the way.

I hate it the job centre because always waiting and there are too much people. People coughing all bubbles and sometimes it comes out. Meemaw telled phlegm. I hate that phlegm. I have never done it I won't ever do it. It's not like sick you can't help it of sick.

Meemaw sitted down but I standed on a edge bit by the window. My feet turned sideways. I could see traffic roundy round the roundabout. I counted red cars fourteen. Spiney counted vans eight.

The last van was Silentnight pyjamas hippo and yellow chick. Very big very small. That is me and Meemaw she said it once. We were by the beds superstore on one day a Friday. She was whole orange very bright and it was summer.

That was the goodest of good days. Meemaw was orange. I had a lolly that was orange I choosed to match Meemaw. I holded it by her face.

This is your colour Meemaw.

You mean my favourite colour?

Your today colour. Of you today.

Am I always a colour?

I didn't say but did a nod. She kissed on my head the top of it.

I was doing remembering that day. A good day. But Spiney said it didn't happen not ever and I was telling a lie. I banged him on the window for a punishment very serious.

Danny stop it! Come here! Look, play with Spiney just here by me, okay?

I had done it wrong the banging but that was the fault of Spiney not me.

The lady had green boots. Buttons on of gold. Very nice roundy. Three and three. Magical of a story.

Ms White? Please come this way.

We went by a desk. A chair for Meemaw and I standed beside.

Can you explain why you are twenty minutes late for your appointment today, Ms White?

Tight in her words in her mouth air a smell of metal. She was not nice. A not to be nice lady of no smile. No smile at Meemaw.

I'm so sorry. We were just about to leave but my son needed the toilet. And then the bus was late. We were on our way. I'm sorry to be late.

Meemaw tried hard and hard. Very sorry so sorry. Meemaw did such many of smiles.

We just couldn't get out of the house. You know how it is sometimes with little ones.

I'm afraid you have an obligation to be on time to appointments, Ms White.

I know. I realise that and I'm sorry I was late but my son had to use the toilet. He's had some issues with…

You have an obligation to be on time for appointments and if you fail to do so then I'm afraid you will be sanctioned. I'm going to have to sanction you today, do you understand?

I've said…

The sanction will be for a period…

Meemaw couldn't tell stop to the Job Centre lady. It was obligation sanction words. But it was repeating repeating. Sometimes you have to stop that Danny because it drives people mad.

Meemaw went still as still. When Meemaw is such still after words you have said a thing of hurtful. Meemaw is going to cry when she moves. Lady didn't know my Meemaw was gone to crying inside. And it would come out next. And maybe a shout.

I regret that this is necessary, Ms White. I regret that this is necessary but you have an obligation.

Meemaw standed up sudden. She turned fast of a swift bird in the sky. Her long coat lifted out of a tail. She was gone fast away.

Fast in the corridor flying. She forgetted to hold out her hand behind. Spiney and me ran after.

Outside Meemaw did big long steps to the flowers. She sitted on the edge crying. We sitted down too. We were three in a row.

Spiney sitted very close of my leg. I sitted close of Meemaw's leg but I didn't touch in case of worse crying. All her colours were gone swirly.

When Meemaw does crying her colours run a mixture. Water in your paint tray. I had paints in the other flat. In the other flat was hard floor and Meemaw could wipe up spills not lose the bloody deposit.

Meemaw crying. I did watching the man the newspapers trolley man. He gived them to people coming over the crossing mostly they snatched them up. Take take take. Pterosaurs swooping.

I readed the papers but it was hard. Trying trying. Three tries then a man stopped close he was on his phone.

Newspaper by me I holded the words of my eyes. Man stabbed in park.

Meemaw not loud crying because outdoors and people would come. Come and ask what and it is none of their business.

But then a person did come. I had getted up I was making Spiney walk all along the edge close to the trumpetty daffodils. Jump over the bin and back again. Faster faster went Spiney and a person was there sudden and talking to Meemaw.

A person sitted close on the wall and talking. I went back. Standed by Meemaw.

I wasn't sure of a man or a lady because short short hair trousers no earrings at all. But then I saw boobies. Boobies and close. Gived Meemaw a tissue from her own packet fat and a new one and we didn't know her.

Please, oh no. Don't worry. Thank you.

Meemaw said it round round. Lady waiting. She didn't say that's enough. She looked at me.

That's a fierce-looking monster you've got there.

It is not a monster it is actually a dinosaur called Spinosaurus that lived in the Cretaceous era more than 65 million years ago.

She laughed. It is not funny or a joke to be said it is the actual truth of Spiney.

Wow! You're quite the little professor, aren't you?

I didn't say. I closed my mouth tight. I looked away by the daffodils. When I looked again her face was pink. Sticky wet.

Meemaw was getted up then and sniffing. The lady putted her hand on Meemaw's arm.

Let me, let me just see what I can do. I can see how upset you are. I've seen you before in there…

She looked at me then. I stared hard.

… and your little 'un. I don't like seeing you so upset.

Meemaw's voice was wobbly of the crying.

I don't like to ask but I just can't… I just can't deal with it now, getting sanctioned, you know?

The lady did nodding nodding hard her head.

There's discretion. There's discretion. I'll have a word. I… I think I can sort it for you. Just give me your number and I'll let you know, eh?

The lady was close close. Smiled big. She did another touch of Meemaw.

No more crying in her Meemaw settled to grey of a stone. A slow colour. Quiet and not more crying.

I wanted go go go. I pulled on Meemaw's hand. I thinked of the library the better smell of it and labels of colours. Orange that means dinosaurs and prehistoric.

Hey Professor! You go easy on your mum, eh?

The lady had spikey hair like daggers. Rubbing on my Meemaw's arm. Too much of touching. I watched her but only in little looks. I did spying on her. I did pulling on Meemaw.

I'll text you soon as. Don't worry too much.

She turned around for going away. Good good. Then she stopped.

Whatever, come back tomorrow and have a coffee with me, eh? My treat. It's bloody grim working in there.

Meemaw tucked her hair by her ear but it came out again and hanged down.

Oh, oh, well, you don't have to do that.

I'd like to. Come on, it's just coffee. Cheer me up, eh?

The words were quiet and broken into each one. Softly soft. Meemaw doesn't like coffee only tea.

Thanks, that's very kind.

She looked away by the roundabout. There was a huffle of wind. Meemaw's hair lifted up like reaching out. I pulled harder.

I'll see you then?

Yeah, sure. Tomorrow.

The lady went away then. I was glad of it. I did three jumps.

Meemaw blew her nose on the lady's tissue. Lots of snot came out I wanted to see. I like it all gloop.

Danny, don't!

Meemaw pushed me away. She wiped then throwed the tissue in the bin thonk.

What happened Meemaw? Have you getted a obligation?

Meemaw did a sigh.

Why do we have to come back tomorrow because you don't like coffee.

Meemaw laughed then. A small little tumble laugh.

That nice lady is called Karen and she's going to try to sort things out so we don't get sanctioned.

What is it sanctioned?

It's a punishment, Danny. Because we were late. It means they take away our money.

I knowed it was the poo had maked us late. I hated that big poo for its evil-doing. And now no money for data and ever lollies or something. Then Meemaw shouted.

The bus!

The bus went roary round the corner gone.

Oh God! Love, its ages until the next one.

Meemaw did a sigh looked at her phone.

Danny, love, it's ages until the next bus and it's too far to walk from here. I'm really wrung out, sweetheart. I think we'd better go home.

I sitted down. I sitted on the wall pushed my feet down hard hard on the pavement. I holded my hands on my ears to never hear more Meemaw and stupid words.

Yahyahyahyahyahyah...

Louder louder to not hear her.

I cried because of today the worst day. No library and the stupid poo. And Meemaw.

Meemaw sitted beside me close. I feeled beside me her bigness. I heared the tupperware even through my hands. I smelled it. I smelled Marmite sandwich.

I opened my eyes and Meemaw had it on her hand. Pink flat hand a triangle sandwich. Meemaw's head looked sideways of want it? No words. Just looking.

I taked one hand off my ear. Taked the sandwich bited it.

I promise you, Danny, we'll get up early tomorrow and go straight to the library. But I really really need to go home now.

On the roundabout past the turn turn of the cars there were yellow daffodils more. I thinked they had come everywhere now the daffodils. I did chewing and the daffodils.

Marmite sandwich was a good taste of home. I thinked of inside my sweatshirt. Home and right smells.

Remember, Danny, we can definitely go to the library tomorrow. We will go tomorrow. I promise.

I looked along the flowers beside. One daffodil was yesterday the next one today the next one tomorrow. They were in a line. The line was a promise.

I unstucked my feet. We went to the bus stop. I yawned a big yawn very stretch of elastic pants wide.

All the way home on the bus my eyes went running in the yellow lines. I hummed a going home noise of quite loud. Not too. Meemaw letted me.

Ha...ummmmmmm...ha...ummmmmmm...ha...ummmmmmm

When we getted off it was seventy eight steps. Meemaw opened the front door and our flat door and all was to still inside. The home smell so good.

Phone Meemaw?

Meemaw gived it no words. Meemaw grey. I went under my sweatshirt with Spiney.

CHAPTER TWO

Jane in the library is the goodest person of the world except me and Meemaw. Jane is wet big eyes dark silvery hair crinkled face. Her voice is rumply-soft quiet like Meemaw's velvety coat.

When Jane talks her eyes go by the floor not staring and we talk of dinosaurs taking turns.

But today no Jane. No Jane in the library and a hurt in my tummy of crying coming and four times of swallowing to keep it down inside. I did pulling but no words. Meemaw knowed it was wanting Jane.

Just stay calm, poppet. If she doesn't come, I'll ask.

Meemaw was still the grey of yesterday. On this morning she had smoked two rollies out the window. No milk in the fridge so her tea a dark dark potion. No milk for krispies. Just crust for toast and crust is too fat.

I squeezed my toothpaste.

Too much, Danny! Come on, share with me.

Meemaw swooped in and stealed some on her brush.

No Meemaw!

I threwed my brush down then gone under the sink. Fluffy of grot on it. Meemaw shouted. We never did teeth.

Get your shoes on then! Christ!

Then no Jane in the library. I sitted on the spinny chair by the computer did kicking the underneath. Meemaw taked my hand pulled me off.

Stop it! Come and look at the books!

No!

Then Jane. Jane sudden. Smelling right of Jane.

Danny! I hoped you'd be in, I've got a surprise for you.

Two hands Jane held up a big book.

This came by in a box of old stock being weeded out of the stacks and I thought I knew someone who might like to have it.

In two hands right out to me because she meaned me the someone.

Walking with Dinosaurs. A book but like on YouTube. The actual thing. I taked it to the table heavy as treasure and thumped it open.

What do you say, Danny?

Chapter one new blood.

Danny, what do you need to say to Jane?

Chapter one new blood.

Thank you so much, Jane.

Thank you so much Jane.

You're very welcome.

I turned to the back because of index that Meemaw showed. Up and down the letters my finger runned the good good words.

Coelophysis Ornitholestes Troodon.

I turned the pages fast fast. But remembering of careful.

Careful careful of the pages Danny.

Jane her hand near not touching.

That's right, Danny. You're a careful boy with the books.

I finded Troodon showed it and words underneath.

See Jane! Fast and intelligent a deadly combination a deadly combination.

I see.

I finded Spinosaurus showed Spiney.

Spinosaurus! See!

I putted Spiney's face on the actual word.

Danny, love, time to go now. Take the book to the machine.

No, no, you don't understand! He can keep that one. It's being chucked out anyway. It's too tatty for stock. We'd only chuck it out.

I looked up.

Are you sure? Do you hear that, Danny? You can keep it forever!

Quiet. I was wanting the book mine forever. I was wanting the book to live in the library. Library is borrowing and the books on the shelf. Orange label of dinosaur and prehistoric.

Jane crouched down not too near. Speaked by the side of me quiet.

Would you like to keep the book, Danny?

I didn't like it then the keep or not.

You can keep the book, Danny. Or you can leave it here. You can choose that.

He might have a bit of trouble deciding, Jane. Decisions can be tricky. Shall we take the book home, Dan?

Library books live in the library.

I can bring it back sometimes. Sometimes to go on the shelf. Dinosaurs and prehistoric.

But it's coming home with us now, yes?

I didn't say more words.

I think that's a yes. Thanks again, Jane. Come on, Danny love, we need to go now.

Meemaw going too fast.

Bring it back sometimes.

Jane speaked slow.

Yes, you could do that, Danny. Bring it back sometimes for a visit. But always take it home again, won't you? Because it's your book now. Let's write your name in it, shall we, to save confusion?

Save confusion.

Jane getted a pen.

Can you do your own name, Danny?

I taked it to do my Danny name she putted White. Then she writed personal copy withdrawn from stock. I readed each word she writed of the pen.

Meemaw maked a sigh. I looked. Browning to brown.

I don't mean to be rude, and thanks so much, Jane. But we have to get going now.

My coat twisted arms inside out hood gone upside down. I was busy with sort it out. Then I heared words of quieter. They don't want you to hear of it.

He's got astonishing reading skills for four, hasn't he?

Meemaw too fast again grabbed my hand. No snatching!

It's not a big deal. It just comes naturally for him. Thanks again! Goodbye! Say goodbye, Danny.

Goodbye.

I thinked why rushy rushy. Book was too heavy so Meemaw taked it for the bag.

We've got to get to the Job Centre again, love, remember?
No...
Come on. You can look at your book when we get there.

***

Outside the job centre we stopped. Better than going in.
Right, I'll text her. Wait just here, Dan.
I did balancing two feet careful on the little wall of the flowers. Putted Spiney's face inside the trumpetty daffodils. Spiney told me whole world gone golden Danny. He whispered it very quiet in my mind. I taked him one to the next of five daffodils. Walked slow away of Meemaw.
Danny love, come here!
The Karen lady had come. Karen lady wearing a blue shirt of tangled flowers on it. Her hair spiked up. Perfume strong as knifes. I holded my nose.
She touched Meemaw again right away touched her shoulder. Then she kissed Meemaw's face. Only I do. Only I kiss Meemaw.
Hi Karen!
Karen pushed her spikes of hair they pinged up spring. Pink sticky again her face.
Hi Natalie! Did you get my text?
I just saw it now. Thank you so much! I can't tell you how much it means. Thank you!
Oh, it's nothing. There's discretion. She owed me a favour anyway.
Well, thank you. Really, honestly, it makes such a difference.
Well, I could tell you were decent. It's not like you were taking the piss. Not like some of them.
Meemaw didn't take her turn then of talking. We take turns Danny. Meemaw looked over by the roundabout Karen smiled at me I looked. Still holded my nose. Meemaw saw then. She pulled my hand down.
Well, look, I've only got fifteen minutes, really. Shall we get some drinks?

Meemaw holded my hand hurry hurry to the Costa. We don't ever go too expensive a bloody joke those prices Danny.

We sitted on silvery chairs a round table of one silver leg.

What would you like? Coffee?

Tea, please.

And what about you, little one?

I didn't say.

Oh, he's fine, Karen. He doesn't need anything.

Right, back in a tick then.

She went inside.

No holding your nose around people, Danny, remember? It can hurt feelings. And Karen's really helped us out. She's really done us a favour.

Karen came back with drinks. Three big cups.

I got him a milkshake. Didn't seem right not getting him anything.

Oh…thanks…

Meemaw taked the cups. All papery cups and lids. My one a straw stucked up out of its middle. I looked at it not touching.

Meemaw maked a rolly. Messy one of tobacco squiggles escaping. Karen didn't smoke she watched Meemaw. She watched Meemaw close like trying to learn of it.

She watched Meemaw's hands Meemaw's mouth. I watched her eyes go zip zip about. Meemaw speaked not looking at me still looking at her rolly.

Try your milkshake, Dan, eh?

I did just in case of nice. But it was yuck. A painty thick and strongness. No more.

I counted seven cars green or nearly. Green is rare.

So, what you got planned for the rest of the day then?

Oh, nothing much. He's just got a new book, haven't you, Dan? They were chucking it out at the library. Show Karen.

I climbed down went in the bag and getted my book. I holded it on my tummy. Karen not to see.

Come on. Don't be mean, show Karen your book.

Karen laughed a slidey laugh.

Oh, don't worry. I'm enjoying what I'm looking at right now.

She putted her hand close Meemaw's by the ashtray. Littlest

fingers touched lied next to each other close. Meemaw did a laugh too. A laugh that was new and of a surprise.

Then I needed a wee. Very urgent. I pulled Meemaw. I whispered.

Wee Meemaw!

Ah, we need the toilet I'm afraid, Karen.

No worries. I have to get back now anyway.

She pushed back again the spiky hair. Maked a big perfumey smell. A attack of smell. I coughed. Meemaw picked up the bag.

Thanks so much for the drinks and for everything. You've been really kind.

Meemaw pushed me gently on my back. My coat stucked on the silvery chair I pulled.

Then it was free and we were going but Karen's voice came sudden. Too loud.

I was wondering if you fancied meeting up again, maybe?

Meemaw stopped pushing me. Meemaw looked at Karen. Swoosh! Very fast very fast all the grey washed over. There was a waterfall on Meemaw of ruby red colour. Ruby red slippers. Very. I never saw Meemaw be it before that colour.

The world was roary then of cars and I was needing a wee. Meemaw and Karen just standed still no talking. I pulled Meemaw. She taked no notice no. Didn't look. Looked just at Karen.

Yeah. I mean, yeah, it's just me and him you know so…

Karen's words came fast tripping over.

Sure! Yes, sure, how about the park? Maybe over the weekend?

Meemaw's words chased Karen's words.

Sure, yes. You've got my number, yeah? Great, yeah.

The wee the wee! I was full and bursting.

Meemaw!

Okay! 'Bye Karen.

We went through the big glass door into Costa.

Inside Costa clank bang of the coffee maker man. Music. Bright white. Too much. I holded my ears. Meemaw opened the door toilet. Inside was quiet.

Long wee splashy in the toilet and Meemaw waiting not talking. The soap was appley foamy fluff I liked.

I washed on a long time. More more the appley soap. Meemaw

looked in the mirror. Meemaw looked looked. Still no words. Water getted too hot. I taked my hands out.

Okay, sunshine, here's the dryer, look. Pop your hands in for a whoosh of air.

I looked.

No! It says blade. Blade is of a knife. Air blade, Meemaw.

I showed the words. Meemaw laughed.

Do you dare me, Danny? Do you?

No!

Meemaw pushed her hands in. It roared! Such loudness. But not a blade of cutting. Meemaw's hands in out. She laughed. Meemaw laughed lots. I holded my hands on my ears tight and waited for it to stop.

***

At home Meemaw gived me have three pieces of drawing paper and that is a lot. I started a comic of stegosaurs. They go over a cliff.

Why don't you use some other colours, Dan? Or your black pen will run out.

I like black. Black is best for all except red sometimes of blood.

Meemaw had a rolly in the big window. All was sunshine and Meemaw ruby ruby red. New colour. I watched sometimes sometimes I went in my picture.

After one rolly and tea gone halfway Meemaw climbed on a chair taked down her precious box.

Precious box lives on the wardrobe. I don't look because of ashamed. Because of a day long ago I was three. Such a bad day. Meemaw put the box up high after. It was biggest big scissors and crinkly paper. I cutted it the precious letter of Meemaw's mummy. The letter of Meemaw's mummy when she was alive in America. Meemaw did dripping tears. Drip drip on it and sticky tape for mending. But the letter gone wonky and some of the words lost.

I went under the cover a long time that day. Meemaw said ashamed. I don't like it now to think. I don't like it the box.

But today was a day of shiny photographs. Meemaw tipped them all slidey out. Meemaw did lifting them up each one and looking. Little laughs.

I did my best stegosaur and a bubble for words. I maked him say oh no! in his bubble. Meemaw leaned over showed me one of the pictures.

Who do you think that is, Danny?

There were witchy people of wild hair.

Don't know.

Meemaw holded her finger by one face.

Not even that one?

It was a person of black bits round their eyes. The person had a open mouth like a roar.

That's me, Danny. That was me way back when and those were my friends. We were having a bloody ball.

A ball is a dance of Cinderella. But Cinderella is a puffy dress and white mice. A pumpkin. Not blood.

I looked at the Meemaw of black bits on the eyes.

Those were my friends, Dan. Those were my friends.

She stroked it the shiny photograph. Her thumb all round its edge and looking like loving. Her eyes blink blink. Strokes like a kitten on its teeny head or me me on my eyebrows sometimes in bed and night night my lovely boy.

I pushed under Meemaw's arms. I lied on her lap put my face in her tummy. Smelled the smell of her. My Meemaw. I wriggled in until she putted the photographs back in the packet cuddled me instead.

Right. Bath time, Danny!

Noooo!

Come on. It's getting late.

Meemaw getted my clean pjs from the laundrette bag. Shaked them hard for crumples. Meemaw getted her baggy laggy joggers old holey t-shirt. Shaked them too. I snuffed sniffed in them the smell of laundrette blue. Thinked of turny machines frothy inside.

Come on then, love, into the bathroom!

Meemaw turned the taps squooged shower gel. Blue in a puddle and turning into white. Good good smells. Nothing wrong at bedtime. Bubbles maked a mountain in the bath tall. White mountain filled up of light.

Always baths now. Shower's gone so broken and too much tiles falled off.

We can't use it, Danny. See, the water squirts out all over.

Even in your eye. Nozzle gone drippy. A drippy wozzle nozzle. Useless of a shower.

We getted in the bath.

Right! Time for an episode of Terence the Turtle! Ow!

Sorry Meemaw. That was for a joke.

No pinching boobies, Danny. Pinching boobies isn't a joke. Listen now and hear what happens next.

Meemaw tells it out of her head. She telled how he went to a island all empty just a tall coconut tree. Terence maked a pulley which is a contraption. He sended Caroline Crab up high to get their tea of a coconut.

Caroline Crab and pinchy pinchers!

Stop it, now. I told you, Danny White.

Meemaw washed my hair careful as careful. No bubbles in my eyes. Eyes shut and my mouth closed up tight. No water getted in me.

Meemaw wrapped me in a towel. I sitted on the bath mat pulled the frayey edge. Maked a long long string. Meemaw standed up a handful of blue of shower gel. Rubby froth all over and in the hairy fanny triangle the smelly under arms.

After tooth cleans and last wees Meemaw getted the bed to flat. Up out it folds. Skeleton of the sofa comes out. Then it's our bed.

Stand back, sunshine, I'm always worried this thing might bonk you on the head.

Are you reading Meemaw in the chair this night?

No, I'm shattered tonight, Danny. Let's just snuggle down.

Meemaw drawed the curtains getted in beside me. I holded Spiney under the pillow he likes it best very soft. In my mind I heared him telling all his night night wishes. I listened. Said I love you Spiney in mind words. Feeled him warmer there.

I putted my other hand on Meemaw's squashy tummy. Inside is bubbles and pops. Meemaw still the red ruby coloured. Like the slippers of sharkle one day on YouTube. Meemaw singed me the song. Somewhere over the rainbow.

Meemaw reached up clicked the light to off. Then she was just the dark shape the smell of clean Meemaw. I closed my eyes.

CHAPTER THREE

In the park is a pirate ship. A sandpit sea. When we go Meemaw sits on the high up slope she can see all the places.

I must stay inside the gates never ever run off outside. The road and the pond are dangers Danny.

Inside the gates I can do swings slide balancey planks go everywhere to the edge. By the fence is a sandy scuffly edge. Lolly sticks. Wrappers stuck in. Mostly I stay in the sand-pit Spiney likes. There are no turns and pushing.

I maked Spiney a cave in the sand underneath the slide. Away from feet. A cave just a little bit bigger than Spiney all round. I slided him in out. No falling down. Again again then another boy came. He watched. Said words very fast.

What's that? What are you doing? What's your name?

Very fast were his words.

Boy! Boy, what's that thing?

He is a Spinosaurus a dinosaur of the Cretaceous period.

This is my robot man from space. See? See, Boy?

It was a robot of one leg.

This is robot man and my name is called Azeem.

We played robot dinosaur adventure it was good and no pushing.

Come on Boy! Come on dinosaur boy!

We runned fast he shouted.

Robot dinosaur adventure!

Dinosaur adventure!

Azeem had a nose runny of snot. He wiped his fingers on it. All sand stucked. Azeem getted a stone from under the bushes throwed it hard in the sand. Sand sprayed up. All on my trainers.

It is the meteorite that caused the mass extinction.

Azeem picked it up again. Throwed down hard.

Boom a bomb!

Meteorite.

Then a lady came of a green coat and shiny shoes.

Come on, Azeem. Time to go. Say goodbye to your friend.

She getted a tissue wiped it away the sandy snot.

Goodbye dinosaur boy!

Karen was up the slope with Meemaw. All the time there. They were near the skinny tree all over white flowers now. The wind blew the white petals all in the air like snow. Like snowing of a cartoon. Meemaw there behind it.

Meemaw was laughing. Karen lying on the grass and laughing too. Karen in a hoody. Meemaw would say put your coat on put your coat on it's a cold day. But no coat on Karen and all the time laughing. Karen and my Meemaw.

I tried to make Spiney a new cave but it went to crumble down.

Boys came said words too fast and shouting pushing. One had a smell of milk. Trainers too close. I getted out the sandpit went up the slope to Meemaw.

Here he is, the professor! How you doing, mate?

Karen looked fast. I looked away.

Right, I'm going to get us some drinks in. Professor, do you want some crisps?

Bounce hair spikes. A little white of spit fired out on the grass. I nodded for crisps.

What's that, Danny?

Meemaw sharkly of the ruby red. I looked at my trainers.

Yes please.

Karen runned down the slope. Bounce bounce her hair spikes. Bounce the hoody hood of her.

Come and sit down, Danny. Listen, you remember to say thank you to Karen when she brings the crisps, okay?

I putted Spiney close my leg on the grass.

Karen getted me salt and vinegar which are best. I yummed them up and only a bit sandy because I remembered to wipe my hands on my coat before I opened.

Meemaw had tea and a rolly. Karen drinking a can of drink

called Coke Zero on it. I watched her gulpy mouth.

Do you want a sip, mate?

She holded it out the can and Meemaw speaked quick.

Oh, oh I don't let him have fizzy drinks. Just water really.

Karen putted the can beside her on the grass.

Fair enough. Sorry, I don't really know what's what with kids his age.

Thanks, anyway, though. I just... I don't really want to get him started on...

No, no, fair enough.

I crunched all the crisps a good zing. At the end I tipped the packet up some went tumble on my coat.

Karen was all the time looking at Meemaw.

Meemaw was all buzz of a bumble bee. Shimmery glittery of the ruby red. Meemaw's head sideways all sideways eyes up down when she blowed out her smoke. It was too much a loudness of looking. I closed my eyes.

Do you like football, mate?

I heared Meemaw laugh.

He doesn't really know much about it to be honest. It's not my thing.

Then I heared Karen laugh.

Not your thing? Well, we'd better sort that out then! I'll bring a ball next time and we can have a kick about, eh?

It was quiet. I opened my eyes. Meemaw not talking. Karen not talking. Meemaw and Karen staring at each other. Meemaw's nostrils gone big as a dragon. Then Karen speaked quiet. Hard to hear in the screamy of the park.

I bet I can persuade you to join in.

No thanks.

Meemaw flicked her ash on the grass. Karen lied down close of Meemaw. I never saw a person so close of Meemaw lying.

Karen taked a daisy from right close of Meemaw's leg by her jeans. She pulled off the thin white petals til just the yellow puffy. She throwed that away.

All sudden I wanted Meemaw to push me on the swing I thinked of the whooshing air. Swing please swing. But no words would come. I pulled.

Danny, just ask, sweetheart! What is it?
I putted my hand round Meemaw's ear. Whispered inside.
Swing Meemaw!
She brushed off the sandy crispy bits.
It's better to speak out loud in company, love.
I hated those words said. Stupid Meemaw. But she getted up.
I'm just gonna give him a push on the swing for a bit, Karen.
Sure.

There was a free swing. Meemaw waited and I getted on. I holded tight very tight of the chains. Not like in the baby swings when you can't fall out. You could fall out. She lifted it high high.

Hold on, Danny! Keep on holding on! Whatever you do don't let go!

For a minute I was holded up and thinking of falling. Falling down and bang on the ground. But then whoosh! I was swinging!

All the trees gone smeary on the white sky. I hanged back my head to upside down.

Shutted my eyes then and it was the feelings. Just feelings of whoosh and go.

I opened my eyes. Meemaw behind me. Her upside down head her upside down head and long hair blowing of the wind. Like octopuses' arms. Meemaw just a lovely head of my Meemaw and love and love.

It was forward backness on on. Meemaw's hands were a pushing machine. I went higher I could see the pond where the ducks and gooses live. I didn't want stop ever to come just Meemaw always be pushing and not ever stop.

But she did. She shouted.

Hey, Danny! That's enough now.

Her hands gone then and always falling lower. Slower. Sad and ending.

I watched Meemaw going up the slope. Karen waved Meemaw waved. Kept on walking on. She flopped on the grass near.

Faces close. Two faces only just a little piece of green grass in between. I draggled my feet on the ground. I draggled draggled my trainers turned sideways. The red coming off all scuffy.

When it came time to go Karen walked all along. On the corner by the pet shop she holded Meemaw's hand of her two hands. Kissed Meemaw's cheek slow. Lips pressed in.

I've had a really lovely afternoon, Nat.

Yeah, me too.

Meemaw's voice quiet and the cars going by.

Karen rubbed her hand up down the top part of Meemaw's arm. Rubbing slow and looking.

I'll message you, yeah?

Meemaw nodded and then sudden a flashing sharkle. Karen smiled.

Then sudden she crouched down. Karen's face close of mine all yuck of the perfume smell. All loud and close.

So, Professor…

Blue eyes of much too. Blueness only. One colour in. Not a mix-up of colours like Meemaw. Not true not real like Meemaw. The Karen eyes sharp. They spiked me.

I won't forget the kick about.

Nose of a bobble it moves. Eyebrows thin archy as a viaduct. All the time stinky shout of perfume smell.

I closed my eyes. Waited. Thinked of go away and go away. I heared her stand up.

I think that's me dismissed then, honey, eh?

Laughing and nothing funny. Go away go away go away.

He's tired, I think. Danny, say goodbye to Karen.

Still my eyes closed. I didn't say of it.

See ya, honey. Really soon, I hope.

Yeah, me too. Bye Karen.

I opened my eyes. Meemaw still. Meemaw staring watching Karen going. Away down the road she getted smaller smaller. I thinked shrink away to invisible.

She went round the corner gone. Meemaw picked up the bag.

Come on then, Danny.

I stopped by the pet shop window.

Can we go in just look Meemaw?

Meemaw doesn't like it she tells it is like a prison in the glass boxes for the kittens. When we stop by the yellow birds Meemaw puts her finger on the thin bars says who the hell would put a bird in a cage. But today not any of that.

Come on then; I know you love it.

Meemaw standed still still in the shop. Gone away. I looked a long time at the creatures.

Best were baby rats curled up together in the corner gone asleep. A tumble all babies together. I putted my face close and maked the glass go white. I wiped of my finger. A one-eye window. I holded Spiney up so he saw them too. In a long time the shop lady came.

I'm sorry, love, but we're closing up. Is there anything I can get you?

Meemaw did a jump grabbed my hand. I pulled. No grabbing.

No! Sorry! Come on, Danny.

Rushing. I don't like it.

***

When we getted home Meemaw gave me her phone and I finded the most brilliant of things on YouTube. It was called *Dinosaur! Tale of a Tooth*. Fifty seven minutes forty one seconds that is nearly a hour. I watched it all all.

There was a man called William Buckland. He was from olden days had a tall hat and a giant tooth and that's how they first knowed dinosaurs existed. The man of the voice on top was American. All up down. He said *they ruled the planet for one hundred and twenty million years*. I said it after. Up down. Again again.

One hundred and twenty million years…

Just of my quiet voice.

The man talked on. More of dinosaurs.

Meemaw was making our tea. Lots of chopping chop chop chop. She getted the little jars spices of smells in them. We can't use them often because of gets a bit pricey. But we like the tasty taste.

There was the one coriander and the ginger and sizzle. All good smells and *Tale of a Tooth* man telling on. Meemaw stirring humming humming. Fizz onions going to golden. All smells of golden in our flat.

Tea time!

Tale of a Tooth, *Meemaw! One hundred and twenty million years!*

Later, love. Time to eat now.

It was of delicious golden the smell. Meemaw gone golden too. She was gone very golden warm. Her hair shiny and smiles. I sitted down on my chair.

Well done, sunshine! Here you go! Veg curry!

It was many of carrots and sometimes hiding peas. We did happy of no talking and I eated lots.

Meemaw humming sometimes.

Right, no bath tonight love. The meter's a bit low.

Tale of a Tooth!

Tomorrow, love. We don't want to run out of data. Come and have a wash.

It was a clothes off wash of a flannel.

I washed hands and face. Meemaw gave me a soapy flannel for wash my bot willy and balls. Last my feet. She did rinsing off because nasty itchy if you leave soap on your private parts.

Not much of talking. It was quietness but still the gentle golden of Meemaw. I thinked of *Tale of a Tooth* and tomorrow. I thinked of it safe in the phone. Then into my pjs.

Right then, pyjama boy, time for another instalment of Terence the Turtle, yes?

Make him to find a great fossil tooth Meemaw! As in the days of the dinosaur hunters!

Hey! Who's telling this story, you or me?

You, Meemaw, but make him!

Meemaw didn't do it but she maked it so Terence went on the train to London. In London to the Natural History Museum where the actual tooth was in a glass case.

That's really true that is, Dan. It's in the museum in London. Maybe we'll go one day.

What day Meemaw? What day can we go?

Oh, God, I've done it now, haven't I? Not for a long time. In a long time when we have the money.

Meemaw tucked me cosy in. I didn't mind of it too much because still in the phone was *Tale of a Tooth* and the man of the up down voice. And one day the museum of London. I did a yawn.

Meemaw lied down beside but on top. Not going to sleep with me tonight.

You know, I was a real dinosaur nut like you, Danny, when I was little. Once we went to that museum I told you about. It's brilliant. It's got loads of stuff, not just dinosaurs. There are animals carved in stone in the walls.

I thinked of stone animals. Then the creatures in the shop not of stone but actual alive.

My dad lifted me up so I could touch one of the stone monkeys and I wished so hard for it to come to life and come home with us.

Did it? Did it go alive Meemaw?

No, it didn't.

Meemaw kissed my head.

When we came out of the museum though, we did have a treat. We had whippy ice creams with chocolate flakes from the van.

I want a chocolate flakes.

Meemaw doesn't let me have chocolate so not fair. Not a good story part like the stone monkey.

It was a real scorcher of a day though, Dan. And I remember a lot of that ice cream melted down my hand before I could eat it. I must have been really little. I don't know.

Meemaw was gone far away and not more talking. Remembering of it. I did remembering too but I didn't know of the people so it was too hard.

Was your mummy there Meemaw?

Yes. Yes, she was there that day.

So then I tried to do remembering of a mummy for Meemaw but I couldn't. I did wriggle and wriggle under the covers instead.

Time to go to sleep, lovely boy.

Meemaw did a snuggly kiss of my neck. Turned out the big light sitted in the chair sideways.

There was thumpy music. Sometimes shouting outside of names and you bastard. I turned over over over.

Settle down, love.

Meemaw sitted her book on her knees open. But not turning pages. Street lights went pop to on in the sky of blue treasure. Pink then orange the street lights go.

Meemaw and the lamp. Meemaw sometimes swooshed sudden to ruby red. Just sitting still not reading. Sometimes to ruby red. And sometimes her eyes closed.

CHAPTER FOUR

Meemaw leaned her head on the window.

It's not going to stop, Dan. I've checked the forecast.

Raining hard as hard. The windows gone to melty. Wind went rattle bump.

Tell you what, how about a pj day?

I feeled a big whoosh of good.

Yay!

I love pj days but Meemaw doesn't say yes mostly. Meemaw telled once of pj days can be the start of a slippery slope.

But not slippery in our flat today. Slippery outside of the pouring rain.

Meemaw wiped the table. The squashy sponge round round.

It's going to be chilly later because of the low meter. We'll have to snuggle in bed and do story mountain, okay?

Okay!

I did a shout very loud Meemaw jumped.

Story mountain is all the books come on the bed. We read them one then another and a mountain maked for our little finger men. Finger men climb it. The conquer of it. Mount Everest. It is the goodest of things.

First of the day though was washing up. All washing up of last night tea time and breakfast too.

Your turn to dry, Dan the man. Here you go.

It was the cloth of the clocks museum came of a charity shop. I like it the big numbers circle of it. I putted it on my face.

Ha! You've got a clock face!

I pulled it tight. All our flat was in the little holes of it.

Come on then, sunshine, that's not drying up is it?

Meemaw holded out a knife going drip on the floor.

I did knifes and forks putted them in the drawer. I did big plates of tea time my small plate of breakfast two mugs of Meemaw two glasses of drinks of water. I worked hard. Meemaw did it all one bowl only of hot because of low meter.

We can just leave the pans on the rack.

Then Meemaw went standed by the window looking. The rain runned down and down.

On the upside down silver pan white bubbles runned too. I touched. Soft. Then I lifted it over over of its heavy handle and looked in. My face inside. I speaked.

A hundred and twenty million years!

It came a good boom.

Meemaw laughed. I looked at her. A still blueness but not dark.

How about a Spiney bath?

Yay!

Just a shallow one… And go easy on the washing-up liquid, eh? That's got to last.

Spiney gets dirty in the world but Meemaw won't let him in our bath. She says very fond of Spiney but too mucky for a bath companion.

He has separate Spiney baths. Separate of himself. I pulled the chair over and standed up on it. Meemaw filled up the bowl to halfway. She did the squeeze of green washing up liquid that must last. Gived me the scrubby sponge.

Not too hard, remember?

Bad of Meemaw to say it. There on the side of Spiney's sail is a place of pinky where I did it. I scrubbed the colour off for a mistake.

I washed in Spiney's toes. In his hand claws my finger diggling. I pushed bubbles inside his mouth by the pointy teeth.

Spiney roared and spitted. He even bited me for a punishment!

No Spiney! Don't you dare!

I holded him underneath the water.

Bad Spiney! Bad!

I pushed hard. Cruelly and hard. I feeled strong but then sudden I was scared.

Oh sorry sorry Spiney! So sorry! Don't be drowned.

I kissed him on his face all wet of bubbles. I looked in his eye a sorry too. He was okay and not drowned.

Spinosaurus were like the crocodilians of today. Spinosaurus went in the water and devoured fish.

Next I flied Spiney in the air. I did Super Spiney. Standed far away of the bed. Throwed him hard. He landed boing! Bounced.

Super Spiney!

Spiney is allowed to bounce he is light. Not heavy like me. I runned to fetch him. Runned back and throwed again.

Oh the bounce! I'm not allowed it the bouncing. Sofa bed won't take it Danny. I runned fast to fetch him. Jumped on.

Danny.

Her warning voice I always know. Even though not even looking. A warning of bouncing. I wanted it so much. Bounce and bounce. I remembered it of the old flat. Oh the bounce!

Meemaw was sideways in the chair her woolly socks on. Feet dangly over the side.

I taked Spiney to Meemaw's feet. Spiney bounced on them. Hard. Meemaw did a sigh. She looked up from her book.

What are you going to do now, love?

Meemaw's finger slippled in the pages. She wanted to go back in. Meemaw reads books of other worlds of space. Meemaw devours them. Four every time at the library.

I pulled tiggy tug her feet fat and woolly. I pulled until she putted her book on the floor.

You're not going to let me read are you?

I looked but no answer.

How about a game of Beat Your Neighbour?

Yes!

Do you remember the rules?

Meemaw getted up she fetched the cards.

Yes! Half each to start. It is twenty-six cards Meemaw. twenty-six cards each and no jokers in.

That's right.

Then it was take turns. Turns like talking but the cards talking. Numbers ones just tell of next please! Best are clubs the bally shape I like and seven is the goodest of them.

Jacks queens kings and all alone aces tell give me give me! You have to. I had lots. Meemaw had to give me. I getted a fatness of cards hard to hold. Meemaw only a thin littleness of her cards.

But then Meemaw had a all alone Ace. Give me give four and I had to. Again again came the kings and queens and all. All my fatness of cards I had to give Meemaw. Then I runned out. None. Empty.

I looked at the cards all in Meemaw's hand. My hands empty of nothing just air. Rage comed up fast and fury. I tried snatching of the cards.

Raaaaar! Give me the bloody bloody cards!

Danny… calm down…

Meemaw holded up her hand high. All the stealed cards up high.

Give them! You horrible poo! You didn't win of me I winned of you!

I pushed Meemaw.

I winned of YOU!

I pushed Meemaw again. She dropped all the cards they fell down. All on the carpet. I grabbed one scrunchled it up.

Meemaw turned around went to the kitchen. The scrunchled card in my hand and stamping. Meemaw filled up the kettle. I stamped two times hard hard. My foot hurted underneath. Crying.

Meemaw bringed back a glass with water.

Danny! Danny!

I wanted to push it away all the water to fall down on the floor. All to wet and a mess. But I looked at it the silver top of it moving. Moving a gentle slosh of it.

Danny, have a drink.

I taked it two hands careful drinked. It was cold and grey flavour. Good. I gulped big gulps.

Right then. Let's count these all back, yes?

We did counting still I was crying just a little bit.

Fifty five… Give me that last card, Danny.

I looked at the scrunchled card.

Oh! Oh, oh! Such a mortal wound! A mortal wound of him, Meemaw!

I holded him in my under arm.

Come on, love, let's pop that one back in and the others will flatten it out. It'll be okay. Let's put it away now…

At the last I kissed him. He was nine of hearts. I was sorry. Meemaw tucked in the flap of packet.

Come on then, I think lunch might help.

***

I watched Meemaw spreading peanut butter. Gloop. She cutted four triangles. Four triangles together comes a rectangle.

I eated them one three two four nibbled down to strips just crust. I maked them be a cross.

Meemaw! Crusts for you!

You sure you don't want them?

No. Crusts for you Meemaw!

Meemaw smiled. Meemaw sitted by the window, smoking her rolly. Yumming up the crusts.

I needed a wee then and it was a long long wee. A splashy waterfall in the toilet. The water gone to yellow.

Okay, I'm turning the heating off, come and snuggle in!

Snuggle in!

I jumped but not bouncing. Not really.

Right, what's first then?

Walking with Dinosaurs!

Meemaw opened it up looked at the words and pictures.

Okay… Seven pages, okay? You choose.

I choosed about the ichthyosaurs of the Jurassic.

They look a bit like dolphins, Dan.

No Meemaw. A dolphin is a mammal of the present day.

Yes, so it is.

After *Walking with Dinosaurs* it was time for a old book. I choosed *A Squash and A Squeeze* and I can read all to Meemaw. Meemaw joined in for repeating bits but I readed the story.

Take in your cow said the wise old man…

I did good reading. My ear on Meemaw's booby. When she joined in I heared her voice inside. She stroked my hair. At the end we went round of it again.

After book mountain I stayed snuggly in bed in cover cave.

You stay warm, poppet, okay? Flat egg, yes?

Yay! Flat egg and beans!

No beans, love. It's a bit of a Mother Hubbard situation.

Meemaw opened the tins cupboard showed me inside.

I thinked of the sweety yum of orange beans. None.

How about you have two flat eggs, eh? I'm not hungry anyway…

Can I have the phone, Meemaw? Tale of a Tooth?

Let's see how we're doing with data, okay?

Meemaw went sweep and swipe and did a nod.

Yep, we're okay. Here you go.

I went on YouTube and looking for *Tale of a Tooth* but it went buzz. It went buzz buzz again of messages for Meemaw.

Let me look, Dan, that might be important.

I holded the phone tight in my two hands. Didn't want to give it but Meemaw's hand came in under the duvet.

Come on. You know what we agreed. If you want to go on my phone you have to give it back when I ask. I'm asking, Danny.

I putted the phone in Meemaw's hand then I peeped one eye at the crack.

Meemaw smiled at the phone she did sweepy swipe to make a reply.

My turn Meemaw!

But she didn't give it back. Meemaw did more sweepy swipe and buzz buzz came more replies. Little laughs. Meemaw sharkling up and I waiting.

Meemaw! Come on!

Hang on…

MEEMAW!

Sudden Meemaw spinned round looked in my peeping eye. Blink.

Change of plan, Dan the man, we're going out!

Meemaw runned to the bathroom I heared water. I stayed under. I putted my mouth by the crack for calling out.

It is a pj day! No going out! Flat egg now. Flat egg please thank you Meemaw.

Meemaw didn't say a reply to me.

I looked out again she had taked her green top out of the laundrette bag and she shaked it. Then Meemaw sniffed her jeans.

She was going very fast getting dressed. I putted my mouth back at the crack.

No Meemaw! No going out! No going out today!

Still no reply I looked again. Meemaw in the mirror her hair brushing. Flying up. All the bright ruby red of her she went close to the mirror rubbed her eyebrow of a finger. Then she came by me. Crouched down.

We're not having a debate about this. We're going out and you're going to get dressed right now.

I started crying. Meemaw very still waiting. She was sharkle red. She was strange not right. Not right. Even my crying she was still sharkle ruby red.

I wanted to change her. I shooted out my arm banged Meemaw hard on her shoulder. She falled back.

Meemaw went to purple deepness fast fast. She reached in my cave grabbed me right round pulled me out all her strongness. Plonked me on the floor.

Raaaaaar!

I spitted. Spit and spit. It went on Meemaw's jeans. I did kicking hard just in the air. Meemaw standed back.

I will not get dressed right now! I will not get it! Horrible poo!

Then no more words just crying. Loud. I climbed back in the bed. I digged in deep under pillows.

Meemaw putted one hand on my sticky out leg of the covers. I heared her talking calm but loud because of crying.

You will get dressed, Danny. You will get dressed right now and I'll tell you why.

I feeled her hand on my leg. I flapped my leg for get off. Meemaw's voice louder.

Because we're going to the pictures!

I went still.

Going to the pictures is a thing of long wanting. Wanting since when I was even three I think. On YouTube I see little programmes Meemaw telled called trailers. In cinemas now and that is also pictures.

Meemaw telled pictures is a room all dark and the screen big of a wall. Seats in a row. All in the dark. I wanted it and Meemaw said one day. One day when you're a bit older. One day when we can get the money together.

All sudden it was one day on this day.

Come on then! Shake a leg, matey, or we'll miss the trailers!

Inside me was a crash of things then very hard. I wanted it the pictures. But this was a pj day. And flat egg. But the pictures. The pictures very exciting the screen big of the wall and darkness.

I wasn't crying then. I came out of under the pillows. I sitted up at the edge of our bed.

Come on then, poppet. Let's get these on.

Meemaw holding pants for stepping in. Trousers and t-shirt and all. Then it was coats.

I knowed something sudden. I thinked I knowed it. I needed to check of true or not.

Is Karen coming to the pictures?

Yes, it's Karen's treat, Danny.

Not Danny's treat. I thinked about Karen then her bobbly nose and loud smell of her. But the pictures. The pictures of darkness and a mighty screen. I putted on my coat.

***

All the way on the bus Meemaw sharkled the ruby slippers. She was bright. Her eyes went twinkle and looking around at the people. Her face opened up and smiles.

I was very hungry because of no time for flat egg. I looked out the window. All the street was nearly night-time. All the drops on the glass were like Christmas lights. One day will come Christmas. Father Christmas chocolate in a advent calendar. Meemaw's birthday.

The glass went to grey of breathing and I did my name. Then I did the tooth found by William Buckland the palaeontologist. Underneath I writed tooth.

Then we were in town. Meemaw holded my hand. It was the dark street and we hurried. I did a yawn.

There were puddles. The puddles were the ripply ripped world of orange lights.

I didn't like the pictures door. Pictures cinema had a blue door that swinged itself open fast at me. But inside was better. Very very sweet smell of cake in the oven. My tummy groobled loud.

The carpet taked my eyes in the pattern. I wanted to stand still and just be in it but Meemaw pulling.

There she is!

Karen lifted up her hands. She had hot dogs three wrapped in white tissues. A cup a straw popping up.

Meemaw and me don't eat hot dogs they are meat and we are vegetarians. One day I asked by the library. It was a van of good smell but Meemaw telled they are of meat. Meat is a animal's actual body.

Hi, you two! I got tea!

Meemaw's mouth very close my ear it tickled.

Don't say anything, Danny, it's just this one time.

Meemaw taked two hot dogs. Karen gived a man a long orange paper of black writing. He teared it and gived it back.

Enjoy the film.

Karen was gone fast through the door. Meemaw squeezed my hand.

Right, come on then, Danny. Ready?

I knowed it would be dark and a big screen Meemaw had telled. But very very loud.

I standed still holded my ears hard. I could still hear music and Vauxhall Corsa a voice. A road on a mountain the car twisty this way that way. So big.

Meemaw pulled. I walked along but not letting go my ears then.

It was tippy up seats I don't like. Meemaw knows I don't like because of being squashed in. But she holded it down and I climbed up for a try. I was doing lots of tries because this was it the pictures cinema. I had been wanting.

A baldy head man was too much in the way. The light was shiny on his baldy head. I twizzled. I tried to get down but Meemaw holded up her hand of wait it's okay. She folded up her coat and I sitted on top. Then it was better.

Meemaw holded out the hot dog. I sniffed. It smelled good my mouth went wet. It had red sauce I love. I taked it.

The noise was louder now with no hands for my ears but I

liked it the hot dog. I eated it fast fast. There was a advert of M and Ms. They are little mans I like. Hot dog was the taste of smoky and sauce and white bread we don't have. It was chewy chewy and yum.

I swallowed the very last.

Braaaaaack!

A mighty burp came in a moment of quietness. Meemaw and Karen laughed.

The film name was there. Called *Home*. A big letter U in a green triangle.

At first I liked it the pictures. It was with aliens and funny. All the people sitted still watched and it was bright big. The voices up down good to hear.

But I was thirsty then very sudden. I looked round to Meemaw for a drink. Meemaw and Karen were doing kissing. They were doing kissing with mouths open like beasts and boyfriends. Devouring.

Very wrong very wrong very wrong. I looked back on the screen my heart thumpa thumpa thumpa.

I wanted home and nothing of this be true. I shutted my eyes and counted. I counted to two hundred then splitting two hundred up to twenty fives and there were eight. I like eight eight is a good and safe number of two circles. Then I opened my eyes slowly. Looked at the big screen. Only look there Danny.

But I was so so thirsty I slided my eyes sideways. Meemaw and Karen had stopped doing kissing. Perhaps maybe they had never done it I thinked. But that was not true. I knowed it. Tears started coming up of crying. I pulled on Meemaw's arm.

Thirsty!

Sorry, love, I forgot to bring water.

I hate and hate it if Meemaw forgets water because then what then what?

Noooo! Meemaw! Water!

Karen leaned across Meemaw with the big enormous cup of a straw sticking out. Sticking it at me.

Hey, Professor, cool it, eh? Have some of this.

I twisted. I tried to get down away out.

Noooo! Out! Out! Water!

Meemaw pressed on my legs.

Danny, stop it this minute! Sit still!

Hissed of a snake and Meemaw's hand hard on me. All the big huge screen runny of tears. I went still. I holded my ears closed my ears. Tears runned fast on my face.

Meemaw's voice whispery. Mouth air warm on my face.

Just have some of this for now, sweetheart, and calm down. Come on.

I feeled the straw touching on my mouth and Meemaw's hand on my cheek.

Come on, sweetheart. You're okay.

I sipped. It was sweet as sweeties and all bubbles. It was a surprise in my mouth. First a little tiny sip. Then more.

You take it. Okay? You hold it, Danny.

I did hold it. Cold. Wet. Such the sweetness and bubbles. I opened my eyes.

I put my eyes sideways watched Meemaw and Karen in the darkness. Sippy sippy sip. Karen reached holded Meemaw's hand in her own one. Put it on her leg. All was cold and trickly running down inside me.

***

Outside it was windy dark. Mans shouted and a motorbike of a roar came by. Karen came to the bus stop with me and Meemaw.

How'd you like the film then, Professor?

I didn't say.

He's really tired, Karen.

Late night, eh?

She came close, crouched down.

Have you had a nice time?

I pulled on Meemaw.

Stop it, love!

Meemaw picked me up. I pushed my face in her neck. Smelled of right and mine. Karen's voice very close.

How about we go down to Brighton on Saturday?

Meemaw's voice was a buzz in her neck when she speaked.

You know I think that's too much.

Karen did a laugh. It was a evil laugh of a baddie.

I'll message you. You know how persuasive I can be.

Meemaw laughed and it was a nearly evil laugh too. I twisted and pushed.

Hey come on now, Danny. Here's the bus!

Inside the bus was yellow bright warm. We sitted by the window me on Meemaw's lap snuggled in.

I looked out peep under Meemaw's arm. Karen was outside. She kissed her fingers blowed it to my Meemaw. I pushed my face in Meemaw's neck again.

Danny boy, are you okay, my angel?

I wouldn't wouldn't look up.

CHAPTER FIVE

Jane was sitted behind the desk at the library.

Hello Danny, how are you?

I'm very well thank you.

That is nice to say a polite boy Danny. Jane is my friend. Not Meemaw today but Jane is.

Jane taked a rectangle of white from a pile. I looked it was a label of the library. She speaked not looking at me.

Watch this, Danny.

She pressed it on a thing beside. It was a black thing with a rolly part that shined.

It's got water in it, Danny. It's wetting the labels for me to stick in these books so I don't have to lick them all. Do you want to help me with one?

I looked at it the thing. I touched with my finger the shiny of it. Wet. Jane helped me hold the label.

Just gently. Let it roll… Right, now press it down.

The label was wrinkled of wetness on a book. We pressed it on. Jane's fingers pressed. My fingers pressed.

Another one!

I taked a label. Rolly rolly on the spinny thing.

Not too much. Danny, now, come on. Let's press it down. Gently…

Another one!

Last one. Last one, okay?

We pressed again.

All done! Thank you, Danny. That was helpful.

Jane taked the books to a trolley. I like them the trolleys but only for library persons to push. Jane taked away the rolly thing too.

I taked one more label pressed my tongue on. Sticky tasty good. I holded my tongue right out label flapping on it. I closed my one eye. Other eye watched it flapping.

Jane sitted down again. She holded out her hand for give it back. I did because Jane.

Paleontologists are dinosaur hunters of the present day.

Indeed they are, Danny. They hunt for fossils, don't they?

William Buckland had just one clue a gigantic tooth that he acquired in 1817.

Did he? I don't know about him, Danny, was he British?

I didn't know of that. I looked at Jane's crinkle face. I like it. She smiled.

I'll look him up…

Jane tippy tapped on the keyboard. I looked for Meemaw.

Meemaw was gone far away in fantasy and sci-fi. I didn't care. Today I had said six words only to Meemaw. Krispies please no yes I did. No was of needing a poo. Yes was sure. I did was brushing my teeth.

That was a actual lie to Meemaw. A lie is not true. True was I putted my brush under the tap and it was gone to wet. But no teeth. No teeth. That was a lie and a trick I did on her a new thing. The trick is inside me. No one can see.

On the bus Meemaw was bright and yellow and

Danny! Triangles in the glass there!

and

See that big black dog?

Meemaw doing tell of nice things to Danny. I didn't say of triangles or the dog.

It was a good dog of pinky tongue sticked out. Jane could have for labels licking.

There's William Buckland, Danny!

Jane twizzled round the screen. He wasn't the actual man in the programme *Tale of a Tooth*. He was just a drawing done in black pen. But his tall hat he had. I putted my finger all around the edge of him. I readed words underneath I knowed.

Megalosaurus. Coprolites.

You've taught me something today, Danny, I didn't know about him. There was another palaeontologist I do know about though. He was called Gideon Mantell. He lived quite near here in Sussex.

Tippy tap again her keyboard.

He discovered the fossil of a dinosaur called iguanodon. I think we have a book about it... Hang on. We do! It's in the adult section though. Shall we go and find it?

I nodded.

This way.

We walked past Meemaw on her phone. Little smiles and laughing. I knowed it was Karen inside. Karen inside I could snatch. Stamp stamp Karen crunched and all squashed inside.

Just over here, Danny!

Meemaw looked up then. Smiled at me. I went to Jane.

The book was of Gideon Mantell and him on the front. The inside words were very small.

Here we are.

Jane holded it open to see.

You don't have to borrow it, Danny. It might be a bit heavy-going. But there are a few pictures, I think.

Jane turned over a page. I touched.

The fossil record.

Shall I pop it here for you? You can look carefully, can't you?

Jane putted the book on the table opened up.

The phone was ringing library phone. Billup billup billup. Jane walked away fast to answer.

I climbed up on the squashy red chair to look. The book words were long sometimes nonsense. I readed them one and the next one. But hard to make them fit to sentences.

I saw carnivore herbivore evidence that means proof. Proof actual true. Then I looked up because Meemaw had come.

Come on, Danny, it's time to make a move.

Meemaw gone floaty light pink. Very prettiful colour.

I want to borrow this book Jane finded for me.

I'd forgetted. I'd said ten more words to Meemaw of a mistake. Meemaw leaned by my head.

Is it not too hard, love?

I didn't say. Holded the book tight closed my eyes. Meemaw's phone another buzzy buzz. I opened my eyes. Meemaw was smiley smiling at the phone like only for me. Smiling only for me of lovely boy. Looking like filled up pinky good.

Meemaw walked away sweepy swiping her finger on the phone. Karen inside. Not looking at me.

Come on then, poppet, bring it to the machine.

Outside was a fresh air sky smell. But sudden my tummy did a fierce pain of grooble. Pain heavy and squeezy. Poo pain. I holded my tummy and went to still. Meemaw looked at me.

What's the matter? Do you need the loo?

I nodded.

I don't ever do a poo in toilets in the world. It is a not good plan.

But my tummy did the fierce pain again. Then came a trickle of wee I grabbed my willy. Squeezed.

Quick!

Meemaw taked my hand whizzed quick quick in the toilets. She pulled down my trousers pants plonked me fast on the toilet.

I holded Meemaw's coat. A big feeling. Big of the grooble pain.

I putted my face inside Meemaw's coat. I breathed of the Meemaw smell.

Then buzz buzz again and Meemaw on her phone! On her phone then and even laughing in the library toilet! I looked up and Meemaw dancing her finger on the phone.

I maked a groan of the wounded triceratops. Meemaw putted her phone in her pocket.

You're okay, love. Just relax… Danny, relax…

I crunched up my hands in the Meemaw coat. I pushed my head on it. I could see again again the Meemaw phone screen flash. Buzzbuzzbuzz.

Karen all the time maked light in Meemaw's pocket. Grooble pains went one another on on. Then stopped. No poo had comed. Meemaw maked a sigh. I looked at Meemaw.

She had a line come in the middle of her eyes. Pink was gone away. She had gone to grey now.

Come on then. Let's go home. Try not to worry about it.

Try not to worry about it.

We washed our hands of the runny soap. Pink as icing. I taked more more. Swirls and lovely it was. More.

Meemaw did sighs and captured of my hands under the runny tap. She rubbed all our hands together all to bubbles. I pulled my hands away.

No!

Rinse it off, Danny, it's not good for your skin.

I pushed up on the underneath of the tap maked a whoosh all of water spraying.

Danny! Stop making a mess! You know that's not okay!

Outside it was a all white sky. The wind and rustly leaves. Spiney did a dance of the leaves in the air.

Spiney can always do poos. He does them in the bed I tell him off. We walked along Meemaw me and Spiney.

Spiney pooed on every garden wall I telled him cheeky beast. Then I flied Spiney all along. Flying of the wind.

Super Spiney!

I runned runned forgetted about poos. Forgetted about Karen in Meemaw's phone. Forgetted everything except Super Spiney.

Super Spiney!

Stop on the corner, Danny!

I stopped. Meemaw holded my hand but no pulling.

***

Two envelopes with windows were on the mat. Meemaw putted them behind the kettle.

Right, you need to be drinking more.

Meemaw runned a tall glass all of water. I did sips.

Come on, love, big gulps. Try to get it all down.

I did seven of sips and putted it on the table. Meemaw did another sigh.

Right. Well that's better than nothing, I suppose.

Meemaw opened a tin of beans tipped in the pan. They were tumble orange in.

Then I sitted by the table went in my jumper for three hundred and seventy two. Swinged my legs and counting.

Here we go then!

Plonk on the table the lovely beans smell.

I had three spoons only of beans and sudden the poo feeling came back. Very urgent it came.

Meemaw!

I runned to our toilet. Pulling my trousers and Meemaw helped.

Calm down, Danny. Calm now!

It came a mighty ship. I did a small of sick too. It was sick of beans. I cried just three tears.

It's okay, sunshine, I've got you. I've got you.

Meemaw stroked my hair I forgetted to still not talk to Meemaw and to be cross.

Meemaw it was a mighty ship and sicky.

I know, love. I know. Let's pop you in the bath for a minute, eh?

Meemaw maked me a little warm bath of myself. She letted Spiney in it too for a treat. Meemaw washed gently. She getted the sicky bits off my face with toilet paper wet of water and throwed it away in the toilet.

I washed my bot of careful careful.

Well done, poppet. Well done.

After I getted out Meemaw wrapped me up in yellow towel. I yawned big and then another one. I was very sleepy like bedtime even in the day.

It's all been a bit much, hasn't it? All a bit much. That was a late night last night and your little system's a bit out of whack.

I thinked whack is hit and hurt.

Let's have a little siesta, shall we?

Meemaw pulled out the bed even in the day. She helped me one leg other leg into my pjs. She taked off her trousers and we getted in the bed.

Cuddled up close in the bed. All my cross feelings were goned away like birds flown off. I heared the thump of Meemaw her heart. It was safe warm. My eyes went droopy droop.

***

I came awake. It had gone dark in our flat. Swoosh and car lights zoomed across the ceiling. There was Meemaw's voice but wrong.

Meemaw asleep talking. All nonsense and strange singy songy. I knowed it was Spanish and wake Meemaw up. Right now.

I shaked Meemaw's arm joggle joggle.

Meemaw! Meemaw wake up!

Meemaw opened her eyes. She rubbed her hand on her face.

Was I talking, Danny? Was I talking?

Spanish words of nonsense.

Oh I'm sorry, Danny. Did it wake you up? Are you okay? Did I scare you?

Meemaw sitted up rubbed on her face again. I didn't say of scared.

God knows what that was all about. Blimey, it's dark… What time is it?

Meemaw leaned down picked up her phone. Then a gasp noise of shocked like tea spilled.

What's wrong Meemaw?

Sudden I didn't like it. All was wrong. It was sleep in daytime now turned to night Meemaw talking all Spanish and gasp.

What Meemaw what?

Meemaw didn't answer. Instead dancing her finger on the phone screen. I knowed it was a Karen thing. I kicked my foot on the bed.

Meemaw putted down her phone.

Danny, guess what?

Kick kick kick.

Stop that, love. Listen, listen, this is a good thing! We're going to Brighton tomorrow for a day out.

Kick kick kick.

Danny! We're going on the train! Isn't that good?

Meemaw's face was Cheshire Cat of the Alice book. Meemaw's teeth in the dark. I thinked of just the teeth left behind.

Meemaw! Meemaw! Turn on the light! Turn on!

Okay, okay, calm down, Danny! Hang on.

In the light she was Meemaw. All of Meemaw but a ruby shine sharkle red again. A explosion.

Hey! It's okay! It's a good thing, Danny! A good thing.

I looked away by the pillow.

Meemaw leaped out of bed. Long legs of skin and hurrying.

Right, I'm going to make us some hot chocolate and pack a bag! Then we're both going back to sleep because it's an early start for Brighton! You're going to love it, Danny!

Meemaw putted milk in the little pan. She getted bread and spreading for sandwiches. I watched then I pulled the Gideon Mantell book out the bag. I opened it on the bed. All the little words close close. I sended my eyes sliding all along. Sometimes I stopped for a word I knowed. Mostly I letted my eyes go. Along along.

Danny? Danny? Danny, I'm talking to you.

I looked up Meemaw stirring. The teaspoon in the green mug. Round round tink tink tink. Then round round the panda mug. Tink. Tink. Tink.

Karen is very special to me, you know?

Meemaw looked at me.

At the moment Karen is very special to me, Danny boy.

I pressed my hands hard on my ears feeled the squish.

Meemaw stopped talking putted the panda mug on the chair beside the bed. She crouched down not talking. Meemaw's waiting face.

Sweetly sweet of hot chocolate came very curly in my nose. I picked up the mug.

Sometimes two people suddenly really like each other a lot, Danny. It just happens, you know? Sometimes it happens like that. Sometimes it happens to a man and a woman and sometimes it happens to a man and a man and sometimes it happens to a woman and a woman. And that's what's happening to Karen and me.

Hum mmmmm

I did the mmmm and gulpy down the warm. Sweet warm and mmmmm.

Danny? I need to know you've heard me Danny. Do you understand?

Meemaw was doing a spell. It was a spell of a hundred words of wicked.

I went louder.

MMMMMMMMMMM!

I gulped. Big gulps fat cheeks of all the warm chocolatey.

Hey, take it easy, love! You might choke!

I holded out the mug.

Empty Meemaw. All gone.

Meemaw taked the mug to the sink. She runned the tap. I turned to a new page. The words went sudden to clear. I heared them in my mind. Then fast they came to my mouth.

Gideon Mantell emerges as a leading light in the new science of palaeontology...

Emerges is comes out. Comes out of a dark place. Dinosaurs in the smoky and dark. Gideon Mantell a shiny man of light.

Meemaw snapped her head round fast to look. She came close crouched down again.

Are you reading from that? Did you just read those words?

Meemaw tried to turn the book round. I holded on tight. Tight tight and no talking. Meemaw did a sigh.

Danny, do you understand what I'm telling you about Karen?

I turned the next page. Meemaw standed up walked her skin legs away in the kitchen. I sended my eyes back in the words. Sliding sliding all along.

Mmmmmmmmmm.

CHAPTER SIX

I was having my krispies. Knock de knock on the door. It was Karen comed to our flat. She standed by the table. Too near. Darkening. Filled up the air all her perfume smell. Under her arms two big rolled up things. She was breathing loud and huff going in my ears.

Only last krispies left now. Soft baby fish krispies swimmed in the milk. I chased chased one and the next. Licked them off my spoon. Spoon was wetty silver milk. No fishes left now. I slurped it spoon and spoon to empty.

Karen plonked the rolled things.

What shall I do with...

Meemaw speaked quick tumbly.

Just stick them over there for now. I haven't said.

They did a cuddle. My eyes slided off.

Come on then, Danny. Go and give your teeth a brush and then we'll be off. I've made some sandwiches, Karen.

Karen did a kiss of Meemaw's cheek.

You're so sweet, baby. There's no need. We can get fish and chips.

In the bathroom mirror I saw a slice of the other room a slice of Meemaw and Karen doing kissing. Moving as beasts of the sea. I shutted my eyes brushed harder harder to make shhh in my head. The whole world to minty. Minty in my nose eyes ears. Meemaw came behind me.

Blimey, Danny boy, don't forget to spit!

In the mirror my chin white as Father Christmas. In my mouth hot fire.

I've been on the train two times before. Best time to Haywards Heath for a treat instead of a bus. Meemaw founded three pound coins in the foldy bed they were from a person before us who was long gone away Danny. Finders keepers! Let's go on the train!

A other time to visit Mick who is my grandad in Hove on one rainy day when his tummy was a ulcer. We saw the sea a square green blue at the end of the road. But no time today Danny we walked fast by. I wanted it the sea but Mick's flat was the biggest biggest telly all day CBeebies and Wotsits from the shop. That was good.

I knowed it the station. I like the platform numbers crissy crossy fence long forever tracks. Karen was carrying the bag. She plonked it down.

Right, you two, wait here. Let's start as we mean to go on, eh?

She runned off up the steps. I wished not come back not come back get on the train no Karen. Meemaw stroked my hair.

Are you excited, sunshine?

I didn't say looked at the silver forever tracks. Feeled Spiney's tail.

We'll have a lovely day. You'll see. We'll have a lovely day, Dan.

Karen runned down the steps. Come back and not disappeared which was a sorry thing.

Here we are then!

She had a scrunchled over white bag of paper. Two cups in a holding thing.

I got you a cappuccino babe, okay?

Meemaw peeled off the lid all a coffee smell came out. She blowed it did a little sip. Meemaw drinked it not liking coffee.

Karen went in the paper bag getted out a huge thing of red jam and icing. Huge and shining of sticky.

How about this, Professor?

Red jam is not good as purple jam but icing I like. I looked at it. Bended down looked underneath.

Blimey! The full inspection, eh? Do you want it or not?

Meemaw taked it. She folded round the paper for a handle for the sticky. Gived it to me.

Thanks so much, Karen. What a treat, eh, Danny?

In Meemaw was a wobble of her colour like clouds in her pinkness. She looked fast in my eyes for please. She said please of no words.

I taked one bite. It was thickly in my mouth. I wanted to open up out it fall but not nice to spit out our food. I chewed it up. Did a swallow.

It's as big as his head!

Karen laughed. She laughed on on.

I putted down the thing on the bench and Meemaw scooped it up quick.

We'll wrap it up for later.

All the time Karen looking at Meemaw her eyes round wet. Nostrils sometimes big. Mouth wide. I thinked she wanted to eat perhaps Meemaw. I standed up taked two steps back.

Stay away from the edge, won't you, Danny? Behind the line!

I taked Spiney did a nod. I didn't say but I knowed it anyway. Live rail. I know of it the live rail.

Meemaw told one day *you never forget anything, Dan, do you? You remember all the safety stuff, you're like a little manual.* I thinked a little man. Dan the man. Don't forget.

Spiney and me walked the stripe of sunshine concrete. Sharkles and straight shadow line each side. We went away far of Meemaw and Karen.

We went to a sign Passengers must not cross the line a walky man a line right through him. Do not must not. Next a sign yellow black waspy danger. Live rail. Zigzag of lightning for electricity. Electricity.

Electricity in the track can zap you killed to death. Just a tiny touch. Meemaw told me invisible to see electricity but it's hiding in the silver forever train track.

I sended my eyes in the track. Shimmering singing wheedle wheedle down along the sharpy stones. Sudden I thinked perhaps hidden electricity might jump in my eyes and kill me. I runned back to Meemaw.

Look, Dan! Here it comes!

The train face came bigger bigger. Stopped. Beep beep beep for the doors a orange light. Karen pressed.

After you, babe.

Not babe my Meemaw.

On the train was a new smell. Greasy grey smell. The windows gone grey too. All over spickled. Covered grey over the world. I holded my nose.

Meemaw looked at me but not cross. Meemaw happy for the sunny day of train and Karen.

It's okay, love, it's just a bit grubby on this tatty old train.

I letted go my nose slowly. Taked small air in to get used to it the new smell. Grey of tatty train smell.

Karen putted her trainers up on the other seat that is rude. Hand on Meemaw's leg touching. I looked close to the grey window to see out of the tiny gaps. Teeny tiny gaps. The world outside.

We rattled off. Rattling rattling. One stop a station Hassocks. Socks in it! I nearly telled but not. I looked at the Karen hand there squeeze squeeze on my Meemaw's leg. No talking but looking at each other. Looking.

Sudden Meemaw maked me jump.

Hey, Danny! Look! Look up, quick, there's the windmills!

I looked up but bang all black in the window.

Aaaagh! Noooo!

It's okay, love, we're just in a tunnel.

Nooooo!

I shutted my eyes. Meemaw came by me I feeled. She putted her arms all around me.

It's okay, love. It's dark because we're in the tunnel. We're going through the hill.

I opened my eyes to peep. In the window Meemaw and Danny. And Karen. All outside tunnel people we were. Looking in.

Danny, you know what? They dug this tunnel more than a hundred and fifty years ago, before big digging machines. There were lots of men cutting all through with picks and shovels.

Words bubbled fast out of me.

Meemaw! Meemaw, did they find fossils when they were digging in the tunnel?

I wouldn't be surprised.

Like Gideon Mantell finded fossils in the digging chalk?

Yes. Just like that.

That was a good thing and better. And Meemaw still cuddling me.

Sudden again we were out in the day and come to a station called Preston Park. Karen getted up taked Meemaw's bag from the high up shelf.

Next stop then.

She looked under her arm at me.

He really is a professor, isn't he? Is it always dinosaurs and that he goes on about?

I looked at the floor my red trainers. Crossed over and mine. Meemaw did me a squeeze.

You love dinosaurs and fossils, don't you, Danny?

I sitted very still for keep safe. No words.

Karen zipped up her hoody putted Meemaw's bag on her shoulder. Yawned very wide. She looked out the grey window her spikey hair on the glass.

I 'spose he'll be starting school soon, won't he, and mixing more with other kids?

The train was slowly down down. We went by the door waited for the light to come inside press. Beepbeepbeep.

Press it now, Dan!

I did. The doors opened clonk.

***

The thing of the pier is it is actual standing in the sea. Metal legs go down down in the water stand on the ground underneath. You walk on the top and the sea under.

I holded Meemaw's coat thinked of the climbing frame in the winter. In the park in the winter. The wooden part went to soft. One day a man with waspy tape banged it away. On it growed bright bright yellow blobs called fungus Meemaw telled. Fungus had eated the wood. If the man not banged it someone could have falled down to the ground. Sometimes hard things can go to soft. They can break.

Under the pier was sea. I didn't have my arm bands from one day at the swimming pool. So if I falled a disaster. I holded tight on Meemaw's coat. Sticked my feet still.

It's fine, love. It's safe and strong. Look at all the people.

I looked at the people. It was still a dangerous thing the pier. They didn't know it perhaps. Under in the cracks the sea was moving. I saw it move and move.

Shall I carry him?

Karen gave the bag to Meemaw reached down like to pick me up. I did a step fast away.

Noooo!

Just give him a minute, K. He'll be all right.

Not okay not okay.

Come on, Professor, be a brave boy, eh?

He just needs a minute.

Inside me was thump. But I looked I saw a fat man. The man walked along the pier. I looked at his feet shiny black shoes. I smelled him vinegar. He laughed. The man didn't fall crack and through and splosh in the sea.

The man went on. I thinked he was a tester of the pier big and heavy. He walked in front of me. To test safe for me and Spiney. I knowed it.

I hopped on the next plank the next.

There we go! Crisis averted! All okay, Dan?

I didn't say.

Funny little lad, aren't you?

Karen putted her hand out for touching my head. I went low quick. Meemaw rubbed on Karen's arm.

After twenty five hops along the planks stopped. They came to a slope instead. Slope to a building. I stopped.

Karen and Meemaw were linked up in their arms. Karen pulled.

Come on, Nat! Let's blow a bit of money!

Meemaw standed still so their arms stretched. Meemaw did a little laugh.

No. It's a waste, K, and I don't really want him thinking…

Karen pulled more. Pulling is not nice.

Oh, come on! Live a bit, Nat, for fuck's sake!

Fuck is a swear word we don't say it because that's rude. Other people might be upset. I whispered it.

Fuck fuck fuck.

Karen grinned big wide. Laughing. Pulling. She slided up

close to Meemaw's ear whispering in. It is better to speak out loud when you're in company. Meemaw pushed Karen in her chest. Meemaw laughed and laughed.

Go on then, you wicked woman! Five minutes.

Victory! Come on, Professor!

Inside the building was yellow red flashing flashing. Smell like metal. Hot too hot. Chings bings wooooaaaaaooooo! Wild fierce machines. Racing car roar. All very around me. Loud.

People were mostly all backs but one a man in the low down racing car. It was a pretend the racing car. It didn't go along. The road in front on the screen. The man twizzled the wheel. Did a crash.

I closed my eyes put my hands on my ears. Still the loud. Still very too hot.

A noise came up in me like a racing car too. Louder louder. Meemaw crouched down. I feeled her hand on my wrist. She whispered at my ear her tickle breath.

You're all right, sunshine. Danny, listen to me, it's just for a few minutes then we'll go outside. Open your eyes, sweetheart. Come on, open your eyes.

Meemaw unzipped my jacket putted her hand on my chest.

You're all right. Open your eyes.

I opened one eye. Karen was by a window a big girl inside. She was a dolly girl of yellow hair dolly eyes red mouth spotty on her cheeks. She gived Karen a pot like marg in. Karen came bouncy on her trainers.

It's only a fiver, Nat. Come on, let's see how we do!

She rattled the pot. Inside was the horde of Sinbad. Lots and many. 2ps too many to count of. I never saw such of 2ps. I opened my other eye.

Watch, Professor! See? We put them in here.

It was called Copper Falls. Pictures of a waterfall. Inside bright light. All moving.

Karen pushed one 2p in a hole. It falled down down down inside. Landed plonk flat on a silver shelf moving. Moving moving. 2p pushed and swallowed. More 2ps falled down on the next place. In out the silver shelfs moving. The 2ps falled down again.

To the edge was such a mountain. I thinked all fall down fall down. But not. All the 2ps squashed up together and none falled. The Karen 2p was losted inside the machine. Gone forever. A disaster.

Come on! Give it a go!

Karen jangled the pot by my face close. I shutted my eyes. Losted and gone.

Meemaw squeezled my hand lots little of squeezes. Like please again please.

Look, Danny, I'll have a try. Watch me have a go. Danny, watch!

I didn't open my eyes. Meemaw letted go my hand. Wooooaaaaaoooo of the machines! Karen's voice shouting.

Bad luck, Nat! They nearly went that time! Come on, Professor! Come on! Your turn! Your turn!

Again the jingly pot by me. Close very close. I shutted my eyes tighter. Then Meemaw's voice.

I don't think this is a Danny game, really.

I thinked outside outside outside. I thinked outside and the noise to stop. The smell the hot to stop.

Sudden came a crashy tumble. Eyes tight shut shut.

Woohoo! There ya go, Nat! Bonanza! Come on!

And Meemaw a wildly tumble of laughing.

I was all alone in the noisy sea. Too much scared. Too much alone. I opened my eyes.

Meemaw and Karen pushing pushing in the 2ps. Tumble and tumble inside the bright. Sometimes crash some falled into the holder places. Meemaw and Karen scooped them. Laughing and laughing. Scooped them back into the pot. Meemaw's hair was all dancey.

One 2p falled on the swirly carpet by my trainer. I picked it up putted it in my pocket. Curled my fingers round. I telled it in mind words you are safe and saved. Scrunchled it tight. Whispered.

You are safe and saved.

Karen holded the pot to Meemaw.

Last two! Come on, baby, what's mine is yours! Together, yeah?

Last 2ps went in. Tumbled down swallowed up. No more falled out. Over and gone. All were lost.

Come on, let's go back outside, K.

Meemaw holded my hand. We went by the edge of the pier.

A seagull on the fence looked with a yellow eye. Then it flied away. Wide wings. The wind was buffy bump. Better. Smell of cold and outdoors and special of seaside.

I let go Meemaw's hand. I holded on the fence. Hard cold. I looked at the sea. All moving waves running. White stripes all along far. I went in the waves with my eyes.

Right! Fish and chips time, yeah? Shall we go in and get a table?

Meemaw standed close to me. I feeled her there but still my eyes away in the waves.

Well, look, I've done sandwiches, K. Let's not waste them. How about just some takeaway chips to go with? He'll be better if we don't have to go indoors again.

Okey-dokey, sweetheart, your wish is my command. I'll get them. Don't go disappearing on me though, eh?

Still my eyes in the white running waves. I heared Meemaw do a sigh.

Come on, love, let's sit on the bench, okay?

Nooo!

Danny, come on the bench, love. We're not going indoors.

Meemaw and me sitted down on the bench. A roof over. I could see the sea but not so close not so good.

Are you having a nice day, Dan?

I getted up again went to the fence to have nothing in the way for my eyes. White stripe waves coming coming in in to the land. I holded the 2p in my pocket. Holded tight of him.

You come home with me. Come to my house not lost in the machine.

Meemaw called.

Danny! Come and eat! Chips!

I like chips best.

Karen had bringed three shiny boxes. I sitted down next to Meemaw. Yellow squeaky boxes tucked in closed. My tummy groobled for hungry.

Karen gived me one big box all to me. The lid popped open. Inside lots and lots of chips and a smell of golden tasty.

Tomato sauce, Professor?

In Karen's fingers was a drippy red sauce packet.

Yes.

Yes what, Danny?

Yes please of sauce.

Karen dribbled red sauce out. All across my chips. Too much! I pulled my chips away. Splat red sauce on the white bench.

Ooh! Whoops-a-daisy! That's enough, is it?

Sorry, K! Danny, just be careful!

Karen putted some red sauce on her chips. Then she throwed it in the bin, licked all her fingers.

Meemaw tucked her flying hair behind her ear. Out it squiggled quick for flying away again.

Keep your chips in close, Dan! There's nothing those gulls like better than a nice hot box of chips.

Chewy chewing the red sauce chip was good. Good in my mouth.

Karen had three cans of fizzy drink. One two three. They were on the bench by her for one each. I taked one. I holded it up at Meemaw for please.

Go on then!

That meaned yes.

Kish crackle she opened it for me. It was red and Coca Cola swirly writing like a wave. Other side Coke. I drinked a big slurp. Woo! Icy icy in my tummy. Sweet and fizz in my mouth. I gulped gulped putted it down on the bench two hands.

But my hands were gone greasy of chips. They slipped. The bench too curvy and thonk it went down on the wooden pier. Splash out came a wave. Splash on Karen's foot.

Karen jumped up.

Fuck! Fuck it! Jesus!

She shaked her foot. Shaked it. Meemaw in our bag quick. Meemaw to save the day. But fast words to me.

Oh God! Oh God, Danny, what have you done?

Meemaw holded out toilet roll at Karen. It blowed in the wind all long. Karen didn't take it she shaked and shaked her foot. The Coke gone on it.

Karen, here! Dry it off with this.

Karen didn't take it she shaked her foot more.

Fuck it! Fuck! I'm gonna go and wash this off in the loo. New fucking trainers! Fuck it!

She runned away through the people.

Meemaw picked up the fallen over Coke. She taked it to the bin pushed it in. She sitted back down started eating her chips. Meemaw chips bare of red sauce. Meemaw doesn't like it. Meemaw posting chips fast fast in her mouth open closed snap.

Beside Meemaw still a closed Coke can I thinked of it. Bubbles fizz cold.

Meemaw can I have the other one?

Meemaw turned round her head fast. She was gone to bright yellow green. Meemaw's voice like throwing stones.

I think you've caused enough trouble, don't you? Just eat your chips.

My tummy went closed full up. No more eating.

I looked at people walking on the pier. One a man with a baldy bald pink head. One a lady with sunglasses very big. Like bee eyes.

It was gone to very bad on the pier. My tummy went squeeze pain. Inside was crying coming.

But Karen came and I didn't do crying. I watched Karen she sitted by Meemaw. Meemaw stroking.

Fuck, that's been an expensive can of Coke. I don't suppose these'll ever look the same.

I'm so sorry, K. I'm so sorry. He didn't mean to.

No, I know. Of course he didn't bloody mean to. I know he just dropped it. I'm not an idiot. He's just a little kid. I get it.

Karen wriggled all her shoulders for get off and Meemaw stopped stroking. Karen's trainer was gone dark of wet. It didn't match the other one that was bright bright of turquoise and white of soft stuff.

I knowed I had to say it too of sorry. Meemaw would want it. I tried it to make it come out. Then it came sudden on its own. Loud.

Sorry.

I didn't look. Feeled her eyes on me.

Oh well, it's done now, Professor, isn't it? I could do with a drink.

Meemaw leaned put her arm round Karen's shoulder for feel better about the trainer that was all my fault. She kissed Karen's face two times.

How about we go down on the beach for a bit?

Karen standed up.

No, I'm fucking freezing. Let's find a pub where they won't mind him.

Meemaw started closing up the squeaky boxes putting them in the bag.

Oh for Christ's sake, we're not gonna want them cold and greasy are we?

Karen throwed all the boxes in the bin. All the chips gone.

***

Meemaw doesn't like pubs. Sometimes dark brown days we come past the pub on the corner and Meemaw is *Look look at them, Danny, all pissing their lives away.*

Men do shouts by the pub after bedtime. Sometimes it's fighting sometimes a joke. Meemaw says beer turns jokes to fighting. Beer is a potion of a witch I won't ever drink.

We walked long on pavements of all people. Meemaw maked me hold hands. Sticky hot hands.

How about this one, Nat? It's a Wetherspoon's, it'll be fine for kids.

It's so busy though, K. Can't we find something a bit smaller?

I did pulling. Pulling by the step.

Okay, whatever. Let's go along here…

Karen was going fast wiggling in out of all the people. Lots of people now and all in the roads. No cars.

K! Karen! How about in here. It looks nice.

Is it a pub?

Yeah, yeah, look.

Okay, whatever. I just need a bloody drink.

The pub wasn't like the corner one at home. This pub was big clear windows flowers on each every table. Little white soft of flowers in blue pots. Wispy of green bits too. I touched gently. Meemaw moved it away.

Leave it, Dan.

There was a lady near of yellow hair piled up like fat strings. She had a teeny dog I liked. It sniffed my leg. The lady smiled.

She likes you. Do you want to stroke her?

Meemaw nodded for yes I could.

I bended down close of the dog. Eyes round and wet. All dark. All dark nose and pointy of a fox. I stroked. Gentle to be kind. Teeny dog had a head silky smooth and hardness of skull inside. It squiggled all about.

What do you want, babe?

Just a juice, thanks.

Oh, have a proper drink! Don't make me drink alone.

I'm feeling a bit headachey, K. Just a juice would be lovely. Orange. Thanks.

What about him?

No, he doesn't need anything. He'll be fine. Thanks, though. Thanks, Karen...

We sitted by the window and Meemaw undid my coat and taked it off.

You be a patient boy now, Dan, okay? Sit quietly.

Karen had a big yellow drink of tall and wet on the outside. The top was white frothy like the sea waves. Meemaw had orange juice. Her glass was round like a Christmas ball. Karen bringed crisps too.

I didn't know for me or not the crisps. Strange and strong. A bad smell. Karen opened them teared the packet down all the smell came out.

Karen did a big drink gulp. She taked a crisp putted it in her wide wide mouth. Smiled at Meemaw rubbed on my head. I sitted very still.

Let's forget it and get back to the fun, eh?

Meemaw was hiding her colour. It isn't a often thing she does. Just sometimes. I looked at Meemaw counted to sixty. Still hidden colour. Karen standed up.

'Scuse me a minute, gotta have a wazz.

I flatted my hair she'd rubbed.

Can I have the water please Meemaw?

Meemaw gave our water to me from the bag. I gulped seven

gulps gived it to her back. Meemaw wasn't looking at me. Meemaw was gone away hiding. She looked out the door in the street.

All the time of waiting Meemaw's eyes were wanting to go in the street. I hoped it meaned go home soon. I thinked of it and hoped.

We stayed in the pub a long long time. Karen had three yellow drinks Meemaw two of the round drinks of orange. I kneeled on the seat looked out the window. A big brown dog was there playing the piano. He taked off his head sometimes. Inside he was brown beard red face man. There were people people people. I thinked of go home.

After long of waiting I went under the seat. Meemaw asked me two times to come out but she wasn't really meaning it. It was just a saying thing.

I heared them talking Meemaw and Karen but I closed my ears of the words and did counting. All to a thousand. Then I finded a crack in the floor inside was grey fluffy fluff for picking. At the last Karen leaned down. Too close. Big face in my under table place.

Come on then, Professor, one more stop before we go home.

Her breath air stinky.

One more stop was Argos a very big Argos. I like all bits of Argos it is very good. Find the number Danny and we check it on the machine then write it on the paper. Meemaw pays then we wait.

We are a number then me and Meemaw sometimes good with a zero sometimes a fivey number not so good. Our number comes green on a high up screen and then it's time for go to collection point A.

Karen did all of it herself. No sharing. Karen did numbers and the little pen and pay and holded the paper I didn't even know what our number. I didn't know! All wrong in Argos.

I kicked the underneath of my chair. Kick kick kick kick.

Enough, Danny!

Meemaw still invisible colour and Argos all wrong.

Karen went bouncy to collection point B came back with a bag. Big and blue of Argos.

Right then, you two, ready for surprises?

Karen gived me a big box. It was of all colours a truck inside. It was bigger than Spiney. She putted it on my lap not even asking. I holded up my two arms for not touching.

I hate trucks cars trains all the playing things that aren't alive. I looked at the box of the truck. I thinked about dinosaurs. In the catalogue might be dinosaurs. A T-Rex which moves or a whole lots of predators in a collection. Maybe a pterosaur.

Wow, Danny! Wow, look at that lovely present Karen got you! Thank you so much, K.

Meemaw holded the box on my lap. Inside me feeled sore like a tumble down in the park. Like a knee all scraped in me.

And then this for you, beautiful lady.

Karen taked out a small box of a heart. She holded it on her flat hand. It was soft darkly blue.

I just knew it was for you.

She opened up the blue heart. Inside was a twinkly golden thing. Shiny in the whiteness light of Argos.

Take it. Put it on.

Meemaw taked it out. A trickly chain curled up on Meemaw's hand. A word of loopy writing. Angel. I thinked it was maked of gold and was treasure.

Here, let me.

Karen putted it round Meemaw's neck.

In a sudden fastness Meemaw flashed her colour. Meemaw flashed the ruby red.

She kissed Karen's mouth. I looked at the Argos numbers all going on and on.

Number 473 to your collection point, please.

A man near coughed a phlegm cough. Karen speaked words quiet to Meemaw but I heared.

Well you are an angel. You're my angel and I'll show you what that means later.

All was wrong in the big Argos of Brighton.

***

On the train I falled asleep. I missed the long tunnel and the windmills again Meemaw had said of.

I waked up getting off at our station. Meemaw carrying me.

Hello, sleepy-head. Down you get now.

I squeezed my legs tight.

Noooo! Carry me! Carry me Meemaw!

Come on, love, You've had a little nap but now you need to walk.

I squiggled around. Karen reached out her arms.

I can carry him if you want.

I went to still.

Get down.

Meemaw putted me down.

Karen didn't go away. She came back all the way to our flat and in.

Karen sitted talking to Meemaw while Meemaw maked pasta for tea. I did drawing on my stegosaur comic. I waited for the time of Karen to go. It didn't come time.

How about I get your new truck out?

Oh, that'd be kind. Isn't that kind, Danny?

I drawed a sharp tooth big. A big sharp tooth even though stegosaur is a herbivore. Karen getted the truck out of its box.

There ya go, Professor!

She putted it beside me. She pushed a wheel on my comic. I moved it away.

All the time Karen and Meemaw did talking. I went in my comic. More accidents for the stegosaurs. And mountains. Mountains and mountains to far away.

There were three plates. Karen staying for tea in our flat. Meemaw had the bendy prong fork we don't ever use.

Mmmm, very nice! You're a great little cook, Nat.

Thanks.

I eated lots of pasta because good and tasting right of home. I did a hum to not hear Karen. I eated my last five pasta tubes one on each finger for finishing.

Ahem, Professor, what's wrong with your fork all of a sudden?

Meemaw did a laugh not a real one.

It's just what he likes to do with his last five pasta tubes. One for each finger isn't it, Dan? It's not the sort of thing I mind.

Karen gulped gulped her water down.

Right, I'll wash up. That was gorgeous, babe.

Karen taked the three plates. Her back by our sink and hot tap on. Squeezy squeeze the washing up liquid that has to last.

Meemaw standed up.

Come on, Danny. Bath time, poppet.

We went in the bathroom she shutted the door. Meemaw turned on the taps putted blue shower gel in. All smelling right but everything wrong at bedtime.

I went to a stone statue for getting undressed.

Come on, don't go all stiff… Danny! What's up, love?

All my clothes off and Meemaw lifted me up putted me in. Meemaw not getting in.

Sit down. Come on, sit down… Do you want Spiney?

Meemaw gived me Spiney I sitted down dived him in the bubbles. Meemaw crouched by the bath looking crowy like on a post sitting. She leaned over swooshed her hand in the water. Swooshed it.

Danny, there's another surprise tonight. Karen's brought you a special puffy air bed and a sleeping bag so you can do camping. You can do camping here in the bathroom tonight.

I looked at Meemaw's hand in the water. It was nonsense. Nonsense Meemaw talking because bathrooms aren't camping. Camping is tents.

Karen's going to share the big bed with me, Danny, and you and Spiney can have an adventure in here.

Up up from my tummy came a great and roary rage. It comed up but stopped right in my mouth like a stopped sicky that wouldn't come out.

I was all in the nude. In the nude in our bathroom Karen in the other room. There is a little lock a slidey metal lock but Meemaw hadn't slided it. Karen could come in. Karen could right now push the door to open.

I thinked of Karen's big hands her eyes on me nude. I didn't want Karen eyes on me nude.

I bited my teeth hard together hard. I taked the wet flannel I bited that too. I sucked the bluey soapy flannel. I pushed my teeth in squeak.

Danny, don't suck the flannel. The soap's not good for you. Give it to me.

Meemaw tried to take it I bited it like a dog. Like the piano dog. No like the tiny dog of the silky and skull. Real and real.

Grrrrrr!

I know it's a bit of a change, sweetheart. It's not for every day, just for sometimes. It'll be fun for you and Spiney to have an adventure, won't it?

Fatness of hot tears comed up and over. Only four tears comed.

Grrrrr!

Come on, love.

My teeth went to chattering. Meemaw taked it away the flannel. Chattering chattering and time to shut my eyes. Meemaw sighed.

Oh, poppet that bath's gone cold, hasn't it?

Meemaw lifted me out wrapped me in the yellow towel. We did pjs. One leg and the other leg.

CHAPTER SEVEN

I reached out. No Meemaw. Bump on my hand. Thonk of edge of the bath. Cold. I remembered in the bathroom.

The bathroom window pattern was broken orange of street lights outside. Still very night-time.

All the bathroom was dark but a little line of light at the bottom of the door. A glowy line and voices underneath.

Spiney was gone low down in the sleeping bag I finded him with my toes. I catched him with my feet lifted him up. Holded him in my two hands.

You're all right sunshine.

I wanted Meemaw. Wanted wanted. But not Karen. I wanted no Karen. I closed my eyes tried to make sleep come back because best to go back in sleep not this awake.

Meemaw had given me her woolly socks in case of cold feet. But my feet were gone to bare. Socks gone lost in the sleeping bag. I squiggled all around feeling. I finded them each one. Slided them on my feet. Big and soft Meemaw paws.

I closed my eyes and then was a noise. The noise was a uh. Then another noise. A moan. It was a moan of a Meemaw headache or starting a bad dream.

I getted out of the sleeping bag quick as I could. Pushing it down wriggling out.

If a Meemaw bad dream I must be there Danny to wake her up. If Meemaw is talking all out loud Spanish I must say its okay Meemaw you were doing Spanish. Meemaw rubs her face says god knows what that was about. Karen doesn't know of Spanish talking and wake her up. Meemaw doesn't want it Spanish talking. Not ever. I know. Danny knows.

The bathroom floor was slippy of Meemaw's woolly socks. I holded on the door handle. All my body shaked. My hand jumped. Another uh and uh uh uh. A great strangeness of sounds.

I thinked about the other side of the door. It was hard but I thinked it to be ready. Karen in our bed curled. A Karen dog gone in the bed with Meemaw. I didn't want to see.

The door handle fat too big in my hand and cold cold. I letted go. No noise of Spanish talking no noise of anything. I standed my hands dangled down.

My eyes had gone to seeing in the darkness. I looked on the floor. The sleeping bag was dark but wrinkles were shiny lighted orange. I thinked get in back in. Maybe Danny. I didn't know. I didn't like it the choosing.

Sudden came a terrible noise. Meemaw my Meemaw.

Ah ah AH!

I grabbed the door handle two hands. Twisted pushed hard. It swinged wide open and I falled onto the floor.

Karen was in the nude. I saw her Karen bot. In the nude is for at home just bath time with your Meemaw. Private parts Danny. I saw.

The bed went tumble. Duvet buffetty dancing.

Danny! Danny, sweetheart, it's okay.

I standed up. Karen pushed her head under the pillow. No Karen just a lump in the bed. Meemaw sitted up tucked the duvet round.

What's the matter, poppet, did you have a bad dream?

Meemaw crackly sharkly. Ruby flashes shooted off Meemaw into our flat. Wasps of the sharkle. Meemaw eyes all round awake shiny.

It's all right, sweetheart, you go and get back into bed and I'll come and tuck you in.

Meemaw's shoulders were bare of a hot day not bedtime. A stripe of Meemaw leg too. No baggy laggy joggers. She had taked them off.

I turned round quick and runned. Fast in the bathroom. But all went sideways in a long slide. A clonk loud and heavy. My head.

I heared it a mighty wail. It comed first then pain. It flashed. It flashed a loud flash and it was in my head. I putted my hand up. A

terrible thing of lump coming big and softness there. Very wrong.
I screamed out a fear.

Aaaaaaaaaah!

Meemaw swooped down. Meemaw a circle of arms all around.
On her lap.

Show me! Show me, Danny.

Meemaw's hand pulled my hand away.

Oh blimey! Oh blimey, you're all right sunshine. It's just a bump.

I scrunched my hands in Meemaw's hair. Crying loud.

Meemaw picked me up runned water in the basin. Cold cold
flannel on my head.

No no no!

I pushed her hand. The wet of the icy and the cold flannel. Cold
finger trickles in my pjs wet.

No!

It's what your head needs, Danny, come on!

I slided my nose on Meemaw in her neck. Snot on Meemaw.
I kicked.

Two more minutes. Just two more minutes, come on.

I heared my crying going quieter wobble. I heared my breathing
in Meemaw's neck. Feeled the warm and snotty of me snuzzled
in. Meemaw sitted on the edge of the bath. Rocked me.

Is he okay?

I peeped. Karen feet bare and then jeans going up.

He's okay he's just got a bit of an egg. He's done worse.

Meemaw taked the cold flannel off.

Ooh, yeah.

She putted it back. Karen did a cough.

*Best thing for him's probably sleep. Back to sleep, Professor,
yeah?*

I pulled tight in Meemaw's hair she grabbed my wrist of stop.
Yes.

Meemaw standed up again. Carrying me. I pinched in hard my
knees. Little monkey Dan.

I heared Meemaw's breathing in.

Honey, I think…

*Oh! Yeah, sure, of course. Of course. Take him in the bed. I'll
crash here.*

I heared the kiss of them. Karen kissing my Meemaw. I shutted my eyes hard. Inside was flash flash of yellow lights.

Meemaw still in the nude she putted me in the bed. There was my Meemaw the boobies long legs hairy fanny triangle of my Meemaw. She finded baggy laggy joggers holey t-shirt putted them on I watched her getting in.

It was warm in our bed warm but smell of the Karen perfume. All the smell on my pillow I turned my head but ow. I slided away from Meemaw. Far to the edge. I lied with the sore place pointed up.

CHAPTER EIGHT

When I opened my eyes there was smell of breakfast. Karen's back by our cooker. I sitted up looked. It was flat eggs cooking splittle pop.

Morning, Professor. Your mum's in the bathroom.

All the things of the night-time were coming back in my mind. Coming in pieces and then a tumble together. I touched my head on the bump. Big and enormous it felt. I needed to see in the mirror to know of it. I getted out of bed.

Meemaw came rubbing her hair with the yellow towel.

Morning, poppet. How are you feeling?

I didn't say anything of words just hurried into the bathroom.

In the bathroom was no puffy air bed and sleeping bag they were disappeared like just in a story. It was the floor like usual.

In the mirror I was normal Danny too. But not when I lifted up my hair. It was a purple lump smooth. It was the bony plate of pachycephalosaurus but slipped sideways on my head. I pressed with my one finger and it hurted.

Danny, breakfast's ready!

I looked at mirror Danny told him in mind words soon she will go.

On the table three flat eggs one two three all very completely wrong. Yellow very bright means slimy over like a eyeball of egg. I don't have it ever.

Toast cutted diagonal that makes triangles. Triangles is sandwiches and four squares is toast. Four squares like windows is toast.

I sitted down on the chair sideways legs not under the table not properly Danny. I holded the chair looked at wrong flat egg and wrong toast.

Karen was big mouth crunch and chewing.

So what's the plan for today?

Chew chew.

How about the park?

That was not take in turns. That was ask and answer all yourself. She looked at Meemaw nostrils big. Chew chew.

I looked at Meemaw. She was hiding her colour again. She cutted a small small piece of toast.

I think it might be a good idea for Danny to have a quiet day just to make sure that head's okay.

Karen did a gulp of tea. Yucky big swallow noise.

How about I go back to my flat and get my laptop and we could watch a film?

I keeped my eyes stuck to Meemaw. Not on her face just her arm her elbow. I sended in mind words of secret. Make her go away make her go away. Meemaw didn't say words. She eated one bite of white part egg.

I've got loads of stuff he might like. Some Disney or something?

She pointed at my egg.

What's wrong with that, Professor?

Thump came in me. I sitted very still for safe.

Oh, he just usually has his egg flipped over.

He what?

He likes his egg turned over in the pan.

Karen had her last bit of toast spiked on her fork. She wiped all around getting eggy yellow and she eated it. She putted her fork and knife together.

Then Karen spiked me. Spiked with her eyes. Hard.

You don't pander to that sort of thing, do you? You're making a rod for your own back.

Well, I don't see it that way, K. We all have things we don't like, don't we?

Yeah, but there's nothing wrong with that egg. It's good food. Eat up, Professor!

Quick sudden Meemaw sended her knife and fork like a pterosaur swoop of beak open. She lifted it away the egg.

I think he's a bit fragile still from that bump on the head. I'll have the egg and you eat your toast, Danny.

Inside me thump wobble thump wobble. I picked up the toast nibbled the edge to mend it to a square.

You're soft-hearted, Nat.

I thought you liked that.

Oh, I'm not complaining.

Karen did a gulp of tea looked at the big window. She putted her foot up on the seat of Meemaw's chair. Leg foot leg it went. She closed one eye in a wink at Meemaw.

I'm not complaining at all.

I suddenly didn't know where Spiney was. Spiney wasn't with me! I hadn't known it and now all inside was panic!

I getted up runned to the bathroom because maybe he had not come in the night. In the flash bump of the head bang I had left behind Spiney. Abandoned.

What's up, love?

Spiney.

Is he not still in bed?

SPINEY!

Stay calm, love. We'll find him.

I was at the bathroom door then my foot one part in and a shout came loud. Shout of a park man to his dog.

Hey!

I stopped. Thump whoosh wooble thump whoosh wobble of inside me. Faster faster. I heared all the feelings very loud.

Professor, you sit down and eat your toast like a good boy. You can't just leave the table in the middle of a meal.

Thump whoosh wobble thump whoosh wobble. I thinked she might come. I closed my eyes. Tears two came out of my shutted eyes. But no noise. She might come.

But Meemaw. Meemaw swooped picked me up.

Come on, we'll find him.

I heared the bathroom door be shut. She putted me down.

Danny Danny Danny.

Meemaw words in my ear very close.

We're going to find Spiney now, Danny. We're going to find him.

I nodded. Opened my eyes. My eyes wouldn't look well. All

wet in the room because of crying. But Meemaw looking Meemaw looking.

Ta-da!

Meemaw lifted up the hands towel where on top of the toilet and Spiney my Spiney underneath! I holded him tight. Tight on my body. His sail on me on me safe and real. Crying came with noise.

Meemaw lifted me and Spiney on her lap.

It's okay, love. You've found him now. You've found him.

I had. Meemaw wiped my face of a foldy piece of toilet roll. Holded it at my nose.

Blow!

I did.

Come on, sweetheart. Let's go back in the other room.

No, Meemaw! Stay.

I tighted my legs round Meemaw.

We can't sit in here, love. It's rude when we've got a guest.

Meemaw tried putting me down but I wouldn't.

Come on then.

Meemaw carried me and we went to the other room.

Karen had her feet on Meemaw's chair. She looked at us. Me and Meemaw together.

Oh, was it that thing he was panicking about? I trod on it in the night. Scared the shit out of me!

Meemaw's voice was gently gently.

You know, that's a lovely offer about the laptop, K. Can we maybe do it next Sunday though? I think Danny's a bit washed out and I might just put him back to bed for a few hours.

Karen getted straight up quick.

Yeah of course, of course, yeah, whatever.

She went and getted her trainers from by the door. She pulled the laces very tight. I saw the one that getted the Coke on it. It was all brown now not softy. Rough and not a pair of the other one. A trainer gone damaged in a war.

Meemaw putted me down. She went by Karen. She touched her shoulder Karen standed up quick.

K, I...

What?

Well, I just…

Karen taked her hoody from the Meemaw peg. She getted the sleeping bag and puffy mattress rolled up in the corner of our room.

Karen slippy snicked the lock to open but her arms all full and difficult. The door went back to shut. Meemaw did it. Holded it open. She touched Karen's arm more and more.

See you soon, sweetheart, yeah?

Karen went sideways out the door like being a crab.

See ya.

Meemaw closed the door.

Meemaw standed still by the closed door. Closed eyes. Meemaw was white first then each moment sinked greyer greyer. Eyes stayed closed. Still as still. A Meemaw statue.

Meemaw!

I runned across the room putted my face in the Meemaw tummy breathed in rightness and smell. I holded tight as tight. Her arms moved. Meemaw stroking my hair. Inside the Meemaw tummy was gurgle of eggs getting digested.

Meemaw can we have a pj day?

Meemaw didn't say. Long time just stroke and stroke.

Meemaw?

Danny, I'm already up. Come on, let's sort the bed out.

When the bed was folded away Meemaw went to still again. Meemaw's hand on the back of the sofa lying. She rubbed the sofa like it was a feeling thing. She closed her eyes again. Two of silent tears came out went fast down her face.

What's the matter Meemaw?

Oh it's nothing, Danny. I'm just being a fool.

Meemaw you're not being a fool. You are being the cleverest Meemaw in the world.

Meemaw did a smile even though two more tears Meemaw wiped with fingers.

Righty-ho then. Let's get you dressed.

It was a careful thing to get my t-shirt on my bumped head. Meemaw stretched the neck wide as a mouth of giganotosaurus.

Gently does it.

I stretchled out my arms.

Now, you need to do something quiet, love. What's it to be? More drawing?

Please Meemaw can I have the Play-Doh please?

Very often times it is no to Play-Doh because it is a potential hazard with the carpet tiles remember Danny. I do remember.

I remember of this was the new flat and I dropped a pinky pink bit standed on it squooge. Meemaw lied a long time on the floor picky picking with a pin. But you can sometimes see of it when it's sunny on the floor. Today Meemaw looked at the floor did a sigh.

What the hell. I don't suppose we'll get the deposit back anyway.

What the hell meaned yes. Meemaw getted the Play-Doh down from the high up cupboard.

I maked a multi-colour nest for Spiney pink and orange. I maked him lots of eggs for his babies to come. Meemaw curled all up in the chair reading. Still grey but whiter.

I tried to make a tiny one of Spiney to have hatched out of a egg. I tried but always too strange and lumpy. Head too big not four of legs.

So I maked Spiney poos. Sausages of Spiney poos. I splatted them on the table with my flat hand. Good. Soft. Warm. I maked them all again. Splatted again.

All the time was drippy tap and Meemaw pages turning. Sometimes I said words to Spiney. I rubbed a splatted poo. On the table shiny smooth. I maked a noise of rubbing. It was better in our flat then.

Sudden a buzz of Meemaw's phone. Another buzz another one. Meemaw putted down her book picked up the phone. Meemaw reading messages all pink pouring in her.

Meemaw pinker pinker laughing. Meemaw's finger dancing of replies. Karen was in Meemaw's phone making pink and laughing.

I rolled again. Splatted each and every poo. Hard smack. Hard.

Go gently, Danny.

Not looking up. Not looking at Danny just shining phone of Karen inside.

I rolled them up again the poos. Meemaw more and more of laughs. I getted the biggest poo throwed it down on the floor jumped off my chair. Stamped on it. Stamped poo down flat on the hairy carpet tile.

Danny!

Meemaw putted her phone down. She came standed in front of me all the light of the window gone. Shadow Meemaw.

What are you doing?

I went fast sideways getted another poo from the table stamped it down.

That's enough!

She reaching out I pushed Meemaw's hands hard. A great roar the roar of the allosaur bursted out.

RAAAAAAAAAAAAAR!

All up up inside of me was storms was fury was fire bombs going boom in my mouth. All coming out was scream to burn of Meemaw. All out of me was monsters slam slam feet of great destruction. Of cracks and broken. All out was smash of windows crack and crack of shelf and bones of a man of a great man a monster. Bones of a great huge beast of capture. All of me was clouds underneaths when they come by the hill on the bus in the big sky. All the light to yellow grey power. The power of it. The crack crack of it. That. I Danny to rip the hill with my teeth. Bite out the chalky insides. Spit spit it down. All raining of white rain far in the sea. That that.

Then a surprise of words falling out.

I hate that bloody Karen! I hate that bloody Karen! She is a horrible horrible poo! She is not to come here to this flat and sleep in the bed and make a disgusting flat egg!

I picked up all every bit of Play-Doh throwed it down on the floor. Rain of poos.

She is not to come here to this flat! I forbid it!

I started round the floor stamp stamp all the poos squashed. But Meemaw moved swift and strong. Meemaw lifted me up round my middle. I kick kicked my legs.

No! No! No!

Twisty all my t-shirt.

RAAAAAAR! No! Na... Meem...

Pushing in Meemaw's neck. Meemaw taked me in the bathroom putted me down closed the door with her back. Standed there.

I runned hard at Meemaw push pushed fists in her squashy soft.

I hate you Meemaw! I hate you! I hate you!

Then crying crying. I hated all the all of it. My words the day. All all of it.

Meemaw holded my wrists pushed. I crumpled down on the floor kicking thud thud on the black side of the bath. Meemaw crouched down catched my feet holded them hard.

You can stop now. You can stop now. You can stop now.

I feeled the warm the strong of the Meemaw hands on my feet. I stopped kicking.

Meemaw's face twisted very sad and crying. Crying crying me too. I covered my face. A long time I was covered my face and crying there. Meemaw sitted beside me. Meemaw cried a long time too.

CHAPTER NINE

At the library was thickness of quiet.

I have to get some stuff done on the computer, Danny.

I sitted at the shiny red top table. A big splash of silver sunshine on it.

I looked out the window. The daffodils gone to dry curly brown. But red tulips had comed. Cups. Shiny as Play-Doh rubbed smooth don't think about that Danny.

A man came picking up litter. A grabby thing claw of a velociraptor for little sharp man. Orange coat dirty of black by the cuff his pole his claw sticking out.

Orange man picked up a packet Monster Munch. I was hungry of them. I had them on one day Meemaw and me at the agent. Waiting quietly to be good. Signing of Meemaw her name and her name. Sticky zing of Monster Munch so good.

No Jane at the library today but a library man. Man as tall as a giant his head by the buzzy light. Pushing a trolley close by me. He stopped.

Hello.

I said hello mind words today. Today a quiet day.

Meemaw leaning looking in the computer. Tappy type very fast. Clicking clicking. Meemaw doing the forms the applications. Obligations.

Outside man went away with his rubbish wheely and broom. I thinked again of Monster Munch. Melty dust and crunch.

I sended a wish of Meemaw to be finished to be all done Danny let's go. I wanted the park. Run run fast. Go in the sand with Spiney.

A quiet day but no room in my head for reading words. No

room for words. My legs had a ache. I standed up. Meemaw still tappy type clicking. Click click fingers fast. Rattle the keyboard.

All around books. I didn't want them today.

In a book of me and Meemaw it would be lots of stories. Chapter stories like Christmas which is also Meemaw's birthday. Like the day we went to Mick who is my grandad. The day of coming to the now flat from the old flat with the zippy laundry bags. The day Meemaw throwed a pancake on our ceiling. All stories I would put in a book. One of Karen just one then the end of it. Karen not in any more. Not any more.

I went to Meemaw standed close. Meemaw still click tut on the computer. It was boxes and next. Meemaw knowed in my head what I was wanting.

Almost done, Danny. I just have to…

Click again. I sitted on the floor by the Meemaw feet. Meemaw's velvety coat hanging down from the body of Meemaw. Curtains.

I maked Spiney put his head in the pocket. He telled me very dark Danny very dark. Then I did taking things out. Meemaw's tobacco. A tissue a little bit of crusty snot yellow on it. I looked close. Keys for dangle jingle. Meemaw's phone.

I holded Meemaw's phone tried to unlock it. From up above Meemaw's voice.

I've changed the code, Danny, so good luck with that.

I tried numbers numbers sometimes it said wait thirty seconds try again. It counted then backwards to blast off. I watched it the phone keeping me out.

Right. Come on then. Time to go.

Still no words today. A quiet day.

***

It was cold in the park. The sun gone. Bubble clouds coming. Grey dark on their underneaths.

Just a quick play, Dan, it's going to tip it down!

I runned down the slope letted my arms fly back. Thonka thonka my feet on the grass. No one else.

No one in the park I jumped in the sandpit. Sand was dotty all over of rain in last night. I maked seventeen footprints.

I finded all bits of twig and three lolly sticks. Maked a fort for Spiney. A fort from a wild west. A cowboy thing of dinosaurs rised up from the ground. Spiney to be sheriff and a star badge on him.

Then big rain drops falled down plonk plonk. Down from the grey underneaths of the clouds. I liked it tonk on my head one and the next one. The air huff of wind.

Meemaw came. She holded out my coat. I tried to not see Meemaw.

Danny! Come on! Coat!

I letted her. Even the hood. Meemaw tighted the hood. Slidy hood things are fiddly but hood is not good floppy. Horrible floppy on my cheeks. I can't see and it buffs on me. So we tight it up.

On the way home was Aldi. It was bread beans apples.

Meemaw can it be Monster Munch or like Monster Munch?
Not today.

She letted me choose biscuits. I finded ones stuck-on yellow.

Outside because of I had been patient I had just one. I eated it sideways. Creamy inside. Scrape scraped with my teeth it was good.

A window envelope was on the mat Meemaw putted it behind the kettle with the other ones. Then Meemaw maked me beans on toast. She had just toast so more beans for me tomorrow.

Meemaw eated her toast one two three four squares like we have. Like is best. She opened the window envelopes. Meemaw was yellow brown green and bright of it.

I ate all my beans except the last one for Spiney. All my toast even crusts.

Meemaw can I have a apple?

Meemaw did a small smile even in the bad colours.

Cut up?

I did a nod of yes.

Meemaw cutted up the apple taked out all the corey bits not speaking. Because of not okay. Not okay and yellow brown green.

Meemaw putted apple on a little plate. All slices maked into a fan. I love it the fan.

There you go, sunshine.

Stroke on my hair.

Meemaw went to her coat on the Meemaw peg. She went in the pocket scrabbling. She went in the other pocket. She went in the bag taked everything out. I was crunch crunch of slicey apple. Meemaw looked at me.

Danny, did you take my tobacco out of my pocket?

No Meemaw.

Sweety juice crunch crunch.

Danny, you were in my pockets in the library, weren't you?

I feeled it the slidey feeling of things falled over. I knowed I had lost Meemaw's tobacco. Meemaw knowed it too. Meemaw turned and did whispery swears at the wall.

I didn't lose it of purpose Meemaw.

I know.

I putted my plates in the sink sitted down with my stegosaur comic to be a good quiet boy. My comic nearly done. One more disaster comes a river washes one stegosaur away. A baby lost. Then it is the end.

Meemaw maked a cup of tea sitted by me on her phone. She did a long message. I knowed it was talking to Karen. At the top it said her.

Meemaw putted her phone down plonk on the table then. Meemaw maked another straightaway cup of tea.

Meemaw can I have another stuck-on biscuit?

Meemaw gived it but no words.

It was the end in my comic. A brilliant ending.

Done!

Can I look?

I telled Meemaw all the story of it and the brilliant ending.

Then Meemaw he is bited. Bited here see? A radioactive ant. He is come to Super Stegosaur to fly. And a costume see Meemaw?

Wow!

But the baby one is drowned dead Meemaw. This is a great sadness.

Meemaw's eyes all the time slided sideways on her phone. Meemaw's phone was lied still next to the window envelopes. Meemaw's eyes sliding on it again again.

Sudden Meemaw maked me jump.

Bloody hell! Let's just go back!

What?

Let's go back to the library and see if someone handed it in.

We never went to the library again again. Not on one day two times. It was confusion and wrong.

Outside was raining swish swish swish of cars and home now.
No.

Meemaw did a sigh.

You can splash, Dan.

I looked at Meemaw her hair hanged down. She was doing a gentle look at me to make me change to yes. To spell me.

You can splash every puddle if you want. On the way back, once I've got my tobacco, we can go twice round the block and you can get as wet as you want.

Straight fast it came out of me.

Yes!

Meemaw had spelled it well.

My welly boots are gone too small and squeezy of toes but I didn't say of it. Meemaw pushed in my feet. Squeeze squeeze. But I liked it then.

Meemaw doesn't have welly boots. No hood even on her velvety coat.

We went outside. The rain went hard on my eyes. I closed them. Meemaw leaded me along. All was swish sounds. Coldness in the air.

Danny! Open your eyes, love, and look at this!

I looked. A mighty puddle all shiver and lights. Upside down buildings. The traffic lights floated in.

Wow! Stay back, Danny, stay back! Blimey, look at that!

Meemaw's bad colours all gone. Meemaw filled of bright green sweeties colour. Of sunshine lime cordial we had one day very strong.

All spikles of wet hair was Meemaw. Shiny eyes. Shine and shine.

A car came speedy fast in the puddle. Up, up! It maked a wave on us. Water dripping down.

Woo! Jesus Christ!

Meemaw was dancey back away holding my hand. Meemaw's jeans all wet. The bottom of her coat wet. Meemaw laughing.

Blimey oh riley, Dan, it's a tsunami!

We runned across hands tight together and it was still red man. Then walk and walk. Rain drippy on.

The library door was shut. Meemaw pulled but stuck shut.

Oh Christ, you're kidding me!

Meemaw pulled again.

I went by the tulips. All the red tulips runned of silver on them. The drainpipes runned water into the square drains of holes. I putted my welly foot under.

You're bloody kidding me!

Meemaw standed her head on the door. Whoosh and whoosh water over my foot. My foot squeezysqueezed inside red welly boot.

It's bloody closed, Dan!

Inside the library was yellow. I standed in the muddy of the flowers putted my nose on the window wetness. The glass all wetness and cold. The books on the shelves inside but no people. Warmness quiet no people.

Then suddenly a surprise my tummy leaped of it! Jane! Jane came walked by the books a piece of paper in her hand looking down.

I pressed my nose on the window cold. Inside was warm. Inside was Jane.

Oh well that's that then. Come on, Danny.

I standed still watched Jane in the library. Best like a YouTube. A good one.

Jane!

Dan, come on! They're closed. Come on.

Jane walking in the library I putted my hand on the window for a spell. Jane looked up in my eyes. I blinked away it the suddenness of it. But I was glad. Jane waved. Pointed sideways. Meemaw taked my hand.

Come on, I think…

Jane on the other side of the door. Behind the rumpled glass. Rattle of a key rattle and there was Jane in the dry warm.

Hello! Hello, Danny! Is everything all right? We just closed at four, I'm afraid.

Jane all folded on her forehead.

It's very kind of you to open the door. I'm sorry to bother you, it's just we were in earlier and I think I might have dropped my tobacco.

Jane smiled.

Michael found some tobacco under the computer table and I did wonder if it was yours.

Jane holded the door wider open.

I can't really let you in to the library proper, but if you just wait here a minute, I'll get it.

We waited in the corridor of spinny things of leaflets. I spinned it spinned it squeee squeee.

Careful with that, Dan!

I taked one leaflet of a castle Meemaw watching.

Just one, Danny, okay?

It said Arundel Castle a castle of a moat and dragons maybe. Meemaw taked a leaflet too. She opened it out like a paper door. Reading fast fast. Ticker ticker eyes. Blue on the front. Welfare Rights Advice.

Jane came back.

Here you go!

Meemaw putted her tobacco in her pocket and the foldy leaflet.

I'm so grateful. Thank you.

Jane putted her hands in her trousers pockets taked them out again.

No problem. How are you, Danny? What happened to your head?

My hood pushed up my hair. The lump was there I had forgetted. Lump to be seen. I touched with my one finger. Not so hurty.

I banged it on the bath.

Ouch! Have you got far to go in the rain? It looks torrential!

Meemaw taked my hand. Arundel Castle in the other one.

Not far really and he likes the puddles. Don't you, Dan?

I didn't say of it. I standed close of Jane. The dry smell and good. Quietness of Jane.

Come on, love.

Bye, Danny. See you soon.

Then we went. Jane rumpled behind the glass. Her red jumper shape locking the door. Gone. I scrunchled up Arundel Castle.

Give me that, Dan, if you're just going to destroy it.

No!

Please yourself.

We stopped at the bus stop even though not for our bus. Under the roof for a shelter. Meemaw maked a rolly.

Spiney drinked fourteen drops of runny water of the glass. Meemaw getted out her phone did a sigh looked out the window too. Her smoke all round her. At the end she squish squashed her rolly. Throwed it in the bin.

Come on then. Home.

We went home the special way. Little roads. Meemaw letted me walk in the rivers. Rivers of the edge with things swooshing by. Crisp packet green and a dummy of a baby.

Water leaped icy icy cold in my welly. Inside gone wet and cold. It hurted then. I cried didn't say.

What is it? What's the matter?

Long walk on and on.

What's the matter, Danny? If you don't tell me I can't know. I don't know why you're crying, Danny.

***

At home I was still crying of it. Meemaw taked off my wellies. Little toe was gone shiny pinkle all on its side. White skin like a teeny worm pulled off it.

Ooh, was that hurting?

Meemaw holded my foot in her warm Meemaw hand.

You should have said, you silly sausage.

My foot in the warm Meemaw hand. She cutted sticky plaster wrapped it on littlest toe.

Your boots have got too small. That's all that growing you're doing.

I didn't say of words but looked at Meemaw for her colour not finding it.

It's okay, love, it's not a wrong thing. We'll get you a new pair next month.

Meemaw went to put the plaster away. I went in my jumper.

We're having a big potato for tea, have a look!

I putted one eye out. Meemaw was holding a fat stoney potato.
It's for sharing, okay?
Is there cheese?
A mouse bite and you can have it.

I keeped my one eye out spied at Meemaw doing cooking. She looked at her phone scrubbled the potato with green cloth very fast. Wiped her hands on her jeans looked at her phone. Stagged stagged the potato five times of the very pointy knife. Looked at her phone.

Can I go on your phone?
You may as well.

Meemaw did the numbers for unlock.

In my jumper on YouTube I finded *Tale of a Tooth* again. Meemaw called in.

Blimey, that bloke's got a great voice, who is he?

I didn't say. Busy. All the words and great feet of the dinosaurs. Meemaw came close close her face just outside my jumper. Eye peeping in the little holes.

Who's your friend, Danny?
Walter Kronkite.
Cool.

Meemaw still standed there.

Will you be a palaeontologist one day?

I am one. I'm William Buckland and you can be one of the other clever men.

Meemaw laughed. Meemaw laughed on on.

When *Tale of a Tooth* was over our flat was the round smell of the potato cooked. A good smell. Meemaw cutted it open. All its hotness came out.

Mind the steam.

She putted a big splat of marg inside.

Meemaw's half was all the black dots of pepper. Mine was better of shiny yellow cheese. Soft melty.

Go on, have the skin too, it's the best bit.

I leaved it on my plate. Meemaw eated it. Meemaw looked at her phone pushed it across the table. She was gone to grey.

CHAPTER TEN

Today after breakfast and bed put away I was looking out the window. A man came to the steps. A Amazon man. He has come before the Amazon man.

Amazon man bringed a cardboard thing for upstairs man to have. Upstairs man is all the time at work so we look after it for him and mustn't open it Danny not ours.

Meemaw was cleaning the toilet. It was the buzz buzz smell of bleach. Don't touch it can hurt your skin. He brrrringed the bell.

Meemaw! A Amazon man!

Meemaw put her head out the bathroom door.

What?

It's a Amazon man at the door.

She pulled off yellow gloves wiped her hands on her jeans. Meemaw opened our door then the other door. I peeped by the crack.

Yeah, sure, no problem.

But fast talking of go away and leave me alone. She scribbled on a little screen.

Cheers!

The man was gallopy away down the steps quick.

Meemaw putted the cardboard thing on the floor by the door.

This isn't for us, Danny. So no touching, remember?

I didn't say. Meemaw went to hurry back in the bathroom. I looked at it the Amazon thing very flat.

Meemaw?

Yes.

Will I have a allosaur for my birthday?

We'll see.

You can get them on Amazon.

Danny, I told you not to go on Amazon!

I went to by the bathroom door. Meemaw went flush of the toilet all bubbles in it.

I 'spose you see adverts… You're a liability now you can read.

It's £12.99 I want it.

I said we'll see, Danny.

Meemaw pulling off the yellow rubbery gloves again. One day I cutted with the scissors and feeled very good. All the fingers falled down in the bath. Meemaw shouted.

The trouble is I don't have the right sort of bank card to order things on the internet, love. We'll have to look for one in the shops.

Meemaw you get the other card the card for on the internet.

It's not up to me, Danny, that's the bank's decision.

The bank is a app not decisions. Meemaw telling nonsense today.

We can see what they have in the toy shop.

I looked at Meemaw for serious and I mean it.

That will be a actual disaster Meemaw no allosaur.

Danny, it's months until your birthday. Let's just see okay?

Meemaw putted away the plates of breakfast time.

Today's a busy day, Dan, I want to see if we can get some of this council tax nightmare sorted out.

Is it a appointment?

It is. But it shouldn't take long. There might be time for the park after.

Not might be. Park today.

Meemaw did a sigh of long air. She was grey not too dark. Swirly.

I think we'd better put another bit of plaster on that toe, love.

I went in my jumper while Meemaw did it.

Keep still, Danny!

I didn't. I maked my foot squirmy. Meemaw holded tight in her warm hand. Nice and hold on. But she letted go again.

Shoes on then.

I did my shoes. Velcros pressing.

Damn it!

Meemaw speaked of dropping something but nothing had dropped. Meemaw looking at her phone.

I haven't charged my phone. Oh, what the hell! Let's just leave it. It's not like I'm in demand.

She plugged the phone in by the kettle very hard. She was pushing the plug and twiddle the little charger into the phone bot. Angry hands.

Meemaw's head hanged down. In her grey came blue too. Meemaw came to a sea creature. Meemaw whale standed in our kitchen. She rocked a very small rocking. Whale in the sea. I watched her a waiting time. It was a strangeness.

We put our coats on and went out. Upstairs man's cardboard thing stayed by my wellies. Not a allosaur in it too flat.

Meemaw's coat has a little line of gritty on now. Gritty on the velvety of getting very wet then to dry. On the bus I sitted close and rubbed it. All the gritty rumpled away. Soft again and better.

At Asda a lady getted on her bot big it falled over the tippy seat. I looked looked. She had a walky stick orange flowers on it and a wheely trolley four wheels. She maked a puff puff noise and smiling.

Hello darling!

A man his little girl in a buggy pink pink. On her head a butterfly. She had a dummy and bottle for a baby. Purple drink in. The man was thin nearly see-through white skin. He putted his hand in the front of his shiny joggers. Rude to touch your private parts in public.

The bus did whizz away quick at the stops. A wobbly old man nearly falled on Meemaw. He smelled of medicine and minty. By the big roundabout I standed up.

We're not getting off here today. A few more stops. Sit down.

I sitted down again. Meemaw had hided her colour all completely. Meemaw was gone far away and not for talking to.

We went to a new place. Five stops more and then get off. It was a new street I never was in. Tall trees leafy shushing on the sky. We walked along. I did jump the lines of mossy green and dark. I liked it that street.

I think this is it…

Meemaw stopped. We went up steps on a big building maked of bricks. Reddy orange and lots of corners on it. Tall.

The door was dark green and little windows maked of colour glass. One broken a piece of wood on. Shiny silver tape stucking it in.

Meemaw opened it and inside was a floor black and white diamonds. This way that way to the edges. I liked it. It captured my eyes very fast. It maked its own noise come in me.

Zingazingazingazingazinga!

Shh, Danny love.

A white door then a room of blue carpet tiles of hairy like home. People on orange seats all around the edge like at the doctor's for waiting.

The wall was big faces of people painted on. People all different coloured of skins. Scary faces of too much teeth. But a rainbow over them and rabbits in the corners of brown and green eyes. Three for each corner.

I have to ask in there, Danny.

Meemaw went by a open door. A desk man just inside. I went to the corner. I touched the rabbits one two three by a old lady. Not too close Danny. But they were good and of a spell. The old lady didn't look at me. Just the one two three rabbits looked of their green eyes.

There was a box filled up of toys. By the box on the floor was a baby. Her legs stucking out and sitting up. Black girl baby with hair shiny shiny banging a Duplo man of a hammer. Not very right to bang him.

Her mummy was there with the buggy and on her phone. A baby is too little for excuse me please. I leaned past taked a lion panda some bricks for a wall. I maked a square of wall and putted them in. Safe in. They telled thank you Danny.

The baby grabbed the edge of my jumper all suddenly. I moved away. It pinged out of her hand. Not mean grabbing. Just a baby.

I looked up and the desk man was in the doorway with Meemaw.

I'm so sorry you didn't get the message. I hope you didn't have far to come?

It's okay. We'll come back next week then.

Yes, yes I'm sure Chris'll be back then.

Meemaw was bluer bluer in her grey.

We do tea in the other room for 50p. And I don't know if you know about the toy library?

Meemaw shaked her head.

You can sign up if you've got proof of address.

Well, yeah, I brought the council tax bill…

That's ideal. Have a word with Elaine.

Meemaw taked me in the next room. I leaved the animals in their safe square I had maked.

In next room were shelves lots lots toys on them like Toys R Us. That was a bad day of Toys R Us. It was the badness of lights. I did kicking there and breaked a thing.

Noooo!

I standed still. Meemaw holded my hand tight did a squeeze.

Just be calm, Danny. I'll ask how it works.

I did trying to be calm and thinking of Toys R Us went away. It was better this place. It had a quiet smell of boxes and Play-Doh. No lights. Quiet not lots people and music.

A big lady sitted by a small table square. She had a big huge mug of tea. Ginger nut biscuits in a packet peeled open. She holded one out for me.

Biccy?

I taked it quick and she smiled. The lady had dark space between her two teeths. Very big round boobies. Curly hair of metal pipes colour.

Were you wanting to join?

It is yum a ginger nut. Hard and good for biting.

Yes, well, I think so. How does it work?

I just need proof of address and I'll get you registered. Then you can borrow two items for three weeks at a time.

Meemaw writed on a form. The lady did writing on a card. I saw it Meemaw's name all upside down.

Here we are then! Want to have a look? Danny, is it?

It was Meredith Centre Toy Library. A picture of a train and a Lego brick. Too big Lego brick. Big as a train. Meemaw taked it back and putted it away in her bag for safe. Cards must always be safe. People can steal you from your cards.

Well, that's you all official now! Would you like to borrow something today?

I didn't say. I didn't know of it all.

What sort of toys do you like, Danny?

Dinosaurs.

Ah, now we've got a multi-pack of dinosaurs somewhere. It has a blow-up landscape for them with a volcano, I think.

She standed up. A standing up mountain. I heared her legs swoosh swoosh of walking.

It's down here if you want to come and look.

Meemaw nodded at me.

Go on, Dan, I'm right here. Go with Elaine.

I went. It was rows of high up shelves. It was a toy forest.

Elaine reached high high getted a plastic packet down. I could see dinosaurs in it! I jumped jumped a noise came out of very exciting.

Weeeeeeeeeeeee!

I touched the packet gently tried not to grab no grabbing Danny. No grabbing.

Hang on the bell, Nelly, we don't want to break this zip! Let me get it open.

I letted go. Elaine opened it up taked out the dinosaurs one and the next one. She standed them along the shelf looking at me.

T-Rex Triceratops Deinonychus Apatosaurus.

Ooh, you know your stuff, eh? There used to be more but they've wandered off over the years.

I looked at them the not gone dinosaurs. I touched. Apatosaurus of a long lovely head. Beany hard. All all of them good. Triceratops horns sharp on my finger.

Elaine pulled a big folded thing from out the packet holded up it like when we do the bed sheets. Big.

The landscape has trees, look! And a volcano. One of the trees leaks a bit so it deflates, but the rest is still good, I think. Shall I show you?

Meemaw came between the shelves.

Danny, there's a bus in five minutes. We'd better get going, love.

No!

I liked it here and Elaine and the dinosaurs. I grabbed them all the dinosaurs. I holded them in my two arms close my body.

No cause for alarm, Danny! You can borrow them today. Take them home and bring them back to me another day, yes?

It's a library, Dan. Like for books, but it's toys. We can borrow them.

No words were coming. Elaine holded out their dinosaur bag. She holded it open.

Come on, let's pop them into the pouch to keep them safe on the journey, yes?

I letted her put them in. But all the time I holded the corner of the packet tight. Tight tight for not losing.

Right, bus! Come on, love. Thanks, Elaine. I think you've made his day.

Outside the day was gone a dream. Tiny bubbles were in the air the trees very dancing inside of me full up. So happy of the dinosaurs. Their actual land in the packet. I had. We were taking them home.

I jumped jumped all to the bus stop. We waited. Meemaw did a half of a smile on one side.

Well there ya go, there's always little miracles, Dan. Little miracles.

***

When we getted home I sitted down straight away still even in my shoes unzipped the dinosaurs. Out they came. I looked in their faces. Each and each was a goody dinosaur.

Their land four square flatness all covered in plastic. Smelled very good. Open open open of the land. I lied on it. It smelled all good. There were floppy bits. Trees a volcano a rock each one attached in. They had mouth bits like of my arm bands for blowing up to fat.

Meemaw help me help me!

I knowed it would be hard to blow. And fiddly the stoppy bits.

Meemaw!

Meemaw didn't say. I looked over and she was pinked. Pinked and holding her phone. Meemaw's fingers fast shaky doing a message. It meant Karen. All in me came cold sliding. And a go away feeling.

I looked back at the new dinosaurs. Good new dinosaurs. But I fetched Spiney.

Spiney said first a battle with the T-Rex. T-Rex a mighty carnivore Spiney not so but he winned. Spiney was the leader then of them all.

They standed in a line to go on the voyage of discovery through the land. But not good with everything flat. I looked at Meemaw. Laughing little laughs in her phone very pink.

MEEMAW! HELP ME!

She looked sudden like Danny was a surprise.

Do you need a hand with that?

It taked long of Meemaw lied down flat on the floor. Huff puff into the trees the rock the volcano. I sitted on Meemaw's back.

Huff puff I'll blow your house down!

Danny, that really isn't helping...

She wriggled all about. I getted off.

At the last all the things were bouncy fat. Bouncy fat.

The dinosaurs hided behind and jumped off. They loved and loved it. A world I never had before. After in a little while leaky tree went bendy over. Not so good. I holded it up but it falled to floppy.

Are you listening, Danny? I said Karen's coming over later.

I didn't say anything of Karen. I maked Spiney do a hard jump. Jump bang boing on the squashy rock.

Go Spiney!

Bang on the ground landed. Meemaw sitted down near.

Look, Danny, I know it's hard. It's tricky in such a small flat. She's not going to stay over though. It's just for a little while after tea to watch a film or something.

Stamp stamp stamp Spiney across the world.

Danny, can you hear me?

Down lied the apatosaurus. T-Rex and Spiney devoured him.

Okay, well I'll take that as a yes. I'm having a bath.

Meemaw went in the bath without me. Meemaw singed songs on YouTube very annoying loud.

I dragged dinosaur land to by our door. I maked a line all of dinosaurs in the front of it. Spiney Apato Deiny Tricytop Rex.

Behind them was the volcano. Boily hot orange on its sides. Orange called lava. Super hot from the earth's core.

I had maked it. Maked it a trap of Karen. Her horrible foot to go in. Lava all on her trainer and inside hurting. Aaaargh! Go back away down our steps. Lava droppy dripping. Hop hop away down the road Karen. Not come back.

Meemaw pulled the plug I heared water google oogle off down the pipe outside.

Beans and bready sausage for tea!

It is my best tea. Meemaw doing my best tea but for badness reasons of Karen coming later. I knowed it. Still it is very yum.

I showed Apato how Meemaw maked bready sausage in the bowl. Scrunch-up crust a slimey egg and grater cheese from a new piece Meemaw buyed. I picked it up the big bit of cheese. Bited in.

Oi, Danny! For goodness' sake!

Meemaw taked it away in the fridge slam. Fatness of cheese in my mouth. Yum and yum.

The sausages sizzly in the frying pan but Meemaw wasn't singing the song of it today. Meemaw was pink of Karen coming and all gone away in her head.

I eated four sausages Meemaw three. All the beans for me for me.

Meemaw washed up straightaway I didn't have to help. All was to be a hurry and tidy away. I stayed with the dinosaurs in their world. At the end Meemaw came.

Wow, it's a great thing, this, isn't it?

Meemaw on her tummy doing looking. Not touching. I didn't say.

How about if I read to you and the new dinosaurs now, eh?

I wanted that. I wanted that and to cuddle Meemaw now.

I nodded.

We curled up. I had all the new dinosaurs. Showed them each every one pictures.

Meemaw's phone was on her lap under the book. Sometimes she taked it out looked at it. I thinked it was a Meemaw egg but not hatching. No hatching of Karen in it.

I went to yawn yawn yawn in strings like paper rings of Christmas.

Come on, tired boy… Teeth!

Meemaw carried me to the bathroom. I wanted all all dinosaurs in bed.

I don't think any of us would have a comfy night like that, do you? How about they snuggle together on the table?

No snuggling! They are a guard!

They standed in a line all looking at me. I got in with just Spiney to hold for usual.

In bed warm. Dinosaurs were one way Meemaw the other way. She smoking her rolly blowing smoke out the open window.

I could hear cars swish swish down the road. I couldn't see Meemaw's colour. But her shape just. On the floor by the door the land of dinosaurs. All very of peace and good in our flat. No Karen had come in at the end. I holded Spiney in one hand. Other hand my willy. All was good.

CHAPTER ELEVEN

I opened my eyes and knowed it right then. The air cold on my nose sleeping bag silky all about trapping. No Meemaw. I was in the bathroom.

Meemaw?

My voice came a crackle not loud enough. So much noise already in our flat. Noise of crying very crying and words in it. Words of wobbles. Sometimes they falled apart into not words. Just crying.

I holded my hands over my ears shutted my eyes. But too loud.

I tried standing up but all twisty going tight on me. Slip slip the sleeping bag silky and dark and the noise.

I thinked of it the bang of my head on the bath. I thinked of the yellow bright pain rushing. The sicky of hurt of it. The lump. I holded to the edge of the bath went slow. Careful. Stepping one foot one foot. The bathroom floor cold on my bare feet. I standed still.

I knowed it must be Karen in our flat. My Meemaw cries quiet. Only sometimes shouting out of Spanish in her asleep.

Bloody fuck.

I whispered a swear of Karen in our flat. It was a bad swear and I meaned it. Bloody fuck of her horrible crying.

I went by the door crack one eye looking. I didn't want any of in the nude. Not Karen disgusting bot. But I looked. I looked. Brave to look.

Meemaw and Karen sitting on the bed in clothes. Meemaw arms rounded Karen crying. I feeled roars coming in me of fury. Rumble umble up up fast. Meemaw had did a lie.

Meemaw had putted me in the bathroom when I was gone asleep. A trick of such badness. Now her arms rounded horrible Karen. Karen of calling me Professor. Karen of saying Spiney that thing. Horrible Karen.

All the fury roar was in my body. Big thunder of it. But deep deep in. Thunder inside but no coming out. I heared my breathing only. I watched at the door crack more.

I couldn't see Meemaw's face because it was wrong way round. But Karen's all red of crying eyes. Piggy small eyes I saw.

You don't, you just don't understand, Nat, what it was like, what she put me through…

Meemaw shushting and stroke stroke.

She nearly broke me. I didn't think I could feel again but then this… You're my dream. I just know, I just know this is meant. Nat…

Crying crying. Meemaw stroke stroked the flops of the Karen spiky hair.

Shh Shh…

Putted her mouth by Karen's ear. Hmm hmm of words close. Rocking.

I didn't want to see of it then. I shutted my eyes counted inside of three hundred. Hands pressed hard hard on my ears all was rushy inside my head.

When I opened it was kissing. Eating kissing devouring. My Meemaw would get eated up. I must to stop it to stop it I holded the edge of the bathroom door ready. I will go in! Then they were apart. Karen words all panting like running up the hill.

Christ, I want you so much, woman…

Dark words of a growl and more the eating kissing. I stepped back in the bathroom. Back in the dark. Away.

I wanted Meemaw *I* wanted my Meemaw but Meemaw gone with Karen on the bed. All my body was shaking very very. Hard my teeth nnnnnng nnnnnng. I crawled back in the sleeping bag. I slided deep in.

Spiney there my Spiney. I taked him down to the end darkness. Sealed. Maked a curve for my back. The boulder of a story cave. To block. A cave of great depth and darkness. Danny and Spiney in. Inside we spelled. Spiney speaked clear in my mind his voice. I whispered it for him.

I shall kill Karen. I shall bite in her throat Danny the blood going to her head. It will squirt out she will be dead. A mortal wound to her.

I whispered back.

Good good Spiney.

I holded him by my face. Tears went on him but quiet quiet. Meemaw must not come. Meemaw bringed Karen. Karen her blue eyes of wrongness such wrongness. I didn't want her eyes to look at me again. Not ever again.

***

It was day time. I was on the puffy airbed. All was quiet in our flat. Just the fridge noise. Cars outside and a horn tooted.

I getted up looked through the crack again. Meemaw awake in the bed. Eyes blinking. I pushed the crack wide. Meemaw holded her finger on her lips be quiet. Then Meemaw curled her finger of come here.

Karen was a lump. The back of her head dark hair. Alive breathing. I standed close by Meemaw. She cuddled me her arms sticking out of the covers. Bare arms. In the nude. She whispered close in my air. I moved away.

Do you want to go on my phone?

I nodded. Meemaw gave me the phone.

Go and get back in bed.

She meaned the sleeping bag the puffy airbed.

I had a wee. Trickly wee very yellow long. Then I getted back in the sleeping bag with Spiney. We watched *Tale of a Tooth* a middle bit. I pressed sound to quiet to keep Karen asleep. She could be asleep a hundred years of a story. I wished it.

My wish went wrong and it was soon and sudden she came.

Excuse me, I need to use the toilet.

Her face was the Karen face of normal not crying of the night. The blue eyes. Spiky hair rumpled up and mess. She standed sideways. I scrambled out up and away. I went in the other room.

Meemaw was folding up the bed. Talking to me sideways and not looking.

Do you want some krispies, poppet?

I nodded.

You'd better get dressed quick, it'll be warmer. It looks like a nice day out there though.

I taked off my pjs quick. Quick pants on because Karen eyes might come. Karen in our bathroom I heared the toilet whoosh flush. I heared the taps. A long time Karen was in there.

I eated my krispies all up. Quick and gulpy swallow. I wanted breakfast all done in case of another Karen flat egg.

Meemaw maked tea two mugs. Hum hum very sweetly. Very brightly dancey pink her colour. The colour of the best scarf of Meemaw. Of stringy and sequins tiny mirrors on. I taked my bowl to her. Speaked quiet in case.

Can we go to the park Meemaw?

Maybe in a little while.

I still had the Meemaw phone. I started it at the beginning again of *Tale of a Tooth*. I sayed the words back to Walter Kronkite the best words.

A hundred and twenty million years ago!

Karen came out the bathroom I looked quick looks.

Jesus, Nat, it's like a bloody fridge in here. Can you not put the heating on?

Meemaw stirring tea.

Bit of a cash flow issue at the mo. It'll warm up soon, though. It's really sunny out there.

Plonk she putted the tea for Karen by her arm. Best big Meemaw smile for Karen. Karen was looking out our window.

Karen sipped her tea. I watched quick looks more over the top of the phone. Meemaw washing up a can for fizzy drink Strongbow. Not ours. A Karen thing. I slided it back to the beginning of *Tale of a Tooth*. Back for the best words.

Fuck! I'm freezing, Nat!

She rubbed her hand on her face. White with darkness underneath the eyes.

Does he have to have that on all the time?

Meemaw taked the phone from my hand. Taked it.

Danny love, let's have a break from that now.

No snatching. No snatching Meemaw. I didn't say of it. I didn't say of anything anything. All words swallowed. Eated up.

I went on the floor in the land of the dinosaurs. Karen was a new smell. Not stinky perfume but a new smell of very badness. Poorly of a toilet or sicky something. Yucky strong.

I putted Apato behind the rock. Apato almost was going to say a thing in my mind. His voice was I thinked low and quiet. I almost heared him.

Then Karen did a cough. Loud cough of phlegm.

I think you might have your priorities a bit off, Nat, if you let him on your phone the whole time but you haven't got the money to heat the flat.

Meemaw looked round from by the sink holding a plate drippy runny of bubbles. She laughed like not actual funny.

We do have the money to heat the flat, it's just a glitch. I got into a bit of arrears with the council tax so we're economising.

I thinked the council tax nightmare. It was a good thing. It was how we went to the centre of the toy library and getted the great goodness of dinosaur land. Karen clonked down her tea.

How much?

Meemaw did another laugh of not funny.

It's not a big deal, K, I'll get it sorted. I just need to agree a payment plan or something.

Karen getted up very fast and my body did a jump. Hurry hurry she taked her jacket from the Meemaw peg. Her wallet was shiny black as a beetle fat. Pop. Inside lots of brown tenner notes.

Ten, twenty, thirty, forty, fifty!

Plonk plonk on the table.

Then she putted on her jacket. Please. I wished and hoped it. Go away.

I won't have you going short, baby, not if I've got spare. Will that cover it?

Meemaw looked at the money. Then looked at Karen.

You don't have to.

Shhhh!

Karen kissed Meemaw but not too of devouring. Whispery quiet but I heared it.

My angel.

My my my Meemaw.

Karen zipped up her jacket zooop. It was a moment of please

please please go. Loud in my mind. I thinked too loud and Karen heared it. Sudden she looked down in my eyes. A hard hit of look.

You need to put some boundaries down for him though, Nat. He's got to understand he can't just have what he wants the whole time.

Inside my ears was whoosh whoosh. I feeled my face gone hot. Tummy tip tip tip. I feared of a sicky.

Oh you don't need to worry about that, K. He's a good lad.

Karen still her eyes on me. Spiking. Sharpness. Hardness.

Yeah, but it's important he understands discipline.

She pulled her spiky bits of hair. Dark points to the sharp eye spikers. All over spikes. All over.

You don't see what I do every day of the week, Nat. People who never heard the word no in their lives and think the world owes them a living.

She tug tugged of her jacket to puff up.

Half of them wouldn't be in the mess they are if they'd been taught a bit of respect and given some boundaries. You're not doing him any favours being so soft.

Meemaw still and watching. Just watching.

I'll see you after work then okay?

Going actual going. Opening the door. Meemaw voice all jollity.

See you later! Have a good day!

Doors bang and bang. I heared her gallopy down the steps.

I didn't look at Meemaw. I maked Apato walk up the back of the sofa over the top down the front.

Danny love, you were a very good boy about last night and being in the bathroom.

I maked Spiney jump. Jump he jumped over the sofa roaring. Meemaw talked louder.

I know I said Karen wouldn't be staying but she was upset when she came and you know sometimes when we're upset we need some extra cuddles and we don't want to be on our own? Well, that was how Karen was feeling last night.

Spiney roared again.

It's difficult for Karen, Dan, because she's never had a child and she doesn't know all about getting along together. It might take her a little bit of time to learn. But you can be patient, can't you?

I looked at Meemaw then. Inside me very hard rocks had come. Hard heavy rocks had come.

Can we go to the park?

Meemaw looked back at me. Her head on sideways of a question. She looked steady steady. Then a sigh.

Yes, yes, we can go to the park a bit later. After lunch, okay?

Then Meemaw spended a long time hoovering. Meemaw singed songs of happy loud as the hoover. And the dinosaurs killed enemies in our flat. All every one.

***

The park was gone warm buzzy of the insects and take my coat off. We went up on the high slope. Tea for Meemaw and Mister Man lolly of orange for me.

We're celebrating the sunshine!

I bited fast for no drips. Ice and ice. I gived Meemaw the stick.

Blimey! That was quick!

Meemaw lied back on the grass. Her book open on the sky.

Inside the gates, remember, Dan.

I thinked I am the little manual remember Meemaw. I didn't say of it.

I runned down the slope did big steps up. Runned down again. Again again. Three four. My knees went to wibbly then so I went in the sand.

Most in the sand were girls of long hair. Yellow brown all long. Special yellow road-digger man coats said Play Days Nursery. All very the same they came round me. Fast talking. Telling things of their game laughing loud. Other things. One looked in my face.

What's he called?

I didn't know if she meaned Spiney or Danny. I didn't say. Then they all went away in a line. Two ladies taked them. All gone. Quiet. Spiney maked tracks and singed.

When it was time for after school lots too much of children came. Voices were louder louder. So much of shouting.

I closed my eyes holded my hands on my ears by the wall.

Meemaw came. I smelled her there. She taked my one hand off my ear holded it. I walked eyes closed with her. I heared the gate clang.

The shouting went quieter quieter. Splinkle splash of the fountain I heared. I opened my eyes.

Isn't it a glorious day, Dan?

Meemaw orange as the lolly. Ducks were there three. Two seagulls pretending like ducks. Sitting up in the water not flying in the sky.

Of ducks I like green shiny head ones. Best is the goose who is grey. Once grey goose must to be catched of two men in a net. I watched them. I thinked they were going to eat him but Meemaw telled me not.

On the next day they bringed him back. Me and Meemaw saw it. One man was growly voice.

You the reception committee?

Meemaw laughed.

Where's he been?

Vet, would you believe? Bit of arthritis in his leg but otherwise healthy.

The men had welly trousers of walking in the water and putting him back.

Today he was on the little island of the pond. Grey goose otherwise healthy.

Next time we come we'll bring them a bit of bread and you can feed them, yes?

I didn't say. I throwed them grass. It went sinked in the water.

Meemaw's phone buzzed and she looked.

Oh! Oh, I hadn't realised how late it was, Danny! Come on! We need to get home!

She holded my hand.

Come on!

I standed still.

Come on, love! It's late, it's tea time.

Her orange washed away fast. Meemaw was swirly in her colours. Yellow green brown coming up wishy washing. Pulled but just gently. I went.

All going along Meemaw was doing big steps for rushing. I

runned beside. Buzz buzz her phone. Meemaw letted go my hand did a message still walking.

Come on, Danny!

Meemaw's coat flappy flap round her legs. Big bigger steps. At our corner Meemaw was puffy.

Poor Karen's been waiting on our step for us after a horrid day at work. Let's run this last bit and let her in quick... Come on, Danny! I'll race you!

CHAPTER TWELVE

Karen standed on our steps with orange bags from Sainsbury's that is expensive. Meemaw mouse scampered up the steps.

I'm sorry to leave you outside! We lost track of time in the park.

Karen putted her arm round Meemaw pulled hard. Kissed on her face. Meemaw was going in her pockets for the key. Then trying to get it in the hole. All the time Karen pulling kissing her. Sudden she letted go.

That's okay, babe, I've only had the day from hell.

A slanty smile she maked.

Sorry. It was so lovely, we went to see the ducks.

Karen picked up the bags went in.

Indoors Karen hanged her coat first on the Meemaw peg. Meemaw coat on top. I putted my coat under where it goes on the floor with my shoes. Karen very sudden loud shouted.

You can pick that up, young man, your mum's not your servant, you know?!

Meemaw's head twizzled fast. Meemaw eyes fast over me.

It's all right, K. We usually just leave his coat there, honey. It's fine.

Karen floppled in the armchair. Eyes closed. Meemaw by the tap with the kettle underneath getting filled up. I standed still.

Young man young man gone on a circle in my head. Nasty words of hardness. Must to say it out to get it out. I whispered. I maked such tiny of a sound.

Young man.

Karen's eyes popped open. Spiked me. She heared me. She spiked me for it.

Meemaw speaking maked Karen look away.

What's in the bags, K?

Meemaw pointing at the orange bags of Sainsbury's.

I told you I was going to cook something tonight.

Oh, really?

I told you, Nat, this morning.

Oh, I don't remember. But that's a lovely surprise!

I pulled the dinosaur land far to the bathroom door flatted it almost. Just one rumple. I lied on it.

Meemaw bringed me a glass of water. I had some putted it on the floor near. Meemaw taked tea to Karen. I watched from behind Apato. He standed on the blowed-up rock of squashy and I peeped.

Cheers, babe. I need this…

She drinked of it then taked Meemaw's hand pulled Meemaw on her lap. Meemaw's tea still by the kettle far away.

I watched them Meemaw and Karen. Didn't want to. My eyes had getted stuck. Meemaw kissed Karen on her forehead for let me go now. Like bedtime. Let me go now. She tried to get up.

Noooo!

Karen had a little voice all squeaky. Her two arms on Meemaw's middle squeezed. Little voice of a baby.

I don't want to let you go.

Meemaw did a squiggle for really let go.

Come on, K! That's enough!

Karen holded on. Meemaw squiggled again then sitted still. Karen holded tight I saw.

Hey, Professor! So, what've you been up to today?

Not looking at me but talking to me. Then sudden she did look. My air all gone. A wee need came. Sharp. Meemaw was looking too at me. In Meemaw's look was say. Was be a good boy Danny.

I've been adventuring the dinosaurs.

What?

I've been adventuring the dinosaurs.

Playing with the dinosaurs, eh? No shit.

She drinked more tea her eyes letted me go. I looked down at the puffy rock. The edges were crinkles. I shrinked tiny and went in a crinkle waiting. Waiting. Hoping. Go go.

Sorry you've had a rough day, K. You must be tired.

You've no fucking idea.

Our flat filled up of shit fucking very rude we don't say. Some people Danny are offended the words upset them.

Meemaw was gone a new colour. Colour of the walls in the Job Centre. Sometimes tea with too much of milk. Meemaw calls it gnat's piddle. Piddle is wee. Meemaw says gnat's piddle. I say it too. Cheeky boy and laughing. Us together. But no laughing now. Stillness. All still in our flat just Karen's arm up down drinking tea. She maked a slurp.

So, I'm doing a chicken curry.

Oh.

Problem?

It's just, I kept meaning to tell you, babe, but we're actually vegetarians.

Meemaw hadn't turned off the tap all the way properly. Trickle drip trickle drip I needed a wee very.

But I bought you hot dogs at the pictures and you ate them! Why the bloody hell didn't you say?

I'm sorry, darling. It was just you'd already bought them…

Yeah, and I've bloody bought five quid's worth of decent chicken now!

Karen's voice gone up like a thumb stuck on the phone. Gone to shouting.

Sorry! I'm sorry!

Karen letted go of Meemaw. Meemaw getted up went to her tea. Meemaw standed by the kettle looked away. Karen's voice came hard words each one hard throwed down on the floor.

It doesn't matter. I guess I can't do anything right for you, can I?

What?

I can't get anything right. If you leave me standing on the bloody step like an idiot, I suppose I should take the fucking hint.

Karen, I don't know what you're talking about, love, we were just in the park. I'm sorry about…

No! You don't want me here or the meal I'm offering to cook for you. I should just go. That's what you want, isn't it? I'll save you the trouble of kicking me out! I'll just go!

All her words came faster faster down a hill. I thinked in my head gogogogogogo! A ratatata gun fired inside me.

But she didn't go. Karen sitted very still. Hanged down her head. Meemaw came beside.

Oh K, love, don't take it like that. I'm so sorry you've had a hard day and we weren't here when you arrived. And now this. How about if we do a veg curry? I've got potatoes in.

Karen didn't say.

We'll pop your chicken in the fridge and I'll make a veg curry, yeah?

Karen did a sigh putted her hand swoosh in her hair. Her voice came quietly again.

Thing is I can't do enough for you, can I, Nat? I help you out. I do the whole day at work, I come back to make you a meal, and it's all not good enough for you, is it? If you don't want me here you only have to say, babe, and I'm gone, I'm gone…

I thinked say Meemaw. Say and gone. Meemaw didn't say. Meemaw was just looking at Karen. Karen speaking more.

Is it because of him? Won't he eat meat or something?

What?

Cos I've noticed he gets every little thing he wants round here, so I just thought maybe it's him who doesn't like meat.

Meemaw putted her two hands up of that's enough now Danny. But not Danny. Karen.

Karen, you're being ridiculous!

Karen standed up fast. Blue eyes big. Shout shout each every word.

I'm fucking ridiculous, am I, Natalie? I'm fucking ridiculous coming round here pandering to you? Well fuck you then! Fuck you!

Karen throwed our green mug. Saily up in the air. Tea flied out like a wing of it. Crack! Green mug hit the kitchen cupboard and falled in two lumps on the floor. One Meemaw cry of a sea gull then the crack then quiet. Just drippy dribbly tap.

I squiggled under the table to against the wall looked at our hairy carpet tiles the tea had falled on. A wet wing. Very dark. Big broken chunky of our mug. Sharp edges lying.

Meemaw came. Came right then. She bended down holded out

her arms. I crawled into the Meemaw circle. She standed us up. We were a two heads creature and Meemaw talking in a voice of a wobble. I feeled in her chest the thump thump.

I think you'd better go.

Karen went staggery at our kitchen table like a old old man on the wobbly bus. Sitted down plonk. Putted her hands on her face.

Karen, I think you should go.

Oh oh oh!

Karen cried it out. Bursted into tears.

Loud the crying! Loud! I holded my ears maked hummmm. Not enough. Loud the words came of Karen in wailing.

I always do this... I fuck everything up! Everything! I fuck everything up!

Karen, I'm sorry but I want you to go.

Karen didn't go. Didn't get up even. Sitted by our table.

I caaaaaaaaan't! I can't bear to... Bear to fuck this up... You're so... So perfect... it's meant! It's meant for us to be...

Karen's shoulders were wobbly wobbly.

I pushed my face in. In my Meemaw's smell. Eyes closed two hands hard on my ears. Counting.

At 132 Meemaw tried of put me down. I pinched on tight. Meemaw bended down to the floor pushed me off gentle. All the time mmm mmm her voice. I loosed my ear just one to hear.

Danny. Danny, love, just wait by your dinosaurs a minute now. It's okay. It's okay.

Meemaw getted Karen's trainers. Her jacket from the Meemaw peg. She crouched down by Karen.

Here. Here you go.

Karen not crying now. Still. Staring. Not looking at Meemaw. Blinked then. I did a jump.

I love you so much, Nat. I'm just so scared, I'm so scared. Please. Please don't.

Quiet her voice. Still not looking at Meemaw but away away like a screen was come on the wall. Like she was watching something else someone else. Meemaw putted her arms round Karen cuddled her. Cuddled her a long time.

Karen looked at Meemaw's face close then.

Can I make it right, Nat? Can I make it right with you? Let me clean it all up and then I could… I dunno… How about if I went to the burger place and got us all veggie burgers and chips and Cokes? Please. I can't bear to leave now without making it right. Please, please let me make it right.

Quiet again but drippy tap fast as fast. My rumpeting heart fast too.

I think it might be best if you just go tonight, K. Just for tonight I think it might be best if we had a bit of space and time to calm dow…

Karen bursted into tears again. Loud very. Waily again.

This is it, isn't it? You're dumping me, aren't you? I've ruined it! Aaaaaaargh!

Karen bumping bumping her head with her fists all closed up. Meemaw grabbed her wrists holded on tight.

Okayokayokayokayokay… Baby, stop it now.

Meemaw maked a big huff sigh her shoulders up then down.

K, look, go in the bathroom and wash your face and I'll get this cleaned up. I want a word with Danny and then we'll see. We'll talk in five minutes, okay?

Karen nodded. Went in our bathroom. Shutted the door.

I runned to Meemaw. Holded on tight.

It's okay, Danny. It's okay. She just got upset. She's just upset. There's nothing to be scared of.

Meemaw picked me up. Inside full as full of wee but Karen in our bathroom. I bited my teeth hard closed. Pinched my willy one hand tight.

Look, poppet, how about if I say we'll have tea with her and then she goes home? How about that?

Wee hurted hurted inside. Then a turn of dark in my tummy a mighty poo I feeled. All the things in me moving. Meemaw whispered.

I know it must have been a bit scary, love, but she's just upset, Danny. She's upset. Sometimes people have lost a lot in their lives and the fear… Oh God, how can I explain this to you?

Scrunched my willy. Whispered in Meemaw's ear very close. Hot. I smelled the smell of my mouth air. I whispered.

Make her go, Meemaw.

Meemaw maked a big sigh again.

Danny, I promise you she won't stay tonight, but I can't turn her out in that state. It's not the right thing to do, Dan.

Meemaw putted me down. Meemaw picking up broken mug I went back under the table. Watched.

Karen came out our bathroom. Her face splotchy of red patches. A sniff. She looked at Meemaw a smile of cheeky like a joke. Meemaw not looking though.

Meemaw busy posting mug bits thunk thunk in our bin. Karen went near. Falled on her two knees.

Watch out! There might be splinters!

Nat, I was an arsehole and I give you my most humble apology.

She swizzled round her knees and looked at me. Quick I looked down.

Professor, likewise.

Meemaw taked her hand pulled her up.

You are a bloody drama queen, Karen Henderson!

Karen smiled very big. Big empty. A gone broken smile. Of our mug broken. I feeled it very sharp.

Karen opened her arms and Meemaw went in them. I feeled the great moving. Earthquake of hurt. Pinched my willy tight. Bathroom door open but I didn't want to get out. And Karen all around my Meemaw. All around.

I'll go and get the burgers, yeah?

Kissed Meemaw on her hair. Letted go.

Okay, you do that. But, K, I don't think you should stay tonight. I just want that clear now and it's not a big thing, it's just I think we could do with a little break. All of us.

Meemaw's voice speedier up and up. To get the words out. Fast. The eyes of Karen round. Blink blink.

Understood. You're right. You're right, babe. And what's the hurry when we've got the rest of our lives?

Karen banged our door banged the other door. Gone.

I scrambled out from under fast runned to the bathroom. I did a sitting down wee waited for it the mighty poo. Meemaw not came to me.

Meemaw!

Meemaw not came. Poo not came. All inside was heavy. All was stopped. I washed hands dried hands all by myself.

Meemaw was by the window her back. Watching out. Not came to me. Not here. Careful and watching.

I getted the dinosaurs lined up. On our table top standing strong. Meemaw turned round sudden. No colour to be seen. Her voice quiet and the drippy tap still drippy.

Are they all joining us for tea? Is it a party, Dan?

I didn't say. I didn't say any of words to Meemaw at all. Brrring the bell and Meemaw went to let Karen back in.

CHAPTER THIRTEEN

This time it was true of Karen not staying. When I waked up I was in our bed no Karen in our flat. A sunny day and Meemaw by the window.

Guess what, Danny? We're going to visit your grandad Mick.

The sun was falled on Meemaw. Her long hair of shines but her colour still strange. Pale of the gnat's pee tea.

Why are we Meemaw?

We'll go on the train again, isn't that exciting? Do you want krispies?

I eated my krispies. Little rain drop of milk falled down from the spoon on its way to my mouth. I liked it raindrops. I maked more and more. Meemaw not looking. Meemaw smoking her rolly by the window. Far away.

Is Karen coming Meemaw? Meemaw?

No.

On the train was the sun flicker flicker through the trees. We speeded by. I went in it the flicker flicker. I maked a flickery noise of it.

Train said no Karen no Karen no Karen to me. Me and Meemaw away on the train. It was a good thing. Right thing.

See the sheep, Danny?

I did I did I saw sheep fat fluffy white in the field then gone again.

Look up quick! The windmills!

I missed them. Always I miss them.

Then bang the great darkness of the tunnel. I climbed on Meemaw's lap closed my eyes. I didn't want to see us be tunnel people. I holded on my Meemaw and waited.

Inside of Meemaw her heart clump clump then the train went to rattttle and we were out. I getted down. I standed by the window until Brighton. No Karen and a good journey. A great journey of goodness.

Come on, Dan, we're changing trains!

Meemaw taked my hand we runned fast in the station of a high up roof. All maked of glass up high and blue sky in it. My feet did a stumble.

Look where you're going, Danny! Look ahead of you! Come on!

I don't like it hurrying. Meemaw knows. And I thinked I don't know of how to change trains I don't know what!

But it was just get on another one. This time we sitted in a two together seat. There was a table flopped down. Squeak push it up. Bang flop down again. Squeak push it up. Bang flop down again.

Bang! Bang!

Enough, Danny! Just sit quietly, love. We'll be off in a minute.

Meemaw catched up the table. I looked out the window and a station man was there with a hat on.

Do you remember when we came to see Mick before?

Yes. I had CBeebies.

What else do you remember?

I don't know.

Right.

It was already time for getting off. And new streets and houses. I saw a seagull eated some pizza on the ground.

I knowed when it was Mick's door. I remembered sudden the liney glass of bobbly pattern. Inside a orange curtain. A curtain in a door is wrong. The door opened and then I remembered of the smell too.

Smell of Mick's house was so sweety smoky. Smell of Mick too.

Hello hello hello!

Hi Mick… In you go then, Danny.

He holded the door wide for come in.

On the other day Mick was all the time in bed. I only saw for a minute. Now he was getted up in clothes.

Mick's trousers were all colours and droopy. His t-shirt colours too and a great mighty one eye in the middle. A eye on his tummy. Mick's tummy round but all the rest of Mick not round. His arms thin white. Hairy of black hair on them. Mick's face very red. His nose at the end blue of tiny lines on.

He bended down. His face close. Too close. But I wanted to look at the face of such strangeness so I didn't shut my eyes.

Hello there, son! Haven't you grown?

The floppity moustache waggled. Very yellow of teeth. Mouth air of such badness. Such terrible badness.

Come along in then! It's grand to have you here.

Meemaw pushed me gentle push for go on. I did. I holded my nose though for the many smells.

The front room had the big telly of my remember. All the air was cloudy blue in lines. Things moving in it slow.

Blimey, Mick! Can you let a bit of air in?

Sure thing, princess.

Nat.

Mick pushed up the window.

Ugh!

His arms wobbled. Meemaw stroked my head.

Danny, sit down, love.

I couldn't. The sofa was all filled up of newspapers books fizzy drinks cans jumper blue with a unravelly sleeve. All filled up.

Meemaw pushed some things together maked a space of green. It was only some little bits gritty. I sitted down there.

A cup of tea then, is it?

Mick was puff puff in his words.

You sit down. I'll make it.

Grand.

All the floor was things over under and heapy up. In the middle were big big boots. Dark and curly. Mick boots.

I looked at his feet. No socks on. Bare Mick feet. Toenails gone long claws. Black at the ends of each. Toes of hair as a werewolf.

I'm not a very tidy housekeeper I'm afraid, son.

I could feel his eyes and still puff puff like running.

You like dinosaurs, don't you?

I nodded.

Your mother, she liked them too. A sweet wee girl with her big eyes looking at those great beasts in her story book. Ha! Like it was yesterday.

Not yesterday. On yesterday was Karen breaked our green mug. Crack and broken.

Mick started making a rolly. All lots of tobacco he pulled out a fluffy green sort. He maked a super-long rolly. Papers sticked together of spit. I watched. Meemaw shouted from a other room.

Jesus, Mick! Is there milk here somewhere?

On the top shelf of the fridge, princess.

He did a cough of horrible phlegm. I hate it phlegm.

Meemaw came back with two mugs. One of flowers she gived to Mick one of purple stripes for her.

Cheers!

Mick lifted his mug up high did a wink. Meemaw sitted on the arm of the sofa by me. Drinked her tea.

I watched the things the tiny things in the blue air. The spaceships of teeny aliens flied in Mick's house. I didn't say of it.

Aaaah! That's grand, princess.

How've you been keeping?

Very well. Very well indeed.

That kitchen's a disgrace, you know?

Ah, you know me, you know me, princess. It's never been top of my list, the dishes.

He did another wink. He lighted his rolly. Click and a orange flame.

Can you at least sit by the window with that?

Sure thing, sure thing.

Mick kept on of big smiles. Smiles at Meemaw and at me. All quiet and a car outside. A long time of sitting. Mick did another cough.

I can't believe my girl's come and brought the little man! I'm made up, I am, princess.

Have you been working?

He squashed his rolly on the window edge throwed it out.

I've been doing a bit of work for Pete. You remember Pete McNally?

Yep, I remember Pete. Total bloody chancer.

Ah, now, he's a good man. He's a good man.

Huh…

Well, he gets the pieces at boot fairs and such. Nice pieces. He's a fine eye. He sells them on the internet.

Yeah?

Well, I don't understand all that side of it. But there's work when I want it. I get my cut. I get a fair cut.

Meemaw looked at me. Her colours all hidden. I thinked all too smoky for seeing colours.

Mick mends clocks and watches, Danny, when the insides are broken. He makes them go again.

Do you want to see, son?

He standed up. Holded out his hand at me for come on. I looked at his werewolf feet. I looked at Meemaw.

Go on. I'm right behind you.

Mick's bedroom was the same of things on the floor. Clothes drinks cans scrunkle white paper of chip shop. My tummy did a grooble of hungry.

Mick scooped all everything sideways with his feet. He maked a path through. The underneath carpet was swirly orange and dark dark red. Swirly like space.

By the window was a big table of no stuff except a rectangle clock of metal. It was lied down dead. Its insides showing. Insides of golden spiky wheels and little silver twists. Many and much of wheels and twists. Small as small.

I take it all apart and when I put it together again it works.

I looked close close at the spikey wheels and teeth very sharp. I touched with one finger a tiny twist.

I know where to put all the pieces. And then it works.

I think Mick maked the dead clocks be alive again. I wanted some in my pocket of the wheels and twists. Wanted.

Meemaw's voice was behind me loud.

Christ almighty, Mick! It's disgusting in here!

Ah come on now, princess! When a man's alone…

I was just looking looking at the shiny insides of the clock. All lied in the sun and I wanted.

You get yourself some bin bags and you clear the rubbish. Get the washing to the laundrette. It's not beyond you.

I never was the domestic type, was I?

Well, there's no denying that.

Mick did another cough of phlegm.

How's your health, Mick? Really?

I touched one again. A golden wheel. The tippy tip of my finger on it.

I'm fighting fit now, fighting fit.

Right. And are you eating?

Oh I am. I'm grand, grand… Shall we go back to the front room? Does the lad wants to see some TV?

I didn't take any the wheels and twists and the lovely pieces. I was good.

In the front room Meemaw gived me the telly thing. I pressed red it was a man doing news. I didn't want it. So much buttons. I was confused.

Have you eaten today, Mick?

Not just yet I haven't, princess.

How about I make us something?

Ah, ah, well, I've not got a lot in just now.

Meemaw getted up.

I'll go to the corner shop.

She holded out her hand. Mick gived her a blue fiver.

You stay here, Danny.

I'm coming too!

You stay with Mick. I won't be a minute.

Meemaw gone. Bang the door. Tears came in my eyes. I blinked them down looked at the telly man. Big pink loud.

Mick maked a new rolly.

Your ma's a grand sweet girl, a sweet girl, Danny.

His tongue was a butterfly on the papers. Eyes Meemaw colour. Green golden flash.

I see her mother in her. Oh, I do.

He getted up went walking all through the floor things. Stopped by a drawer.

Look! Look, son!

He pulled. Tug tug of too much stuff in the drawer.

Here, look at this…

A glass hard photo of a lady face. He holded it to me for take. I taked it. I looked. The lady was in black and white. Her hair a big tumble of fat curly dark. Her face white. Eyes big big and dark as blackness.

That's my Isabel there. Did you see her before, did you?

I shaked my head.

I see her in your ma, son. God knows I do. Just as she was in London that first summer. A Spanish princess sitting there in a pub on the Euston Road.

A princess. Mick is all the time saying of a princess.

I never knew a woman like her. Not a day goes by I don't think of her still. Did you see her before, did you?

I shaked my head again.

Ten years of my life. Ten years and I never once regretted it. People said she was a handful. You've got yourself saddled there, Mick.

Another cough of the most horrible of phlegm.

But she was a grafter though. She was. When she was well she was a grafter. And then when your ma came along, well... Oh, I never once regretted it... I never... Even after... And people had said. They said you've got yourself saddled there. But they couldn't see her heart, wee man. They could not one of them see her heart.

I looked more at the photo lady. You can't see of people's hearts because they are inside. Inside the rib cage is the heart a tireless pump. We had it in a book of human body.

Click then bang the door. Meemaw suddenly back and all panting of running.

Telly man saying now over to Thomas with the weather. Meemaw puffy in her words.

I'll make us all an omelette, okay? What have you got there, love?

I showed Meemaw the lady of a princess and a heart. Meemaw went still. Thomas on telly said a weather front sweeping across from the south-west.

I was showing the lad your beautiful ma, princess.

Meemaw turned. She went to the kitchen calling.

Can you come and find some plates from that great heap then, if we're actually going to eat?

Meemaw and Mick gone I tried to make it CBeebies. But I getted more news people. Mans ladies different colours but all saying of news in the world. Sometimes a car bomb.

I pressed red button for blackness. Big telly closed its eye. Quiet.

I looked at the lady again. A princess and a heart. She didn't look of a mummy for Meemaw. No colours in her. Too smooth face. I thinked it was most probably not and was a mistake. I putted her back on top of the drawer stuck open. All so many things.

I tippytoed in the things. I looked. Four different of fizzy drinks cans smelled stinky yuck some had little dribbles in. I didn't drink because horrible. Sometimes rolly ends in clonk I heared them knocking inside and smelled them.

Danny, come and get some food!

I went in the kitchen.

It was nice omelette Meemaw maked of fat soft yellow warm. Mick had fizzy drink a big can. He did a burp.

Pardon me! How are you keeping, princess? Are you managing?

Oh, we're okay.

I wish I could do more for you, you know I do.

Mick cutted a big bit of omelette pushed in under the droopy moustache. Wobble wobble of chewing. He eated five bites. I watched. Some omelette left he pushed his plate away. Leaned back in his chair. Meemaw putted down her fork.

Actually, I've met someone, Mick. It's early days though.

Oh! A lucky man, a lucky man!

Erm, it's a woman actually.

Oh! Well, that's all the same to me, princess, all the same to me. I'm never one to judge, am I? Never one to judge.

He drinked a long drink.

Just so long as she treats my princess well. That's my only concern.

I spiked my last omelette bit. Devoured it. A great allosaur. But still hungry.

She's called Karen. I don't quite know... I'm not sure but...

Mick did another burp.

Well you take it easy, princess. Take it easy.

Mick getted another fizzy drink from the fridge. I pulled on

Meemaw's sleeve. Whispered.

Can I have a fizzy drink?

No, that's for grown-ups, Danny.

What's that? Is the boy after a beer now? Ha!

Of course he's not. He doesn't even know what it is!

Meemaw was flash to sudden purple. Snatch snatch the plates. I looked at the leftover Mick omelette. I grabbed Meemaw's sleeve.

Can I have that?

Meemaw did a sigh. Flop the omelette down on my plate she took the others to the sink. Running taps she speaked to me louder for hearing.

When you've finished that you can go and watch telly.

Mick and me went in the front room. Mick finded a programme of *Doctor Who*.

I think this'll be right up your street.

It wasn't in our street. It was of a spaceship of the Tardis. Meemaw likes it space.

Mick falled fast asleep. He did snores that were such loud I couldn't hear of what the tv people were saying. Just the snores. I waited for Meemaw to come and it be time for home.

CHAPTER FOURTEEN

Right, so we change trains again, Danny, remember?

The high station was gone no room for running. It was all legs and wheely bags of handles. I stopped still and Meemaw picked me up. A loud voice of a bing bong hurted.

Oh, great!

I pressed hard on my ears but the bing bong voice still loud.

Meemaw pulled one hand for a crack. Speaked in.

The trains are up the creek!

I didn't know of it. Creaky door in the haunted house. I didn't know. All was loud and too much of people.

We went to a edge. There was a bench we sitted on it. No other person. The bing bong voice stopped. I letted go my ears.

Let's just sit here a minute.

What the creek, Meemaw?

There's a problem. A signal failure and everything's gone wrong.

Oh.

The signals are like the traffic lights for the trains. They say when it's safe to go, and one has broken.

Broken.

Bang! Crack in two bits sharp sharp on the floor. Green mug killed.

Yes.

Up above was a number seven sign. I like number seven. I saw it all along number seven number seven and good.

Then came a man on our bench. The man was too much shiny things. Shoes black tie blue. Hair very of sticky shine. He eated a sandwich with green bits coming out ticky tacky chew chew in his mouth. I watched.

Danny, look at that seagull with his crisps!

Meemaw pointed. Seagull with Doritos blue ones packet. Its head gone inside.

Haha! Isn't he a cheeky one?

I looked back at the man. Ticky tacky chew chew. Huff. Egg falled plop on his trousers. I watched. He getted up and went away.

Outside the blue fence was a place of lots lots of flowers big in buckets. All colours. Names I don't know what.

Meemaw all the flowers are they flowers of the park?

Oh, Danny, you wouldn't believe it, sunshine. They fly them all around the world in planes. Some of those roses probably come from Africa.

I believed because Meemaw said it. They flied in planes. Planes all filled up of the flowers.

I wanted to look close of the flowers. I slided all along the bench to the end. Meemaw was gone grey blue grey. Meemaw was gone still. She talked quiet. Words came floaty along the bench to me.

They are all dying, those flowers there. In fact they're dead already. All you're waiting for is the colours to fade.

Can I look at the dead flowers Meemaw?

Ha! I suppose so. Just by the fence there, Danny. Go in a straight line to there and a straight line back. Okay?

Yes.

It was a blue fence of tiny teeny squares. I looked through one hole one eye. A lady had a dress of green and buttons. Words on her booby too small to read. Flowers lady was rolling up flowers in a parcel maked of paper. Paper round the drippy ends but not good not waterproof. She sticked sticky tape. Scree it went. I liked it. I wanted to pull screeeee.

There was a good smell of them of the flowers. Green. Wet. A all around smell. Meemaw said dead. I thinked of was it the smell of dead? Flowers lady rubbed her hand on her back and looked at the big clock of the high up station. I can't read it round face clocks. Mick mends them back to life but you can't of flowers. I don't think you can.

At the last a train was for us. We getted on it. Already no seats for Meemaw and me. I standed my face on Meemaw's legs. She holded my shoulder for joggles of the train. Joggle this way that way the window just a slice because a fat man there. I saw green bushes and trees gone smeary fast. I feeled a strangeness of wobbly sick. I maked a noise of it the wobbly sick. To keep it away.

Nerrrrnerrrrnerrrrnerrrr.

Meemaw stroked my hair.

Hang on, sunshine, not much longer now.

Spiney was in the bag. I needed him for the wobbly sick.

Spiney!

I can't get to him just now, love. You can have him when we get off.

I maked the noise of the wobbly sick louder.

NEERRRRRNERRRRNERRR!

I pushed my face in Meemaw's leg. Then the train went to our station called Burgess Hill. Meemaw had to touch people on their backs but it was okay because of excuse me.

Off the train all the air was gone to cleanness and better.

Let's just stop a minute, Danny, and get sorted.

Wobbly sick inside me still but not so much. All the air cool and moving. The sky white bright.

Take some good deep breaths.

Meemaw finded Spiney then right away. I holded him of great love and of Meemaw too because she gived him. We sitted still and all was better at our station of Burgess Hill.

Then it was walking home. Me and Spiney. Treading on only lines of pavement.

Come on! It'd be nice to get home before midnight.

But not cross not grey blue grey now neither. Some paler of yellow. The softness in her now. Me and Meemaw.

By the Kasbah shop sudden there was no more wobbly sick. All gone and I was very hungry. Men were there. Four men of bronze colour hair black laughing loud. One pushed the other one. More of laughing. Smell of dinners.

Meemaw can I have chips red sauce Meemaw?

I wanted it chips red sauce.

Not today, love. No money for that.
Chips!
I standed still.
Danny…
Chips chips chips chips.
I was crying then. I was hungry for chips. Meemaw did a sigh picked me up. I did push Meemaw one on her booby. Just one push.

Let it go. Come on. We're nearly home.

Rumplty bump of Meemaw walking on and me having a carry. I stopped pushing putted my head on Meemaw's shoulder of lumpy bone. Rumplty bump. A yawn came.

Sudden I remembered Karen standed on our step with orange Sainsbury's bags. I shutted my eyes in case of it.

When I opened we were by our steps and no Karen. No Karen. Our door of dark blue called navy. Its gritty edges part. Its golden letters flap.

It was dark in our flat. Leftover of Karen stinky perfume maked a quiet noise smell. Maked a itch in my body of wrong. But Meemaw putted on the light and the itch went away.

I runned all round our flat three times. I jumped over dinosaur world and I singed out.

Our flat our flat our flat!
Not too loud, Dan! Upstairs man!
I remembered him upstairs man and I was kind. I quieted it.
Meemaw washed her hands. Started of making me toast.
Marmite Meemaw!
Marmite, what?
Please!
I went for a wee. It was big and long. Then I went upside down on our chair watched Meemaw doing upside down walking about. She maked tea she cutted my toast in four for windows.

Meemaw give me my toast here I can do practice of upside down eating.

No. You might choke. Come to the table.

I sitted at the table Spiney too. Swinged my legs. Very good toast of home. Home water in white mug with the dark line inside.

Meemaw by the window her smoke going out in the air. Picky

picking at flaky paint very naughty because mustn't pick it Danny the deposit.

Danny, you know, more than anything I want you to be free. You do know that, don't you?

I thinked of free. Meemaw meaned not prisoned up.

I am free Meemaw.

You mustn't ever make your choices in life because you think you need to look after me. Do you understand what I'm saying, Dan? Do you hear me?

It was a silly Meemaw thing. All silly and words fast. I looked at picky picking Meemaw her eyes gone shine and fierce to me.

You're telling about nonsense Meemaw. Meemaw looks after Danny for ever ever always.

Meemaw maked a big suck on her rolly talked in funny voice of holding in smoke.

You get one go, one go at life, and every time you compromise, every time you hem yourself in...

Huff out the smoke came of Meemaw's nose. A dragon.

... you find the choices narrow. You find the world shrinks down.

World shrinks down I didn't like it.

Don't say of that Meemaw!

Meemaw's words came fast more.

There's traps, Danny! Traps you don't even see.

Then gone to quiet. Meemaw throwed the rolly end out the window. Grey blue grey very. Meemaw putted her two hands on it the window. Two hands flat. Looked out.

Like heffalump traps?

What?

Heffalump trap Pooh falls in. The jar on his head for a monster. Piglet is scared.

Meemaw laughed. Meemaw turned quick came and picked me up. Meemaw swinged me round.

Help! Help! It's a horrible heffalump!

I liked I liked our flat all to spinning.

Help! Help! It's a horrible heffalump!

Horrible heffalump!

I wanted it for a long time then and long. But Meemaw stopped.

Let's have a bath.

In the bath I stretched out on my tummy. Long as a ichthyosaur. I swimmed in the seas of the Jurassic. Meemaw squeezed up at the end.

Bloody hell, Dan, you're a bath hog these days.

Can we go swimming Meemaw at the swimming pool can we?

We'll see.

We can.

I putted my hand down on the bath bottom pushed up. Actual swimming I was.

We'll see, love, I don't really think my costume's decent any more and it costs a lot to get in.

We went once. We had M and Ms yellow packet after outside. Hair wet and some trickles.

Meemaw washing my hair then. Singing of the little fishes swam and they swam right over the dam. Boop bap diddle daddle wadum choo. I like I like it choo.

Drying my toes Meemaw's phone buzzed. Buzz again again three times buzzing. Probably Karen I thinked. I looked at it the phone. Karen in it. I thinked plop in the toilet but then no YouTube no *Tale of a Tooth*.

You go and get snuggled down, love. I'll be there in a minute.

Bed was cold first but only for a minute. I turned it over the duvet end and I maked a head nest of pillows. Waited for Meemaw in the cosy. Spiney on my cheek. All the flat our flat of our things not the wild sea of Mick's flat. I thinked about Mick his room little gold wheels of watches I wanted. His twists and curls of tiny. His joggle moustache when he eated the omelette. His orange curtain of the door flappy flappy.

***

I waked up very sudden of the big shout. Meemaw doing loud words of nonsense of Spanish. Thump thump arms and legs in the bed like fighting. I slided away. My inside gone thumpa thump too. A bad dream of Meemaw just a bad dream. I joggled her arm.

Meemaw! Meemaw! Meemaw you're doing Spanish Meemaw!

She went still.

Oh! Oh!

Meemaw turned on the light. Meemaw's hair gone wild as a storm and sweaty for a temperature.

Sorry! Just give me a minute.

She getted water. Had a drink. Rubbed her face lots lots of her hand. Light of yellow in our flat but outside it was still night-time.

What did it mean the Spanish Meemaw?

I don't know, Danny. I was asleep, wasn't I? It happens in a dream.

It wasn't in a dream it was now in our flat. Not a dream. I didn't say. I did a yawn.

Do you need a wee, love?

No.

Meemaw turned off the light then opened her phone. I saw its eye. Its bright eye of light. Bright in the dark. Meemaw did a gasp.

What?

Oh, it's nothing. It's just Karen's been messaging while we've been asleep.

She didn't know you were asleep so she was messaging.

Meemaw didn't say anything for her turn.

It's night-time Meemaw for sleeping but Karen didn't know it.

She did know, honey, but she says she wanted to talk to me anyway and she has managed eighty three messages' worth of one-sided conversation.

I didn't say anything of my turn then.

I 'spose that might be called dedication or something.

Meemaw putted down her phone. I scootled close snuggled in. Warm smell of Meemaw. Her booby. I lied still I looked at Meemaw's face. Her eyes open very wide. Orange street light in them.

CHAPTER FIFTEEN

Floppy tree was gone completely to flat in the morning. In the way of Rexy for his running. I lied on the floor tried to blow it. It hurted in my face my head and nothing no fatter. I shouted.

Meemaw!

Meemaw was gone in the bathroom of shut door. No reply to me I shouted louder.

MEEMAW!

It was just the door shut no coming Danny no flush. I dragged it the whole world by its corner to the bathroom. I opened the door went in. Meemaw on the toilet her knickers and jeans down.

Meemaw the tree has gone to flat. Blow it up.

Danny, I've told you not to disturb me when the door's shut. Just wait outside.

Blow it up Meemaw!

In a minute. Wait for me in the other room.

Blow it!

Danny, you need to listen to me right now. You go in the other room, you shut the door and wait. Do you understand?

I standed still. Meemaw putted her face in her hand. Then all of a sudden a roar a roar of giganotosaurus.

Daniel White, get out of this room right this minute or I swear I'll take the bloody thing back to the toy library!

I throwed it. I throwed it hard at Meemaw but it folded itself up the whole stupid world. Crumpled down on the floor. I runned away went under the table.

Under the table is a long long scratch perhaps a giant claw maked. A piece of chewing gum but gone hard as the fossil tooth of William Buckland. The red line I drawed one day underneath in my pen Meemaw doesn't know. She doesn't go under.

I thinked get all my pens do the whole under of the table all scribble. Maybe push shove the table over. A fallen beast. Then better better get the lighter of Meemaw's rollies makes spark and orange flame. Burn burn the table up in fire make a good revenge of Meemaw.

I wanted it. I wanted all the crackle burn of it but the lighter always in Meemaw's pocket of her actual jeans. I can never get. Stupid Meemaw.

I heared flush and the tap of washing hands. Meemaw's legs came by me.

Meemaw making toast I smelled it the hotness. I peeped. Meemaw doing peanut butter toast. I wanted it the drippy taste of it sweet nice.

Meemaw's legs came close. She bended down. Meemaw holding out the plate of four of the peanut butter toast. I taked it. Meemaw sitted on the floor not looking at me. Tea in our blue mug. Meemaw's tea maked curls. She blowed to cool down. Sip of it.

Sunshine, we're going back to the centre today. The place where we borrowed the dinosaurs.

My tummy twizzled over.

Do we have to take them back?

No, no, they don't have to go back for a few more weeks but I need to have the appointment I didn't have last week.

I looked at Apato. He was near my leg. I loved Apato. Today he didn't have to go back.

Meemaw finished her tea. I eated all the four of toast.

Right then! Shake a leg.

I lied down on the floor Meemaw washed up of breakfast things. I shaked my one leg lots lots until gone to heavy hurted.

Meemaw's phone was up above on the table I heared it do a buzzy dance. Again again on the table very loud. Meemaw came and picked it up.

Ah right, change of plan, we're stopping off at the Costa for a coffee with Karen before we go to the centre.

I kicked my hurty heavy leg on the floor.

No!

Meemaw bended down looked in at me.

Come on now, Danny, don't give me a hard time today. Let's just get out the door.

I want to go to the centre.

I thinked of the lady of round boobies dark between her teeths. She might have a other thing of dinosaurs. Meemaw could ask. I wanted that. No Karen no Costa no. I kicked kicked kicked.

Meemaw getted up was putting things in the bag bustly fast all around our flat. I peeped. Too fast for see her colour so I didn't know it. Meemaw bended down again looked in at me. Sudden purple.

Danny! Get out here now, right now because we need to go. We need to be gone right now!

No!

Meemaw standed by the door. Just her back. Meemaw doing many of swears. Whispers coming louder. Then Meemaw a deep breath. Shoulders come up high she turned round came to by me again.

Danny, come on. You can have another milkshake.

It was a milkshake of poo. Karen poo. I don't want it milkshake! I want to go to the centre!

We are going to the centre. First to the Costa, then the centre. Danny, listen, first the Costa then the centre.

Not first the Costa.

Christ!

I rolled my lips in my mouth pinchy. No words to escape not one to more come.

Meemaw's phone buzzed again not a message buzz. A on on buzz. Meemaw putted it by her face.

Hello, K.

Meemaw went by the window looked out. I slided on my tummy my head out from under. I watched. Meemaw's hair lifty just brushed. Her coat on ready. I heared a teeny voice a shrinked down Karen inside Meemaw's phone. On on the teeny voice.

Oh dear, oh baby… Well you can if you like, but I told you we have to go out… Well if you like, if you like of course… Yeah, we can go a bit later.

More the teeny voice. Meemaw flattening on her hair of flying up.

It's just a…it's an advice place, you know, about the council tax…

Meemaw sitted down by the table. The teeny voice on on on.

Yeah, okay. Yeah, see you soon.

A ambulance of neenaw went down the road. Blue flash flash on the window.

Well you got your wish, Danny, there's no need for us to go to Costa now.

I didn't say anything. Looked at Meemaw very brown brown of appointments and we're late of obligations. Very bad colour. I was sorry of my cross. I went to Meemaw cuddled her arm.

Karen's coming here, love. She's thrown a sicky.

Ugh!

I thinked of sicky thrown. Bucket of sicky thrown might go on me.

Why?

She's having a hard time at work. Anyway, she's coming here.

She mustn't do throw a sicky in the flat Meemaw it will go on the carpet tiles.

No, no not throwing sick. It means she's pretending to be ill.

Why, Meemaw? Why pretend?

So she can leave and come here instead, Danny.

Why?

Meemaw closed her eyes like blow the candles make a wish.

Why, Meemaw?

I don't know, Danny, okay?

Meemaw stayed sitted down at the table. Still in her coat for going out but not going now because of Karen coming. I thinked of the centre.

I went to get the dinosaur world. I pulled the world right to underneath the table. Spreaded it out. It filled all up. The table underneath came the sky of dinosaur world. Mine. Not for anyone else to get in. I lined them up Deiny Apato Rexy Spiney Triceytop at the front of the world.

Meemaw still sitting in her coat doing staring.

Meemaw! Meemaw I need the pillows for more mountains. Meemaw!

Brown as a tree. Hard. No words.

Meemaw!

What?

Snap crack her head turned.

Meemaw can I have please the pillows?

She getted up fetched them for me but no words came. I putted them one each side for a protection. No way in. The great peaks of the Himalayas. I lied on my tummy but inside grooble pain. A warning. I sitted up.

The bell brrrrring and Meemaw went.

Her smell is a enemy. In my world snaked her smell.

Hi, baby.

A slickity sound of kissing I didn't look. I holded one hand Spiney one hand Apato.

Bloody hell, I just had to get out of there. It's a fucking nuthouse. A total fucking nuthouse.

I peeped. Karen on our sofa all flopped down. Meemaw under her arm very smalled and low. Karen shirt was the tangle of flowers one. Sleeve rolled up her arm bluey of veins I wanted to bite. Push it off Meemaw.

What did you tell them?

Migraine. I do get them. I'm telling you, Nat, you would not believe some of the bastards we get in there. Total fucking losers and nutjobs and we have to pretend like anyone would give them a fucking job.

Meemaw wriggled.

Do you want a tea?

If I'd wanted to, you know, I could have sat on my arse expecting the world to pay me, but I never bloody did. My dad would have dragged me out by my fucking hair anyway.

K!

Meemaw said it sudden interrupty like wrong things on the bus or in the shop queue.

What? What's your problem?

Nothing. Nothing. Do you want a tea?

Jesus.

Meemaw getted up. Filled up the kettle.

Danny, do you want a drink of water?

I didn't say. Karen taked off her shoes black shiny. Throwed them by our door. Thonk thonk! She stretched all out her legs. I watched close Karen. I heared the smell of her.

Then the eyes looked in past the pillow mountains and spiked me.

Hey, Professor, what you up to?

I didn't say.

Cat got your tongue?

Meemaw bringed the tea.

Here you go, babe.

Karen taked the tea.

You can take it easy now, yeah?

Meemaw sitted down. Karen putted her arm round again. Leaned. Leaned all on Meemaw kissed in Meemaw's neck.

K…

What? What is your problem today, Nat? For fuck's sake, I thought you wanted to see me!

Meemaw squiggled getted her tea. Meemaw's hands shaked. Some tea tumbled out a splash on Meemaw's jeans.

Of course I want to see you, you know I do. Just take it easy, eh? It sounds like you've had a hard morning.

Oh, fuck off.

Quiet then. My tummy groaned a big grooble pain a twisty one. I said mind words go away poo not now it is not a good time for heaven's sake.

I thinked hang on Danny hang on the bell nelly.

Meemaw getted up throwed her tea down the sink. Meemaw didn't want it the tea. It was just of Karen coming I knowed. We should be gone to the centre now me and Meemaw.

Look, Karen, I want to be supportive, sweetheart, but it's not my fault if you've had a hard morning. I didn't do anything. I told you that we need to get to the appointment at the centre anyway, so maybe it'd be best if you went home.

Oh, yeah, the centre. You're going to that fucking centre full of losers and users. That's right. You'd rather be there than here with me. I get it. I fucking get it, Nat.

K, look…

I fucking gave you money, Natalie. I gave you fifty quid to sort out that council tax. Was that not enough? Where else do you owe money, eh? You'd better tell me what sort of mess you've got yourself in.

No!

Meemaw shouting proper to angry.

No, I'm not fucking having this, Karen. I didn't ask for that money, you offered. You offered and I'll pay every penny back if that's what you want.

Karen getted up went across by Meemaw and sudden I knowed that poo was going to come. I pressed hard on my bot but it was a twisty hurt and no stopping it.

I maked a wail noise. A wail came out from the under-table world.

Waaaaa…

Danny, what's wrong?

Meemaw came quick by the table looked in past pillow mountain.

What is it, sweetheart?

I cried. No words to be said. Karen there Karen blue eye monster looking at me. Meemaw reached in. Meemaw lifted me up I putted my face in her neck. Flick flick in neck skin very fast. A bird flick fast inside. I twisted in Meemaw's arms tried to press on my bot.

Is it a poo?

I nodded. We went to the bathroom. I heared Karen's voice loud even though my crying.

Oh, for fuck's sake! Isn't he old enough to go to the toilet by himself?

Meemaw pushed the door bang closed. I couldn't say words pointed at the slidey silver lock. Meemaw closed it. Meemaw pulled my trousers my pants sitted me down the pain so mighty coming coming.

My legs went to trembly trembly. I squeezed Meemaw's arms no crying then just pushing. All the loudness of it in me but Karen's shouts louder.

I fucking get it, Natalie! Don't worry, I understand you don't want me. Never mind what I've fucking done for you. Just take, yeah? Fucking take from me and do me over. You're like every other fucker, aren't you? I told you I loved you. I fucking told you I loved you, you bitch!

Then bang bang so loud. Bombs at our flat. Bang bang on the bathroom door. All pushy pain stopped. Poo stopped.

Bang! Bang!

Each every one maked a jump inside Meemaw and me holding on holding on. Door shaking of each bang I thinked she will come in.

Bangs stopped. Meemaw crouched by me still I feeled the bird flick faster in Meemaw's neck. Meemaw arms tight around me.

Then it came a great cry.

Aaaaaaaaaaaah!

It wasn't me. It was a terrible of pain cry. Of a T-Rex wounded by horn of triceratops. Death cry of a mighty beast in our flat. Here in our flat this very day. But it was Karen.

Again again came the cry. Meemaw whispering whispering.

It's okay, it's okay, Danny.

I squiggled off the toilet into Meemaw's lap she pulled up my pants my trousers. Meemaw rocked rocked rocked. Whispered.

It's okay. It's okay.

Cry stopped. Karen's voice then muffly breathing. Right by the door must to be close at the crack. Inside me whoosh! A rushing of run! My legs heavy strong for go! But we were prisoned up.

Nat, Nat, Nat, I'm sorry, baby, I'm sorry. Open the door. I'm sorry. Nat, Nat!

Meemaw mouth so close my ear.

It's okay, it's okay, you're okay, Danny.

Meemaw tried to slide me off her lap. I clinged on clinged tight of Meemaw. I thinked not to open the door Meemaw. Keep the lock slided. But I couldn't make words come.

You just curl up here.

She pushed me off her lap to underneath the sink. Meemaw pulled off her velvety coat covered my front of it.

Just snuggle here for a minute. You're all right.

Under the sink was white pipe where water trickles away. Grey fluff on. Meemaw's green sock curled in there lost. I pressed in tight.

Meemaw her hand on the slidey silver lock. Meemaw looking

in me. In my eyes. She sended a message you're al right Danny. She opened the door.

Karen on the floor too. Curled up on her side arms round her head. Meemaw crouched near stroked Karen's hair. Karen bursted into crying lots of ugh noises no words.

You're all right, K. You're all right. It's okay, baby.

I shutted my eyes. Inside my head behind my shutted eyes I was triceratops. I was. I plunged my horn in Karen. She was lied down on our floor. Like right now here now. But slain by triceratops. By the mighty beast. Dead.

CHAPTER SIXTEEN

Meemaw pulled our duvet up round me. Round me walls of soft. Sitting in a cloud. Really I was in the armchair. Meemaw and Karen on the sofa for talking.

Karen and I are going to have a chat about some grown up things, Danny. Here, you go on my phone.

She gived me her phone of her shaky hand.

Cloud walls thick only little bits could I hear them. Quiet voices the sometimes ugh of Karen. Words hard of bitch broken fucked up came in the walls.

I watched all *Tale of a Tooth* and then finded another one *Tale of a Egg* but not so good. Still the man though. Walter Kronkite man. His voice strong as big steps across the land. If I had a million of pounds I would go far away in America with Meemaw find the Walter Kronkite man. We in a car in the desert to dig up bones of the most mighty allosaur. Karen wouldn't know where. We gone in America. Karen would never and never know.

I was thirsty. Inside the cloud it was hot. I didn't want to look out but my hair sticked on my head sweaty. So thirsty I had to.

Karen's head on Meemaw. Meemaw stroking her hair. Meemaw looked at me.

Are you hungry, love?

I didn't say. All was too much strangeness for talking.

Night coming. The sky purply purple and street lights come on already. All the day gone. Going to the centre gone. All in our flat was stopped and closed.

I looked at Karen. Her eyes stucked on the floor. Wet in them of crying. Hands tighted up in Meemaw's t-shirt. Crab pinchers. No pinching.

I thinked of the wailing of her and looked at her mouth. Lips pink and fat. She opened them just a little bit. But then it was Meemaw who talked.

Let's see if we can't sort out some food, eh?

Meemaw tried to stand up. Karen maked a noise.

Nnnnugh!

Holding tight on. Meemaw falled back to sitting down. I didn't want to watch more of programmes. I didn't want to watch of Meemaw and Karen either.

My tummy did a hurt I stayed still for what if poo came its way out now? What if poo came in the cloud all white white? A terrible disaster.

K, come on, baby. Let's all have something to eat and things will feel a bit brighter, eh?

Karen turned her face in Meemaw's booby said words I couldn't hear.

Sudden she reared up from the depths.

Argh! Fuck 'em all, eh Nat? Fuck 'em! I'll go and get us some food and a few cans, eh?

She was standed up getted her jacket on looking of wild in her eyes.

Oh! Well I've got some rice and a few bits, K. We could just eat that. I've got an onion.

Fuck all that hippy shit food, Nat. I want a burger. I'll get us burgers and I need a fucking drink.

Karen sniffed little sniffs rubbed her face of two hands. She looked all round then a horrible smile. Bared its teeth the mighty beast. I saw them white white in the dark. All the time darker darker in our flat.

She putted her hand in our pot of the keys. Taked them and holded up jangling.

Won't be a tick!

She went out our door banged the front one hard. Loud for disturbing upstairs man.

Meemaw turned on the light. Her brown was swirls she came quick to me picked me out of the cloud. All things letted go in me.

Meemaw! Poo!

Crying tears came hard of raining. Meemaw runned to the toilet sitted me on it. Then no stopping the great of it. Meemaw rubbing my back I crying no words not words then plop. Plop again. I holded Meemaw's hands.

Why? Why Meemaw is Karen why?

Shhh shhh shhh, my lovely boy. It's all okay.

There was a time a piece of still time stopped. Whee whiney in my ears I heared my voice my teeths all tight together and then a funny voice.

Tell me why Meemaw. Why Karen I hate.

Meemaw holded my hands.

Oh Danny, Danny boy, she's just…

The front door banged. The bathroom door open and Karen coming in now to our flat in to our flat. Me Danny on the toilet private a private thing!

SHUT THE DOOR!

Calm down, calm down!

Trying to get off I pulled toilet roll trundled a great white long of it. Bang! Meemaw slammed the bathroom door.

Lock! Lock! Lock!

Meemaw slided the silver lock. All my breaths fast I wriggled off the toilet.

Hang on there, Danny. Hang on!

She wiped blood very red I cried out. So mighty had been the poo it had breaked me.

It's okay, love, it's okay. Poor little love.

She gived me more toilet roll of blowing my nose she wiped all my face. Pulled up.

It was two actual worlds in out flat. Karen in the one world. Me and Meemaw in the other. I didn't know of how it would be next. But Meemaw had done it the slidey silver lock.

Me and Meemaw washed our hands of soap. Warm soft as a whale it was and all in my body was lightness. I feeled of floating. My bot was very sore but a lightness.

But the other world there very close. The other side of just our bathroom door. I thinked of Karen before how she came to the bathroom door with whisper words and bangs. I thinked she will come again. But the slidey silver lock is there he is on our side. He is to keep us in the safety.

Meemaw helped me dry my hands I was gone too still to do it. I was just my eyes moving this way and that and in me a wondering of what next. Sudden I knowed she would do it. A great mistake. Meemaw pulled back slidey silver lock. She taked my hand leaded me out into the other world.

Karen at our table her jacket on. Brown bag of paper folded over beside her.

Sorry about that, K. Bit of toilet trouble. All sorted now. What did you get us?

Meemaw reached out to take it the papery bag and Karen grabbed it up. She threw it hard hard across the room. It flied and chips falled down. Thin chips falled down in the air. Landed far by the door.

Meemaw taked one step back she looked at me. Me and Meemaw looking at each other just one splitted second then CRACK! Karen throwed a can of fizzy drink in that very moment. It hitted straightaway the kitchen cupboard.

Three more in a hoopy thing of holding she pulled. One then another she throwed them whizz past Meemaw's head. CRACK! CRACK! CRACK!

One was bursted. The fizz of it the drink coming out. Karen was standed up her hands hanging down each side. Her hands fists open fists open. Then still. All to still.

Meemaw came by me holded my shoulder bringed me at her legs. I feeled Meemaw's legs wobble wobble wobble.

I don't care why you did that, Karen, but you can go now.

Karen taked one two big steps her face close by Meemaw. I shutted my eyes. Hissing poisonous fangs.

You know perfectly well, you fucking bitch! Slamming the door in my fucking face!

Wha…?

You're a fucking two-faced bitch, aren't you? All lovey-dovey, care about you, Karen… Then you do that! Treat me like some crazy piece of shit you've got to lock out.

He was just on the toi…

I get it, Natalie. I get it, don't worry. You're just one more lying bitch. Pretending I mean something so you can fuck me around. Fuck with my head. I get it.

Karen, I…

Oh, yeah, I get it, don't worry… You don't give a shit about me. It's all about him. Well, guess what, sweetheart? I don't give a shit about you either.

Meemaw's legs went stagger stagger back. She holded tight my shoulder and it hurted. Karen was doing pushing. Pushing of my Meemaw.

I don't give a shit about you, bitch!

Push. Meemaw another step back we falled both together on the sofa. Karen turned round fast. Flat door slam. Front door slam. Gone.

Meemaw was jump jump in her body all and a little squeak came out. She holded me tight tight.

Me in the Meemaw circle but jump and jump of her body. In the window was us. We were a reflection. Dark dark outside. Meemaw and Danny were gone to tunnel people.

Meemaw holded my head by her mouth. Kisses and kisses on my hair.

My precious boy, my precious boy… It's okay, it's okay.

Meemaw's mouth was hotness on my head. Meemaw smelled the underarm smell of her.

Sudden Meemaw jumped up.

Fuck! Fuck, keys!

She went by our table.

Oh, thank Christ! Thank you, Jesus!

Holding our keys in her hand. Meemaw kissed the keys again and again. Meemaw sitted down and putted her head on the table. Then Meemaw was crying but not Danny. I watched. I watched Meemaw then the door. Then Meemaw again.

CHAPTER SEVENTEEN

Spiney was almost swallowed today. In the morning in the bed I saw his hand going down in the crack when Meemaw was folding.

STOP!

All Meemaw's body did a great jump.

What the hell's the matter, Danny?

Spiney's in there!

Meemaw heaved hoed it back to flatness and I rescued him. Meemaw sitted on the edge of the bed like forgotten it was time for putting away.

Meemaw went to still. Very brown. Even eyes closed like gone to sleep but sitting up. I looked at the brown of Meemaw. The still of her.

Meemaw can we go to the library?

Meemaw didn't say.

I taked Spiney to the window. In our street are the houses of odds and evens. We are the odds the other side evens. Meemaw says sometimes count the odds Danny. I do. But evens is actually better.

Across along is the Kasbah shop of the men and yum smells. In the window two things turn of meat we don't eat.

I could see the bus stop of the not often bus. Two people were doing waiting. A lady of silver mirrors for glasses and a man fat tummy. He had a blue shirt stripey of the football.

The bus came they went in. I thinked it was a predator the bus. It devoured the people. It went to Haywards Heath or somewhere somewhere Meemaw says.

But not today. Meemaw not saying anything today. Meemaw's

eyes were closed. The black eyelashes straight on her face were little caterpillars. Meemaw's nostrils were roundness of in and out. I thinked boo Meemaw. I didn't say because unkind. But I thinked boo and wake up.

I heared a noise outside. I looked round and a man was on our steps. The man had a yellow suit of bright daffodils yellow. He had all in his arms flowers so fat and big. Brrring! It was our bell our bell!

Meemaw!

Meemaw's eyes opened. Meemaw's eyes blinked at me.

Who is it? Is it her?

It's flowers Meemaw.

Christ.

Brrrring the bell again.

Meemaw get it get it the door!

Meemaw standed up slow slow to see the yellow man. She went to our door and getted the flowers with signing and no words. She putted them on our table and sitted down again.

The flowers came in a bubble. All the bubble was full of water the green ends of the flowers in. Some little leaves of curly too. I touched with my finger. It was strangeness. Hardness the bubble.

A scrunched up part had a ribbon round. The ribbon was the pinkest pink of icing. I went closer. Leaned over. I touched with my tongue on the pink pink of it. But nothingy taste.

The flowers were many many many. Pinky purple blue they were and sorts. Best was purple with a line of yellow on them. Added on like painting but real.

I went in them all. My face in and the smell of the greenness. And sweet of donuts or pancakes of Meemaw with the sugar on. And all the brightness. The brightest brightness that had ever come in our flat.

Meemaw opened a teeny white envelope and taked out a thing inside. A message. Meemaw stared. A long time of staring like lots of reading.

What does it say Meemaw? What does it say?

Nothing.

She lied the card down on the table and went to our armchair. Meemaw sat in it sideways. Meemaw looked away from the flowers. I thinked I couldn't look the other way in our flat today. So brightiful were the flowers. They filled all up our flat and it was song. The flowers maked a song on our table.

Meemaw there's so many!

Yes.

Still not looking.

Look Meemaw! So many!

Yes. There are so many flowers, Danny.

She did a quick look. It was little and low. Away again quick like it was hot. Hot to look. Like it was burning in Meemaw's eye. She looked away. Then closed her eyes again.

But not to me the burning. To me they singed their song. Oh Danny! I loved it. I climbed right on the table Meemaw didn't say no. Meemaw eyes closed still. I pushed right into all the smell. I did touching of stroke pinch squeeze squeeze. I putted my eye on the sweetest sweet. Brown heavy dust was there like ladies on their eyelashes. A sticky tongue part shined and shined. I putted my arms right round to cuddle and cuddle the flowers of bright.

Meemaw's crying was behind her hands but I saw. Shake shake shoulders. I heared the first sniff and I went. Meemaw had gone to curled up. A curled up flower not comed open. She was tight in. I climbed beside Meemaw and did patting.

Shh shh. There there.

Meemaw cried of the shaking shoulders but quiet. In a little while she looked out. Pink hot face and snotty.

I fetched long long of toilet roll but when I getted back she was curled up again. I squiggled my hand in the curl of Meemaw holding the toilet roll. Meemaw did a laugh. Meemaw uncurled and wiped her eyes. She blowed but still tears keeped on coming out. Tears running fast like chasing.

Danny, I…

She stopped again and no talking.

What I Meemaw?

Danny, oh my Danny boy, why? Why am I always a fuck up? Why? Why is my life such a fucked-up mess?

Meemaw said it fuck.

I thought for one brief moment there, Danny boy, for the briefest of moments, I thought that someone rated me. That someone cared about me, Danny. Someone who wasn't just a bloody heap of broken bits. Someone who'd maybe got their life together. And thought I was something. That someone thought I was something.

Meemaw stopped talking. She snapped her mouth in a straight line. Pulled me on her lap. Then did a sigh.

Oh shut up, Natalie, for Christ's sake.

Are they from Karen Meemaw? The brightiful flowers are from Karen Meemaw?

Yes, they're from Karen.

Does she think it's your birthday this day?

No. They are a way of saying sorry, Danny. On the card she says sorry.

Meemaw had said it was nothing on the card. She had done another lie.

Over past the flowers were our kitchen cupboards. I looked at the great damage of Karen.

I getted up and went to the cupboard doors. To the hurts of the fizzy drink cans hitting them. Minty green was chipped away black underneath showing. I rubbed the hurts with my tippy finger. It was bad damage the agents will hate Danny. Wave goodbye to the deposit now sunshine.

Meemaw I don't want Karen to come in our flat again even if she sended a sorry. Even the flowers.

Meemaw getted up she went to under the sink and taked out the fat roll of black sacks for rubbish. She teared one off with her teeth. A swift predator. She flapped it the mighty black wing. Meemaw was a pterosaur swooping. The black wing swooped she spreaded it flat. Meemaw taked the flowers. She lifted their bubble. Lifted all their brightiful colours. She sitted them in the black. Then Meemaw prisoned the flowers up inside.

I smelled the smell of plasticky of the black sack. I like it. I do. But all the sweet bright gone.

Meemaw pulled off the top of our bin our swingy bin. She pushed the black sack down inside. It filled it up almost almost at the top and not bin day yet. She pushed the lid on again.

Meemaw picked up the tiny white message then. She stared and stared. Putted it down on the table and went sudden in the bathroom.

I went to the table and looked at it the white message. It was writing of blue pen. Blobby fat. Words loopy of mess I couldn't read. Just one word Karen I readed. It was huge big of too much space. All the other words were squashed.

I taked the white message and looked close of my eye at the Karen. I did a spit of actual spit on and rubbed my finger round round. I did more. Then I taked the white message by the radiator and pushed it down the back. Down the back is fat grey dust and spiders. I hoped for spiders and their poo on it.

Meemaw came back.

Meemaw shall we go to the library and you can get new books of space?

Meemaw blinked one blink.

We can see Jane at the library.

I really wanted to go to the centre where the lady of round boobies was. And maybe more dinosaurs. But that was the plan of yesterday and yesterday went to very bad. Very wrong.

I thinked of it yesterday. Of the crack of the cans. I runned to Meemaw holded her legs. Meemaw blinked one more then sudden speaked.

Yes! Come on, let's get going.

We went to do our teeth.

Because Meemaw had forgetted breakfast she maked me a folded of toast for on the way. I liked it. I thinked it was the best of a breakfast for the walking along the pavement lines. Walking along the lines and foldy over toast was good.

At the corner my toast was gone and I holded Meemaw's hand for crossing. On the other side I singed a song.

Tale of a Tooth Tale of a Egg! Tale of a Tooth Tale of a Egg!

Meemaw was slow. She letted me sing on on in a round of spiral forever. Sometimes in my head it came the crack of cans on our cupboards. I singed louder then.

At the library Meemaw sitted down by the door.

I'm tired, Danny. You go and look at the books.

I went to the shelf of orange labels. Dinosaurs and prehistoric. All books I knowed. One was Eyewitness Guide. A tear of page 16 a bad person did. A name of Adam writed in it too.

I stroked all the teeths of the T-Rex and Jane was sudden there to surprise me.

Hi Danny! How are you today?

Hi Jane! How are you today?

Jane putted a big pile of books on one little table.

I thought of you the other day, Danny. I saw a documentary about evolution and there was a lot about fossils.

Jane was doing putting them away the books. Each here or there of the colours and numbers.

Charles Darwin's theory of evolution was a challenge to the Christian men of his day.

It surely was!

Jane crouched on the floor by cooking. She has good eye crinkles. Very quiet I heared her smiling. Heared it in me.

Jane looked over at Meemaw. I looked too. Meemaw's hair was very tangles of just waking up. Jane waved at Meemaw. Meemaw lifted up one hand but a not wave. A still hand.

Well, I need a coffee now. See you soon, Danny.

See you soon Jane.

Meemaw called out loud.

Come on then!

Meemaw had forgetted of being in the library. Meemaw speaked a loud voice when always we are quiet in the library. And she had not getted books. She was brown. Such brown.

I went by Meemaw because time to go already.

Outside was very windy wildness. Bothery of my hair which is gone long and in my eyes. All the sky was flat bright white. I runned tree to tree along.

Each every time I touched the tree trunk I said a swear of mind words. This was a spell I maked from the library to our flat. I maked a long line of spelled trees for me and for Meemaw to always be safe. By the traffic lights Meemaw holded out her hand.

We need to get some veg, Danny.

That meant the shop of the man.

No!

The shop of the man is not good and Meemaw knows. Not good because the man pinched me on my face and laughing. He said many of bad things. Cry baby and boys don't cry. We don't go. We don't go in it now the shop of the man.

No Meemaw! Not the shop of the man!

Look, I just haven't got the energy to get to Aldi today, Danny. He won't hurt you. You just stand behind me.

I stopped still on the pavement. A dog was there. A dog of squashed face. Tail curled up of a piggy. I holded the pole of the piggy dog.

No!

Okay, okay! For Christ's sake! Stay there then. But don't move a muscle, Danny, okay? Don't move and keep looking at me. I'll be back in one second.

I did look at Meemaw. I looked in the shop. Meemaw was inside the big glass. Meemaw getted tomatoes and went by a man with a white hat. Meemaw paid. All the time Meemaw holded me in her eyes. I holded back. I was brave. I was alone but I was holding.

Meemaw came out and we went along.

Such was the brown and slow of her and then a big jump. Buzz buzz buzz of a talking call lighted up in her phone. Meemaw looked. Then she pressed the button and her phone went to dark.

CHAPTER EIGHTEEN

One day in the old flat Meemaw and me maked scones. Round crinkly cutter we pressed down and it maked shapes. I liked it the cutter and the shapes. I eated one but not cooked and Meemaw said no more.

After we eated cooked ones. Such of golden smell. A melty of butter golden too. Golden trickle with white in it. I holded Spiney and he drinked a sip of it the melty.

On these days of bad colours I think of it the scones day. We can one day have it again. I will magic it. But first a day of Karen gone. A day of Karen dead.

When we getted home from the library Meemaw putted new paper and my pens on our table.

Danny, love, I'm whacked. I need a little nap. You just do your drawing and I'll curl up here.

Meemaw taked a bed pillow but in the chair.

Don't go asleep, Meemaw!

Love, listen, I need just a little sleep, I…

I didn't like it Meemaw asleep and not me. In the daytime and not me too.

Please be a kind boy.

In Meemaw's eyes were tears for crying come but not out yet. I didn't want it the coming out.

Okay. You can go asleep Meemaw.

I drawed a giganotosaurus spiked by spears of aliens. In real there was at no time humans and dinosaurs coexisting on the planet we call home. But aliens might have came in their crafts. Flown away before death and fossilising of their bones. Or the alien bones were maked of metal or ice to melt away. No one may know this.

All was very quiet in our flat and Meemaw still. Meemaw's hair all on the pillow.

I drawed only the spears of the aliens. I didn't draw of the aliens because I didn't know of their look.

Meemaw did talking strange and sudden. I told you I told you. Very fast. Meemaw's eyes still shut then bang! It was a words explosion of Spanish. Gobble obble nonsense words of Spanish. Faster and faster.

Then Meemaw was crying. Tears comed out of her closed eyes and Spanish words lots like talking but asleep. I looked. I standed up and looked at Meemaw my heart a hard clunk of it. A newness. Very strange asleep crying. But I was brave and kind too. I went close by her. I patted.

Meemaw Meemaw wake up!

Meemaw's eyes popped to open. She sitted up quick looking all around.

What, Danny?

Meemaw you had a bad dream and Spanish.

I'm sorry. I'm sorry.

Meemaw wiping her eyes. Her runny nose on the back of her hand. No tissue and that's yucky Danny.

She pulled me on her lap.

What sorry Meemaw?

She did a hiccup noise of the crying.

Sorry…

I thinked she was sorry of the noise maybe but no upstairs man in the daytime.

It's okay Meemaw. You didn't disturb me.

I didn't disturb him. I didn't disturb him.

Meemaw squeezy round my middle holded me. Rocked and rocked. I liked it the rock rock but Meemaw holding too tight I didn't like. Too tight squeeze for breathing even.

Meemaw! Too tight!

Sorry.

Meemaw wiped her eyes more. Sniffed. No more of crying. Then a more gently cuddle and Meemaw humming the singy song of row your boat.

The doorbell maked us both jump in our two bodies at once. It ringed one time then two times fast and bang bang bang. Then the shouting.

Nat! Nat! Nat, baby! Nat!

Meemaw sitted very still. She was stopped on pause. No rocking no song. The bell ringed on on brrrrrrrringbrrrrrring.

All was loud of an emergency. Karen. My heart such hard bangs it maked a cough come. Meemaw holded tighter tighter.

Then a terrible fastness of noises came tumble down. The front door opened and upstairs man shouting.

Oi! Bloody hell!

Bang! Bang! Our flat door bang of Karen. Karen. Louder of shouting than before. Close close came she the beast. Upstairs man shouted too.

Natalie! Oi, Natalie!

Meemaw standed up put me on the floor.

No Meemaw! Don't open!

But Meemaw went. She opened our flat door a little bit. A slice of upstairs man there. His half face.

Look, can you sort this out? I'm just getting home from work, I'm not having all this!

Sorry, yes. Sorry.

Karen was behind the upstairs man pushing pushing. He turned round.

All right mate! Do you mind, eh? Eh?

He pushed Karen back. Then he went. Upstairs man went. Meemaw opened wide our door and Karen came in our flat.

I runned to under the table. I sitted in the middle of dinosaur world. The trees rock volcano all gone to floppy and no good. I putted my arms round my knees. Spiney inside and safe.

The smell of Karen so horrible strong. She speaked in slidy words of such loudness.

NatbabyNatI'msogladtoseeyou. Oh my baby!

Meemaw standed back one two steps. Karen putted out her hand wobbled one step then sitted thump on our sofa. Meemaw holded up her two hands.

Karen, you need to be quiet! Quiet, yeah? You can't piss him off, he's a friend of the landlord.

Karen starey staring. Then she rubbed her face one hand.

Sure sure sure sure.

Do you want a coffee?

Fuck! I didn't come for coffee, Nat! I came to tell you how much I love you baby, how much I... I can't lose you, don't make me lose you, I can't!

Keep it down, okay? Keep it down.

Karen did a burp.

You need to drink some water.

Meemaw getted a glass all filled up. She holded it out for Karen. The silver top was sloshy shlosh and Meemaw's hand wet of it. Karen didn't take it. It shaked and shaked in Meemaw's hand.

Can you hear me, woman? I love you! I'm telling you I love you! Is that fucking nothing to you?

Shhh!

Meemaw sitted down next to Karen. Water shaked shaked in her two hands and splash splash on the floor.

Karen pounced the cunning predator. Pressing trying kissing of Meemaw. The glass dropped down on the floor. Meemaw was doing twisting her head. She tried getting up and Karen catched my Meemaw's hand.

Karen! Karen, stop it!

Pulling. Hands stretched. Inside me I feeled it a stretch too. It feeled of pinch and hurting.

Waaaah!

Karen maked a Karen wail then sudden letted go. Meemaw falled onto the floor but getted up quick.

Karen! I can't have this! You know I can't have this. You must be able to see this isn't okay. I can't have this with him here!

Karen maked another wail another. She banged her fists on her head.

Three big clumps came on the ceiling from upstairs man. A shout of him.

SHUT UP!

Meemaw standed close to Karen again but hands behind for no catching me.

You have to be quiet, K. K, you have to be quiet.

Karen speaked in a hushed down voice. It was dryness and fastness.

All I've done is love you, can't you see? Is there really nothing there? Don't you understannatnatnatnat…Aaaaaaaaaaaaaagh!

Wail again. Long wail on on. Upstairs man maked another clump.

You've got to go!

Meemaw shouted it loud over the wailing of Karen. Karen was quiet. Sudden all to quiet.

I heared only drippy tap. One two sniffs of Karen. Her head hanged down sniff one more. She looked up at Meemaw. She speaked very slow clear for listen to me Danny. No crying.

I'll kill myself. If you don't want me I'll kill myself.

I saw Meemaw's face the sideways of it. Her body so long. The thin of Meemaw. The bones of Meemaw there I saw. I thinked of it a new thin a new colour too. White of bright light. Silver white. I never saw it before that silver white.

Did you hear me, Nat? Do you understand what I'm saying? I'll kill myself.

Meemaw didn't say of any words. All quiet again.

I thinked. I thinked I didn't know of kill myself. How can it be kill myself? Kill is the roar teeth bite or stagged or shot of a gun. Sometimes runned over or electric on the train tracks. All of the things of killed chased in my head and then I thinked of kill myself and I didn't know.

I wanted it all to go away. All the pictures and words of it go away. I pressed my hands flat on my ears heared shh of the inside of me. But then shouting again. Karen.

I'll do it! I'll do it like a shot! What women have done to me, Nat… You know, you know what women have done to me! And now you. So I'll do it! I will! Is that what you want? Is it?

Meemaw was fast hard of a train on the tracks. I never saw her be it before. Meemaw runned at Karen. Meemaw grabbed Karen's arms did pushing pushing to the door.

Get out! Get out!

Upstairs man clump clump again.

SHUT THE FUCK UP!

A whirly windmill of arms. One hitted on Meemaw she falled onto our chair her hair spreaded out. Her face gone under.

Karen was quiet talking again. On and on no spaces no turns.

I'll fucking do it if that's what you want I'll fucking go now and do it. End this now fucking end it if that makes you happy. Does that make you happy?

A long time Meemaw didn't get up. I maked a noise then. I squeaked a noise I didn't mean to. It comed out by its own self. Karen turned round to my world the dinosaur world under the table.

I get it. I get it. You don't want me you've got him you've got him so you don't want me I get it.

Meemaw standed up. Meemaw pushed her hair back of her face. I saw the one red side of Meemaw's face of the hit Karen did. I saw it the purpley of lines and all over fat red. Meemaw's eyes bright alive. Not killed. Not dead.

Meemaw standed between Karen and me. Me under the table. She speaked calm like it'll be all right like it's not a disaster Danny. But she was speaking to Karen.

Let's go out. Let's go out for a walk, honey. Let's just go for a walk and talk and get some alone time, eh? A proper talk, okay?

Meemaw touched Karen's arm. All the room was smalled and far. I thinked of the arm and the hit. I slided right far back under under. The wall hard on my back.

I wanted to get Meemaw and pull her in under. I should have done that. Maked her safe if I could. Meemaw looked at me. Meemaw was a advert lady smiling. A lady of the sidebar not real.

You'll be all right for ten minutes, Danny, won't you? We're just going for a walk.

Meemaw holded Karen's arm and maked her walk. Meemaw taked the keys from the pot.

See you in a bit, Dan.

Bang of our flat door. Bang of front door. I was Danny alone.

Then I feeled it the wet on my dinosaur world. All across dinosaur world was wet of wee. It had went on my socks all everywhere.

I closed my eyes counted but only to seventy eight because then crying had come too hard. I dropped Spiney. I grabbed him up holded him by my cheek. But Spiney was slippery of wee. Wee on my face now and very wrong.

The day was going to evening. Upstairs man's telly said news where you are. I was under the table in dinosaur land but all of wee.

All the time it was darker I thinked of minutes. It is seconds 59 then one minute. But nothing showed me numbers like YouTube or station clocks turning over time.

I didn't know of ten minutes gone yet. Didn't know if Meemaw will come or Karen too or never ever Meemaw come back again. I holded round my knees and crying more quiet. It was cold. I came out.

I went to the bathroom taked off trousers pants socks throwed them in our bath. I finded my pyjamas bottoms and putted them on instead. Come on Danny it's not a disaster. I thinked of accidents of wee Meemaw always says it.

I standed up on tippy of my toes to get the basin tap. A big heave of it and plug in. Then soap. I washed my hands and holded Spiney under too. I rubbed him too much of the soap and it wouldn't come off. I wiped him on the towel for the best try. Not too bad.

Come on then Spiney.

It was gone to actual dark in our flat. I standed by our window watched out in the street.

In the orange light I could see. Seven cars came fast by. The Kasbah of turning meat so bright it was its red name. Inside was one man. No persons were at the bus stop. A person of a hoody came they walked past our steps. Another a lady of bright hair in a big up pile on her head. Nobody was Meemaw.

Crying had stopped in me when I was washing Spiney but back it came sudden and I couldn't stop. I thinked be quiet Danny because of upstairs man. If he came with Meemaw not here would be so very wrong.

I wished two things. I wished Meemaw back and I wished Karen be killed. I didn't know of kill myself but I thinked she could be dead in the real real world. Underneath a bus or lorry of heavy load on the busy road.

Then I saw. I saw them both Meemaw and Karen coming along. Holding hands they stopped by a dark car of no colour. All colour of the world was gone to strange in the night. They did kissing.

My body was gone to wild of shaking. I holded the edge part of the window. My feet cold on our carpet tiles were hoppity all by themselves. Like dancing. Karen was closer closer but my Meemaw too. Meemaw. I wanted such and such my Meemaw.

Meemaw rubbed Karen's arm. Meemaw her head sideways nod nod nod. Then she letted go. She walked to our steps.

Karen was by the car still. Meemaw came up the steps. So close so close my Meemaw I putted my fingers on the window.

She waved at Karen one time then again. Again. Karen walked away down our street. She crossed over. Front door opened and Meemaw was coming in our flat.

She turned on the light.

Danny! Danny!

She was looking all about all about. I runned then like a train on tracks too.

Meemaw picked me up. Both each of us crying then. Meemaw and Danny. We tumbled on our sofa.

CHAPTER NINETEEN

Morning in Mick's flat is different because all the sea of things there. If I wake up and Meemaw is gone from the high up bed I must call to Meemaw because we don't know half of what's on that floor Danny. Meemaw comes from the kitchen and helps me get dressed. Helps me put on my trainers get down.

Meemaw has maked a clear end of table in the kitchen I sit with the book. My own book of *Walking with Dinosaurs*. Meemaw gets breakfast. I have round egg all shell taked off cutted in two halfs with yellow circles in. No flat egg because Mick's fry pan is broken of a wobbly black handle he burned.

In all days here Meemaw's colours are hard to see. She is actual Meemaw but always hidden colours.

Meemaw doesn't eat dinners just me and Mick. He says grand princess. Meemaw goes back in the kitchen more cleaning.

Meemaw told me a story of a man called Sisyphus who always pushed a stone up a hill. Always it rolled back down. Meemaw told me that in Mick's house she is like the Sisyphus man.

I said Sisyphus should have maked a wall first to stop it rolling back down. Maked the wall first Meemaw. I showed Meemaw on my drawing. A hill. Round wall of bricks a circle round the top he could push in there keep it up.

Meemaw said don't you ever lose that excellent instinct to plan ahead Danny.

I maked the hill a prison for a bad coelophysis. He hitted a other one and now they must prison him up there for always.

We have been here three mornings. One two three not at home.

This morning Meemaw was still in the big bed with me when I waked up.

Hey, Dan! Morning!

Meemaw!

She cuddled me.

I curled in the smell of her. Better than the Mick flat smells.

We need to get up, love. I have to go up to Haywards Heath today. Mick's going to look after you.

The sunshine was come in one part of the three window. It maked the orange curtain very glow and a orange rectangle lied on the floor all bumpy across the things.

No Meemaw.

Meemaw was warm soft of her boobies beside me. I smelled it in. I maked a good hum of it. Hum of loudness.

Hummmmmmmmmm… Hummmmmmmmmm…

It's not for long, love, but I need to go to sort things out.

I stopped the hum.

No Meemaw.

Went back in the hum.

Hummmmmmmmmm… Hummmmmmmmmm…

Look, Danny, I have to do an important thing.

Louder came the hum. I feeled it buzz in my nose. Meemaw touched my face.

Danny, listen. Listen. Are you listening?

I shaked my head of no. Still the loudness of the hum.

Hummmmmmmmmm… Hummmmmmmmmm…

Meemaw sitted up then she finded Spiney in the bed by her she standed him on the pillow. Loud her voice so I would hear.

We're waiting for you, Danny. We're waiting for you.

I went upside down my feet by Meemaw's tummy pushed.

Noooooooooooo!

Coco Pops, Danny! If you sit up and listen I'll get Coco Pops from the shop.

I thinked of it. I wanted them. I saw on a advert chocolatey. I sitted up.

Right, this is what I'm going to do. I'll get on the train and go to Haywards Heath. That's the one after our station and where the bus takes us for the Job Centre. I'll walk along the big road by the roundabout and I'll wait by there for it to be time for Karen to come out for lunch.

NO!

Listen! Listen, Danny. I'll wait for her to come out and then I'll tell her she can't come to our flat ever again.

NO!

It's okay. It'll be okay.

NO!

Danny, Danny, I need to tell her so we can go home to our flat. To make sure she won't come again. Do you understand?

The orange rectangle had moved across more slanty on the floor.

No Karen!

That's right, no Karen in our flat again, but I need to go and tell her, Danny, don't I? Because we need to say clearly to people, don't we? We have to be clear with our words, don't we?

I thinked kill myself. I thinked hit. I thinked of the cupboards the minty green soft of our cupboards broken. Underneath was black.

Nooooooo Meemaw!

Meemaw holded me. I went in close hum again.

Hummmmmmmmmm… Hummmmmmmmmmm…

It'll be okay, Danny. It will be okay. I just need to go and get this sorted out properly.

I thinked no but I didn't say it any more. I didn't say any more of words just the hum. It getted to a lovely growly growl I went in.

***

After breakfast of chocolatey goodness Meemaw came low by me. She stroked on my face.

This is something I can sort out, Danny, I promise you. I just need to go and speak to her when she's sober and calm, so I'll wait for her outside the Job Centre at lunchtime and then I'll get it all clear, come back and fetch you and we can go home.

I looked at Meemaw didn't say any of words.

I know that's too much to follow, love. Sorry. Listen, what I'm telling you is I'll come back later to fetch you and we'll go home and no more Karen visits, okay?

Still I didn't say any words. I thinked never did Meemaw leave me. I didn't want her to. I thinked of me and just Mick in the flat. All wrong.

Meemaw standed up and flashed white silver bright sudden. I thinked she must go. Go to face the enemy in a mighty battle.

How about if I make sandwiches just right, and leave them wrapped in silver foil? Aaaaaand look! I've got you a whole new pad of paper and new pens so you can do a new comic to show me when I get back!

I couldn't make words come and not crying. I nodded. I thinked Meemaw must be brave and I too.

Thank you, Danny. Thank you for being a grown-up boy and understanding. It's going to be okay.

Meemaw went to the yucky Mick bathroom. I heared her brushing her teeth.

Another badness of Mick's house is no Meemaw phone. Meemaw has maked her phone gone to black all the time. I said is it breaked Meemaw and she said no. I said or all data gone and she said I just need some peace for a bit Dan we didn't have phones when I was little you know.

I want YouTube and *Tale of a Tooth*. I think of it sometimes the boom bigness of the Walter Kronkite man. The music and the zoom in I love.

I thinked it might be gone off YouTube. Once a thing I liked of a Phantom Cat was gone off YouTube and Meemaw said bad luck Dan.

But I think of it *Tale of a Tooth*. I hope for it holded inside in the black and waiting for you Danny.

Here I have my *Walking with Dinosaurs* book Jane gived me. At bedtimes I have a book of this house Meemaw finded on the shelf. It is of fairy tales I don't like much but Meemaw told it was hers of when she was little and is special.

I like the pictures anyway. The pictures of woods very dark. And a girl of no feet where a woodcutter man chopped them off. He chopped them off with a axe because her feet went spelled and would never stop dancing in red shoes.

And here too is the big enormous telly but not always CBeebies because Mick wants other programmes.

Meemaw came. Ready and her shoes on. Meemaw showed me sandwiches wrapped up for me. I looked at Coco Pops Meemaw had buyed. Sitting there by the sandwiches.

Those are for breakfast only, Danny. You leave them alone, yes?

I didn't say.

Meemaw fast rushy she putted her hair back by her ear.

Look! I got you a bottle of water too, Dan. Flippy lid!

I like flippy lid. Meemaw knowed.

I'll be back by three. Look, here… When the little hand points at three and the big hand on twelve. Okay? Come in the front room now.

Meemaw holded my hand for walking along the corridor. I thinked she will be back. I was wet in my eyes but not crying because be brave.

Mick was on the sofa. A sea beast on the rocky shore. He was inside his cloudy smoke that always Mick has. A man and a lady of the telly said escape to the country.

I'll be back by three, Mick, okay?

Sure, sure, we'll be fine, me and the wee man.

Meemaw telled wee is small. That is funny wee is small. I said it lots lots until Meemaw said enough. But today was not of laughing. Today was the very serious day of Meemaw leaving me.

'Bye, Danny!

Bang the door. Meemaw gone.

I sitted in my clear square. Meemaw maked it for me my clear square of nothing. It is carpet flat for my pad of drawing and nothing of might be dangerous. I like the nothing. I touch the nothing. My hand in the middle of it. My square. My nothing. My fingers spreaded out. One two three four five.

Mick did a big fart. It went rump fump. Loud and on.

Pardon me!

He huffed on the sofa. He was twisty. He pulled his trousers they had went in his bot.

I drawed six boxes for a comic all straight lines only a bit leany on the one side.

Sometimes drawing goes like reading but I am making the story come. I make the creatures do the story. No one in there just me. No one. It is a good thing. All the boxes are mine.

I drawed T-Rex with bubbles of thinking. He thinked I shall kill the evil enemy. I did all the writing. I Danny. I maked the story come out of me.

Meemaw wasn't saying do some colours on it Danny go on go on. I didn't do colours.

Then there was strangeness on the sixth box. On the sixth box I wanted blue blue blue of a sky and I did it. It was a good blue of all open in my hand. I maked it fill fill fill. Blue was the thinking of the T-Rex when he knowed the enemy was gone. All gone away. I went to the edge to the line. Very careful. Only one place over.

Mick maked his snore noise. Snonk snonk snonk gah. He opened his eyes. Closed again.

My feet were gone tangly uncomfy in my square. I taked off my shoes putted them on the sea of things. Floating on top. My two shoes were boats.

I have never knowed of so much sleep like Mick. And not much getting up. I said to Meemaw she said he is poorly of too much years of fizzy drink in the cans. And long rollies and sadness.

I looked at the red red face. Mouth open droopy moustache over. I thinked I will drink just water like before Karen and the first of Coke. I will not to smoke rollies because smelly of stink. But how to be not sad? How can you not sad if you are?

Meemaw doesn't drink cans but smokes little rollies of Meemaw. And sad sometimes. Crying sometimes.

I must watch Meemaw doesn't go to poorly. I did a round circle of red a drop of blood on my comic. Coloured careful the red.

I thinked I must watch Meemaw and see her colours. But here in Mick's flat they are too hard to see. Meemaw is hiding them her colours.

Mick did another fart. His long rolly was gone out in the ashtray. His silver square lighter by it. I thinked I wanted to hold it in my hand nice smoothy flat. But Mick maked a piggy noise loud so I didn't go near.

I went for a wee. I went careful in the sea of things. I went all to the toilet by myself.

Meemaw cleaned the toilet of Mick's house the first night. It smelled very of yuck and poo was in it. Meemaw getted squirty bleach don't touch. She wore yellow gloves. Still it has a thing in. Crusty thing. Meemaw says it is limescale like fossils. A ancient toilet. I don't like the seat black toilet white. They are not matching. Very wrong.

But this a wee only so I standed up. I did good aiming not much drips. Tap was too stiffy hard to turn so I rubbed my hands on my trousers for getting off germs.

My sandwiches were in the kitchen. Wrapped up like birthdays and a surprise. I holded them. A squashy parcel. I thinked of Meemaw and goodness. Then I saw the knife.

I didn't know a knife first. It was just long and yellow the handle part. It had silver circles on I liked. I pulled it out. Out out slided the knife a mighty blade at the end. Not a point but breaked so jagged teeth. Very good. I did a shiver.

I holded the knife close by my eye. Then I holded the knife straight and maked it of me. It was my weapon.

Get back! I shall stag you!

My voice speaking. Danny in the flat. In Mick's flat. Sudden I thinked of Karen but it wasn't. It was me pretending only. A silly billy Danny don't be scared.

But I dropped it the knife. It falled down on my foot then off. Boing a trampoline. I was surprised.

Then came a hurt. It was a burning hurt. A rush of hurt.

I had touched it a knife of danger. A great mistake. I picked it up and slided it back in the heapy heap on the table. Hiding.

I holded all behind my teeths. Breathing hiss hiss I looked at my foot. On my sock my lighty grey smooth good sock had comed a flower. Red rose wet. Blood.

I sitted on the sticky ticky floor and pulled off my sock. The top of my foot had gone wet of the blood. In the middle the cutted part was a mouth. Like a mouth but very small. I touched it. I pulled the open mouth and more blood comed out.

All was thumping. My head inside twizzle. Tummy gone to sicky. I bunchled up my sock and holded it on. Better. All gone disappeared the blood.

I stayed still counting to 5356 a great longness of numbers. But then I thinked of Meemaw coming.

I thinked of Meemaw. I wanted Meemaw not seeing not

knowing.

I went in the bedroom to our bag. Inside were my socks of blue that is navy. I looked again at my foot. Such braveness. Foot was gone to not so wet. The mouthy cutted part gone thick sticky ticky blood.

I pulled it on the navy sock. No bloody was there. My foot looking all not broken and not cutted. I liked it. Better. But inside was still the stingy zingy feel.

I holded the sock of the red blood flower. It was a wrong thing. I looked at all the sea of things and thinked of throwing it in. But Meemaw has eyes of discovering so I thinked no. Then I thinked of the toilet.

In the toilet still my wee yellow from not flushed. The yellow and the crusty limescale. I throwed in the sock. It lied in the wee water sinking. Redness sinking in yellow wee.

I holded the handle with two hands. I did all my great strength of a mighty giganotosaurus. Whoosh in the water. Waterfall! Bloody sock went dancing dancing then gone.

Then the water was clear and still in the Mick toilet. Just the crusty of limescale knowed the sock had gone by. Meemaw didn't know of it. Only the limescale knowed. Only I knowed too. I feeled it close. A secret.

I taked my sandwiches in my clear square. Legs crossed hurty foot holded under safe.

I eated all my sandwiches. Sicky feeling gone. Peanut butter and softy bread. No crusts. I went flip flip flip of my bottle. The lid flip flip and good water I liked.

On the telly a black lady said of economic forecast. I looked at Mick asleep still. He did a piggy grunt. I thinked of Meemaw and Spanish talking. Mick did a cough of bubble phlegm. Then he opened his eyes.

Havin' your dinner, little man?

I did a nod.

He smiled and shutted his eyes still smiling.

I was going to make a comic of episode two the revenge. I started a T-Rex. His hand of two fingers very good. But then I went to sleepy. Heavy heavy. My clear square was gone very hot in the sun. I curled in it. I curled as a sleeping beast.

***

Meemaw touching me was a surprise on my shoulder.

Hey, love! Danny!

Too rough. Pulling.

Meemaw!

Christ! Christ, you scared me there, sunshine! Did you just nod off?

I sitted up all of confusion of the Mick room. But Meemaw had comed back. Meemaw back. Such goodness. I holded her tight.

Mick waked up too. He sitted up rubbed on his red face.

Cup of tea, Mick?

Grand.

I getted up from nothing square and followed Meemaw in the kitchen. I thinked of it the knife but hidden. Gone in the table heap.

Meemaw filled up the fat low kettle. It knocked and rattled of heating up. Then it clicked to off.

Meemaw did you tell Karen no coming?

Yes.

Can we go home?

Yes.

After cups of tea and more rollies all the things of ours were packed in our bags. Meemaw slided in my pens last. She looked at Mick gone droopy eyes on the sofa again.

Right, well we'll be making a move, Dad.

I had forgetted of Mick being the dad of Meemaw. I thinked of the lady in the hard photo in the drawer. She is Meemaw's mummy but gone to dead.

Meemaw lifted me up. Mick standed up and kissed me. It was horrible of his mouth air. The moustache on me like a animal.

Cutted foot was dangling down in my trainer now. Going tumpy tumpy inside. A strangeness but not a bad hurt.

So you're sure things are okay now, princess?

Meemaw did a sigh.

Yes, everything's fine. And it's Nat, Dad.

Nat. Sure. Nat.

He sitted down on his sofa again and a big yawn. Inside Mick's mouth are spaces of no teeth and darkness.

We'll be seeing you. Thanks for… Well, thanks.

Don't be a stranger, princess.

The door curtain joggled when Meemaw closed the door. She stopped still by the top of Mick's steps. Still carrying me and our bags by her feet.

Come on Meemaw! Home! Home!

Hang on, love. Let's get sorted.

Meemaw putted me down and picked up the bags. She taked a big big breath and letted it out slow.

Home!

We will, we will go home, but let's just pop down to the beach, Dan, and have a proper look at the sea. Shall we?

Meemaw taked another big breath and filled all up blue. Filled up of the blue I drawed in my comic. Blue of the sky and the sea. Bright blue of my actual Meemaw.

Yes!

Yes to the sea?

Yes to the sea!

We runned along together. The bags joggling on Meemaw. My foot tumpy tumpy in my trainer and I didn't care.

CHAPTER TWENTY

I stopped by the edge of the stones.

Come on, love! We can go on the beach. It's fine, come on…

The beach was a slidey down of crunchy crunch stones. We went on it Meemaw holding my hand.

Whoo! Mind how you go on the pebbles!

We stopped where it was flat again.

In the sea there standed a skeleton of black. It maked a shuddery inside me the great skeleton. I pointed but no words.

It was a pier like the other one but it burned down.

I looked and looked. It standed alone in the sea. It was just its bones. Gone to dead.

It used to be grand and have buildings on it like the other pier does. A long time ago though. It's a bit sad now, isn't it?

I thinked of the other pier and being on it. I thinked of the Karen day and the Coke that fell and went on her trainer and the Argos and all of that day. I liked the bones pier better.

Come on, Danny, let's go to the edge.

We getted near it. All trickle rumples of soft soft coming. Fast and sometimes closer they rushed.

Meemaw pulled me back. She laughed a surprise.

We sitted where the sea didn't reach us. We sitted on the pebbles that were warm of the sunshine day. The warm holded inside them. The sun was going low down nearly in the far off sea. It maked a path of golden sharkly. I blinked.

Meemaw looked at the sharkly of it. She was doing big breathing in and out. Her hands were stretched and stroking all the pebbles. Stroking like a furry cat. Like my back at bedtime. The pebbles turning and Meemaw stroking. Stroking like love.

We're going to start again, Dan. We're going to get that plan in motion.

What plan?

Meemaw looked at me like a bad thing.

Don't you remember our plan, Danny?

Go home?

No, no, the grand plan! Don't you remember the grand plan?

It sounded like something I had knowed maybe once. Maybe in a book.

Jesus! Where've I been, Danny? Where the hell have I been that we stopped talking about the grand plan?

You've been in Burgess Hill Meemaw.

Meemaw laughed. She picked up one of bluey grey pebbles squeezed it in her hand. I saw the squeeze. Then she throwed it. Meemaw throwed it it flied like a dark bird the bright sky behind. Then it falled. I heared it plop far in the sea.

I holded a blue grey one too. Very warm round. I thinked *Tale of a Egg*. I thinked of inside it curled a dinosaur warm. Asleep not borned yet.

Meemaw putted her hands on my face and holded it.

Danny, there is a plan and it isn't all about traipsing round Burgess Hill and taking any crazy old shit that comes our way. We don't have to take crazy shit because that's all that's on offer.

I wouldn't take it shit! Shit is a poo! It isn't on offer!

Sudden Meemaw letted go of my face and leaped up like a adventure starting. She runned to the water edge.

Come on, Danny!

A man looked. He was sitted on a orange towel with no t-shirt. On his body was swirly of hair.

Meemaw stopped. She hopped pulling off her boots. She throwed them up the beach one two. Higgly piggly they rolled down their socks inside. Hanging out tongues.

I runned too and standed behind Meemaw. She bended down taked all handfuls of the stones from by her bare feet. It was wet there. Meemaw toes on the shiny stones.

The grand plan, Mr Dan, is to get ourselves some money somehow and get away from here. Get away and see the beautiful world before they come for you.

She started to throw them the stones the pebbles. Plop plop plop and grabbing more up.

Before they slap you into school; start slapping on the labels.

A big stone went plop very deep. I thinked of it sinking but Meemaw talking on and fast.

Highly intelligent, socially awkward, bit of a loner, pinning you down.

Meemaw bended down again scrabbled up more stones more. She throwed them one another in the water. Each a word. Each stone taked a word far out in the sea.

While

plop

you

plop

are

plop

still

plop

free

plop.

The sea swallowed up every one. I knowed this was a certainness of Meemaw. This was the grand plan.

Grand plan grand plan! But Spiney! Spiney too! Meemaw if we go in the world Spiney must come!

Of course Spiney will come. Spiney's family. We are a family of three: you, me and Spiney. Don't you worry about that.

I picked up a pebble of big brown. It was heavy. I throwed it but not high. It went twizzle round fast over the sharkly surface. Not far but along the path that had comed of the golden sun.

Come on, Danny, have a paddle!

Meemaw did dancey into the water her arms reached out.

Come on!

I bended down did my velcros tried to pull it off my trainer but the world tipped. I falled over on the stones. Meemaw swooped. She lifted me up carried me up the stones hill. She sitted me on the dry. Pulled them off my trainers then my socks. Then a great gasp.

What's happened to your foot?

It was very white my foot but another red flower of blood had comed. Hidden by navy sock but now there. Sticky of dark red on my skin. Spreaded out down to the edge. Not wet not wet but wrong. I pulled it hard from Meemaw's hand.

I'm not cross, Dan. Just let me look.

I thinked not. I thinked of squish my foot underneath forever.

Does it hurt? What happened?

Meemaw's hair lifty in the wind. I looked at the water. I wanted it.

I had a accident of a knife.

Meemaw putted her hand on her eyes.

Christ. Let me look, Danny, come on.

I slided out my foot. Meemaw looked. She holded it in her warm Meemaw hand. I closed my eyes to not see her looking.

I thinked she would make me say of it. I thinked of the blood sock in the Mick toilet swirled all away and gone. I thinked of the secret of it. I didn't want to say any words of it. I didn't ever. I would not. Meemaw did a sigh.

It's okay, love. Come on, open your eyes. It's just a small cut really and it's not even bleeding now. It'll be fine. Come on.

I didn't open my eyes. My foot in the warm Meemaw hand. I didn't want to open. Meemaw's voice went on. Talking on.

I should never have left you there but I won't again. I won't ever look to him for anything again.

A seagull did a loud shout they do.

Come on!

Then I was lifted up in the air. I opened one eye. So bright! I maked a noise weep weep. I clinged tight on. Meemaw was walking in the sea.

I opened both eyes looked in front. It was all just the sea to the edge of the world. There was a line of dark blue on light blue. So light it was nearly to white.

Across the sea there's France, Danny. It's not far. The world isn't so far away. It's not so far at all. Dangle your foot down, the one that's not hurt.

I dangled. It was cold. Cold icy. I liked I liked it the fierce of it! Slosh slosh. I wriggled.

Put me down Meemaw! Put me in! Put me in the sea!

She did. Meemaw did. We standed. Meemaw holded my hand tight. The sea came. It went on my trousers edge swish swish. I looked at it all the moving light. The stones few and far between under the sea then. Soft mostly. Soft of the Meemaw velvety coat.

Feel the sand, Danny? We'll stand on a thousand beaches with sand that stretches on forever.

Forever. I thinked yes. I thinked I wanted forever with Meemaw.

CHAPTER TWENTY-ONE

It was dark when we getted to our flat and it stayed dark inside because the electricity was gone to the very end. Even the end of the emergency fiver.

Meemaw carried me in putted me down on the bed. It was still bed shape from when we went away.

We'll just get to sleep, sunshine, and in the morning we'll get up and get going.

I didn't know if Meemaw meaned to the world or to the shop for charging the special key. But then a big yawn came push out my mouth before I could ask of it. Then I forgetted asking. I just wanted to shut my eyes.

We didn't do teeth pjs or anything. Meemaw just taked off her trousers and slided in beside me.

***

When I waked up I was scared of a dream but it flew away fast. So fast I didn't know of it just the frightened feeling it had leaved behind.

A noise was of a buzzy bee and Meemaw was sitting up fast.

Oh! Oh!

She bumped my head with her arm.

Ow! Meemaw!

It was Meemaw's phone buzz buzz of a talking call. She reached onto the floor picked it up I thinked good good it is on I can watch *Tale of a Tooth* when she is finished.

The curtains weren't closed. Street lights still on not proper of day time yet. Grey sky. I heared a van just one on its own. A seagull. More birds too. All shouting out and still not proper day time.

Meemaw was saying and saying on the phone.

Yes. It is, yes. What? Well I'm not next of kin, no... Well she's... Yes, yes I do know her. What? Oh, god!

Meemaw held the phone beside of her face a long time. I couldn't see her colour. Meemaw held her head in one hand.

Yes. Yes, I'll come. I'm coming.

Meemaw flopped her phone down on the bed. On its screen down it lied. Still I didn't take it. Meemaw looked away from me and no talking. But something she'd said. She'd said of I'm coming.

What Meemaw? What is it?

Sometimes in a story there is a terrible curse there are red shoes. The girl taked the red shoes for the dance. Then they wouldn't come off until a chop. A chop of her very feet. That was it in my runaway dream of the night. I knowed it sudden. Very sudden very real. That was the dream I had.

Danny, we have to go to the hospital.

Meemaw getted out of bed putted on her trousers again. She was holding her phone at the floor for the light to find my trousers too.

Why?

Meemaw grabbing my feet to put my trousers on. I kicked away. No grabbing.

Why Meemaw? Why do we have to go to the hospital?

Because Karen is there.

Meemaw was holding hard hard my feet. I thinked again of the axe chopping. Chopping off feet. I went still. I letted Meemaw get my trousers on.

Meemaw putted on her boots putted her hair into a pony tail. She pulled it tight. I didn't like it getting up still in night-time and all a rush and a hospital.

No hospital! Not the hospital!

Just be quiet, Danny!

Meemaw bited me with those words. I hated Meemaw then.

My Meemaw doesn't do all the time be quiet be quiet of mean mummies on the bus. My Meemaw doesn't do pack it in stop it get here.

I watched her then jerky fast. She went to the high cupboard getted something out of a tin. My eyes were too filled wet of tears for seeing. I looked away. I looked out the window. The sun was just coming winky over the roofs across the road and in the leafs of the still trees.

I did a yawn. My tummy did a grooble too but I didn't listen. The tears went away. No crying. I wondered of it.

Meemaw talking a loud voice on the phone.

Can I have a taxi to Flat 1, 6 St Martin's Road please? Yes, as soon as possible. That's fine.

Meemaw shaked her coat put it on. She putted my coat on me with no words. Toot car outside. All rush.

Come on!

She holded my hand we went fast out of the flat. Bang of the door too loud for upstairs man.

I have been in a taxi on one day when we were very late for the Job Centre. This one was a more smelly taxi of green smell and the man drived away when Meemaw still putting in my seat belt to the hole. He was a mean taxi man.

Meemaw!

It's all right! Just wait.

Meemaw mean too in the hissy voice of a snake. Kind Meemaw gone this day and hissy snake instead.

The seat belt was all the time going on my cheek. I pulled it away holded it in my hand tight and wishing. I maked a wish for Karen to be dead at the hospital. You can be dead at a hospital. But I was all sudden scared Meemaw could see in my head. I looked round but she was looking out the window. She was not in my head and knowing.

I looked out the window too at the streets of not much people in. We stopped at traffic lights for red. Beside us a man was pushing up silver covers from a shop. He had a long pole of pushing.

The sky was blueing of a sunny day. I thinked about the world and going in it. I thinked we could go right now not to the hospital after all not.

But then we were there. Meemaw gived the man two purple twenties taked back a brown ten.

In all my life I never was in the hospital except when I was getted born. I can't remember that. Meemaw told me I was a bit the wrong way round and I getted stuck. They twizzled me and pulled me out of Meemaw's fanny triangle. Then I was born and alive.

But never after have I gone in the hospital and when we came I didn't like it. It was slidey doors and a long corridor. Meemaw talked to a lady in a glass box.

Then pulling pulling all along.

No Meemaw! No! Nooooo!

Danny, come on! Stop it! Stop it!

Then no talking more. Just pulling. And no windows just walls walls walls. And smells very bad. Noise just of me crying.

At a next door Meemaw ringed a doorbell. A man in blue pyjamas came. All was smells. Lights were hum. Above my head voices.

It really isn't appropriate. Is there no one else with you?

No!

We have some very ill patients in here. Will he be quiet?

Meemaw crouched down sudden beside me.

Danny, you need to be quiet in here because people are ill. People are ill in here and you have to be a kind boy and be quiet. It's okay. Look, it's okay, sweetheart. Just blow…

Meemaw holded a tissue for me. Meemaw to kind again. She stroked my hair her hand gone shaky. Then she standed up.

Okay? Quiet enough for you?

The man letted us in.

Inside the door it smelled very. I holded Meemaw's hand tight tight. We went in a teeny tiny room. A kettle on a table. One thin orange sofa and a chair of wooden arms and a orange seat. It creaked when Meemaw sitted down. She holded me on her lap. Blue pyjamas man standed in the doorway.

If you wait, I'll tell the doctor you're here.

I putted my forehead on Meemaw's coat. She didn't move any of herself just still as still. I tried to see her colour. I couldn't see anything of it. All the time was the horrible smell. The light a very blue white buzz buzz light. I wanted to go home. Home.

There was a bang of a door I did a jump. Meemaw holded me tighter. Another man came in purple pyjamas.

Ms White?

Yes.

He sitted on the edge of the orange sofa very close. Very. I pushed my head more into Meemaw. His voice quiet slow. He was a tortoise sort of man.

Who's this?

He meaned me.

This is my son, Daniel. I didn't have anyone to leave him with.

Daniel, would you like to go with Simon to play with some toys?

I didn't say. Inside of me was hard thumping. I burrowed in Meemaw. A mole digged in. I scrunched her coat tight.

I don't think he'll go. You'd better tell me what's happening.

Well, if you're sure.

Yes, just tell me. Please.

The tortoise voice was nice. I liked it. I peeped at tortoise man from underneath Meemaw's arm. He was a man of bronze colour and darkness eyes. I could see black dots of beard making in his cheek.

Well, Ms Henderson took quite a quantity of her prescription medication and we're going to need to watch her carefully for a few hours. But she's conscious. And she's out of immediate danger.

Meemaw's body did a little jump. Then another one quick after.

We understand from her that you are her partner?

No.

The no was alone and loud. Like a burp.

Oh! Oh, we were lead to believe…

No, we had a brief relationship but…

Then it was quiet no talking.

I wriggled my head so I could see the window from underneath Meemaw's arm. There was a blind maked of white stripes all lined up. I could see little slices of green grass and blue sky. A weeny plane crossed the blue one at a time. It maked a white fluffy line that joined them up.

Do you know if there's anyone else we should perhaps have informed?

Tortoise man talking again. I looked.

No, there's no one, as far as I know.

Tortoise man nodded his tortoise head slow up down. Up down.
Would you like to see her now?

Meemaw putted me on the chair even though I did a hard cling on. I did no talking. In the hospital it was best no talking.

Danny! Danny! Danny, look I just need to go and see Karen for a minute. It's just down the corridor. You'll be fine. You just sit here for a minute. Look, you can have my phone.

Tortoise man was watching us. Very still eyes. I looked in them once. I letted Meemaw go.

Your mum will be back in just a minute, Danny. You just wait here, okay?

He and Meemaw went out. Then I heared him in the corridor.
Just in there. Keep an eye for a minute.

Blue pyjamas man looked in the door at me.
Okay?

I did a nod. He went away.

I looked at the stripy window again. I thinked if I came very tiny I could go through the gaps of the white stripes and then out the window. But it was shut and all the air still.

I was in a buzzy room of horrible smell. Outside a door of high up handle and doorbell. No way out. Meemaw gone with the tortoise man.

I sitted still. I sitted and waited and wished hard for Meemaw.

Blue pyjamas man putted his face at the side of the doorway. He smiled at me went away again. I wished for Spiney but he was in Meemaw's bag on her shoulder. I was without Spiney. Without Meemaw. I picked up Meemaw's phone.

The phone was gone to black. I pressed the button on the side for on. Nothing no light no lock screen just still black.

The light on the ceiling buzzzz buzzzz and too blue too white. I thinked I feeled sick or something something wrong. Maybe it was because I wished Karen would be dead. Maybe this was a trap place for a punishment for evil doing. This was a witch's trap place and horrible smell and Meemaw gone. I standed up. All was panic of fear inside me.

The corridor outside wasn't long. At the end of it was a door of dark red splitted in half. Glass bits at the top and through them another room of hospital. I walked slow to the door thinked I would run back if blue pyjamas man saw me. But no one came.

At the door I could see through the glass bits if I standed up on tippy toes. Inside were six bed things of bodies on and machines. Hospital machines there.

Light inside there wasn't the bluey white. It was more dark. I peered in the murky gloom of it.

At the very end I saw my Meemaw's long hair her coat. Next to her tortoise man standed and in the bed a lump. I knowed it was a lump of Karen.

CHAPTER TWENTY-TWO

The Costa at the hospital was like the Costa of town but squished into small with little windows. Hospitally smell hiding under coffee smell.

Meemaw getted a tea and I had a bottle of orange juice of a straw. A eggy sandwich for sharing.

At the next table was a girl in her actual pyjamas. Pink with a unicorn of sharkle on the front. She had a tube right up her nose. Meemaw pulled on my sleeve.

Danny!

Can we go home now Meemaw?

No. Not just yet.

She was a colour now. A colour had comed to Meemaw as she sipped her smoky tea. It was brown. Her words were floaty far away. Not just yet were words that went floaty over the top of her tea away in the air. No more words.

I liked it the eggy sandwich a lot. I eated it fast even the crust that was shiny soft. I looked at Meemaw's half.

Here, have my bit, love.

She pushed the plate nearer me I yummed it up too with a sippy sip of cold orange juice. Unicorn pyjamas girl was getting picked up for a carry. She was big as big as maybe eight. Big for a carry.

Danny!

Meemaw pulled my arm again. It meaned not look.

Meemaw started fiddling in the bag. She was making a rolly inside for a secret. Dancing hands. Little bits of tobacco coming out on the table. Then she standed up.

Come on! Bring your juice.

We went out slidey doors to a bench place round the corner. Meemaw lighted her rolly up. I sitted on the bench and drinked icy cold orange.

There was green green grass. On the other side a silver fence then road and cars. Meemaw did a long suck on her rolly. Then she rubbed her crunckled forehead. Her knuckles on it. I thinked of Karen hit and hitting her horrible Karen head.

Meemaw blowed out her smoke.

Meemaw can we go now?

I told you, no.

Not actual cross just steady brown quiet. Her voice hard to hear in the outdoors of cars. A bird in a tree by the fence was very loud of shouting in bird words. Blackbird. I finded it with my eyes. Yellow beak blackbird.

Then Meemaw maked a noise I hadn't heared her ever make before. It was sort of ugh. But low of a man or a monster. Then Meemaw was shaky all over. Meemaw's arms shaked and shaked. Her rolly jumped jumped on her knee and her knee doing jumping too.

Meemaw!

It's… It's… It's all right, Danny love, I'm… just…

I slided right up close on the bench. Meemaw putted her arm round me. All of Meemaw's body was jump jump. Her voice wobbly.

I think, I think we'd better…

But she didn't say better of what. The cars on the road away past the silver fence were whoosh whoosh. We sitted and the noisy blackbird stopped shouting. He came down by our feet.

Blackbirds are my best birds because I know of them and their yellow beaks. But Meemaw telled that's just the man ones of yellow beaks. This one was a man one. It hopped and looked at us with the beady eye. Then flew away.

Meemaw still shaky but only little gentle now like leafs up on the tree. I thinked of going in the world. I thinked maybe we should go now because this hospital had maked Meemaw go to ugh and was not good. And Karen was in it.

Spiney?

I holded him by my cheek my other cheek on Meemaw's coat. I thinked hard for a minute of the world and go. Then I went just in the sunshine. My eyes going droopy and a hum. No more thinking of it. It was hard.

Meemaw's song was a surprise. Meemaw does singing sometimes of bath time when we're drying toes or sometimes washing up. But not in the world. And never she has ever singed a song of Spanish before. I knowed this was a song of Spanish because I couldn't hear where words started or stopped and all was nonsense. Meemaw singed it very quiet.

I closed my eyes but no sleep came because of outdoors sounds and too much space. When Meemaw stopped I sat up straight opened my eyes. Still all day time and busy whoosh on the road.

The sun went away behind a cloud. It went a chilly breeze too.

Let's go!

Yes!

We getted right to the front door of the hospital where was a man in a nighty. He had a pole on wheels. The man was smoking his rolly. He winked at me.

Meemaw standed still not looking at the man. Looking at the wall. The man speaked to Meemaw his voice came out a scary croak of a frog.

Are you all right, sweetheart? Are you lost?

Meemaw didn't say. Meemaw stared at the wall like reading words but there was no sign. Then she picked me up. All was very fast as a surprise and we were back in the hospital down the long corridor. Meemaw going so fast. Coat flying. Me flying too.

NO!

Still Meemaw went on.

No no no no! Meemaw I want to go hooome! No no no!

A lady walked by looked at me. I pushed Meemaw's shoulder she bumped it on a door. We went through.

Danny!

Meemaw speaked through her closed teeth of fury. She stopped still.

I was of fury too. I was crying. Snot running on my mouth I wiped it in a whoosh across Meemaw's shoulder. Some went in her hair. I was wriggling fighting to get down. Meemaw putted me down.

I almost very almost runned. But I didn't. All about was hospital. There was the long corridor in front us behind us. Doors to other hospital parts. There was smell.

So I gripped on Meemaw's velvety coat and cried. Meemaw picked me up again and taked me in a toilet that was there. It was still horrible but just us in there. And a lock.

Meemaw washed my face patted it of a piece of blue paper thing. I stopped crying. Then I did a wee. Long and splashy in the toilet.

I know this is hard, love, but just hang on and we'll go home soon.

Then she picked me up again and we flied down the corridor and I was gone to flop and no more crying. No more.

We ringed for to go back in the doorbell door. A lady of blue pyjamas came. We went in the little room and Meemaw putted me on the orange sofa.

We have to wait to talk to the doctor again, love. Here, you lie down.

Meemaw folded up her coat of a pillow and she sitted in the chair. She putted her arm across my tummy. Spiney by my nose for helping with the bad smell. I falled to sleep.

When I waked up purple pyjamas tortoise man was there on another chair right close to Meemaw. I did a big jump of shock. I sitted up fast and squiggled over to Meemaw's lap. Meemaw just scoopled me up but looking at the tortoise man still. They were talking. He had eyes of such darkness and his slow tortoise voice.

Psych are of the opinion that she is safe to be discharged as long as there's some support available at home. So I need to know if that's something you can offer?

Meemaw didn't say anything.

She'll have a referral on discharge and hopefully a follow-up appointment soon.

I pushed my face in Meemaw. She smelled of underarms. I felt her thumping inside.

Obviously I don't want to pressure you if you're not comfortable with this.

Well it's not much of a choice, is it really?

Well, the only other option is to section her if she really has no support. But, to be honest, I don't even know if psych will consider that given this seems to be her first such incident and she's not showing any signs of intent to harm herself now.

Meemaw pulled me closer on her lap. Tight arms.

I haven't known her long.

No more talking for a minute. Tortoise man coughed.

She'll get a psych referral and that appointment should be in the next few days, so she is being offered some ongoing support.

He putted his tortoise head sideways. Tortoise voice slow. Gentle to Meemaw.

We'll keep her in tonight. On the ward. Just to monitor for twenty-four hours. Then we could look to discharge her tomorrow afternoon, if you could be here?

He was looking at Meemaw. All the time looking. Meemaw looking at the floor. I looked at the floor too. It had little shiny sharkles in the grey. Sharkles of diamonds. Meemaw's voice was very quiet when she speaked the word.

Yes.

CHAPTER TWENTY-THREE

It taked Meemaw and me ages to get home. It was nearly to night-time again in our street.

But the shop was open. Meemaw putted three pounds on the electricity key. She buyed a small squishy of bread called Hovis that had a orange sticker of too much. 99p not 69p for big like Aldi. That was end of all the money in Meemaw's purse again.

Our flat looked funny like a dream when Meemaw putted on the light. Like gone away for ages. It had its own smell I don't hardly ever notice.

Meemaw filled up the kettle opened the fridge. Inside all white bright nothingy except a tiny of milk Meemaw throwed it down the sink.

The dinosaur world was still under the table. I crawled in looked at it. The wee was dried up I thinked it was good that Meemaw would never know of it. I sniffed close for smells. It was okay just a little bit of sticky.

Rex was the only visitor dinosaur standed on his feet. I maked Spiney go each to each to help them get up. Then they standed in a circle by the volcano.

Spiney said you're all right my fellows let us face the great battle! But Rex was angry. He bited Spiney's jaw because of all the long time we had been gone away. Spiney battled him down though. Spiney holded Rex tight until he stopped fighting. Spiney was victorious. Then they came out in a parade to go all the way to the window to look out for the enemy and I heard the low ugh noise again.

Meemaw was curled all up in the chair. Small small small.
Ugh! Ugh!

Shaking. Curled up like a snail.

I halted the dinosaurs. I squeezed in the thin space by Meemaw's leg.

It's okay Meemaw, it's okay.

Her brown hair the only bit of Meemaw head to be seen. I patted it.

My tummy was going groobly groobly all squished up. I knowed it was a poo. I ignoring its calling for a long time because of always other toilets. Now that poo knowed we were home and it was going to come.

I putted my face by Meemaw's folded in head. I whispered.

Meemaw! Poo!

She didn't look up. Meemaw didn't say anything. I whispered again.

Need a poo Meemaw!

But still Meemaw curled so I went on my own.

Pully light thing is broken off too high up for a reach so I leaved the door open. Light came in the crack. Not so scary and I sitted on the toilet. I waited. There was a great pain of squeeze of ow. Then it stopped.

Meemaw!

Not too loud because of Meemaw curled up and small. But she didn't come. Instead another pain. I cried a little bit of crying. Then the door swinged more closed sudden! All by itself of perhaps a ghost! Dark came and swallowed me and the pain again. A great push of fear in the dark and still no Meemaw.

Meemaw!

Louder but still she didn't come. I couldn't get down because now now the poo was coming. It roared in my tummy roared out my bot with a sharpness and splash.

For a minute I waited. All was fizzy in my ears. My eyes trying to see shapes in the dark of the bathroom.

Meemaw I'm finished! Meemaw come!

Meemaw didn't come. I slided off. There was some paper I wiped one time. I looked close in the dark to see of poo on the paper but I couldn't see it. I thinked what if I look close get poo on my nose? I throwed it away the paper did two more wipes of new bits like Meemaw. Always new bits.

Pulled up my pants and trousers banged down the lid. Tried to flush. Handle so hard. Only little dribbles of water came not proper whoosh to carry off the poo. I gived up.

Quick as quick I did cold tap splished my hands in the water for germs. Then runned back into the light.

Still was Meemaw curled. I climbed in next to her putted my face close for a whisper.

I did it Meemaw.

She didn't come out. Meemaw was still. I heared the little dryness of breath in out in out. I snuggled up closed my eyes sended in all of love to Meemaw in the curled up place.

But Meemaw stayed curled up and I getted off. I maked the dinosaurs go on on with the expedition. All my body feeled better better of a song inside of me even though Meemaw curled. So I singed all good words of *Tale of a Tooth*.

A hundred and twenty million years ago clever men clever men! One clue a tooth! One clue a tooth!

Spiney leaded them in the mission. It was all to the window. They lined up on the edge looked out at the world all darkened the street lights orange.

A van went by fast I couldn't see of all the words just one. One word was glass and a picture like glass broken. Shot out into separate daggers.

I thinked of Karen in the hospital her spiky hair. I thinked all the night would come and she was far away far away and that was safe. But then I thinked of Meemaw and tortoise man and I knowed tomorrow we would go back again. Because Meemaw had said a yes. I thinked it meaned go back again.

When I looked round Meemaw was uncurled staring at the door. Her face closed no colour.

Meemaw can we go in the world tomorrow?

Meemaw didn't say anything.

Meemaw can we go in the world not back to the hospital?

Meemaw didn't say just sitted. I brought all the dinosaurs by her feet. The dinosaurs roared each one at a time to Meemaw. Then Spiney standed on the chair arm and speaked in his voice right to Meemaw. He doesn't usually speak to Meemaw. But Spiney speaked.

I can battle the enemy and we can go in the world!

Meemaw waked up sudden. She looked at me all come back.

Are you hungry, Danny? Do you want some peanut butter toast?
Yes.

But she didn't get up. Just stared at the door again a long time. I waited. Then Spiney speaked more.

You must not ever see Karen again you can go into the world!

Meemaw curled up again. I had done it wrong. I shaked Meemaw's arm.

Can I have toast Meemaw? Meemaw!

Meemaw didn't come out just a small voice all curled in.

Give me five minutes, Danny.

Five minutes is not long but this was long. I taked the dinosaurs back to their world and standed Apato on the volcano for a emergency. Rex and Spiney saved him. Then I was so hungry so so hungry.

Meemaw still curled and when I came close to her I knowed she was asleep. Meemaw asleep is special slow in out. I can snuzzle in her arm still the in out is the same. I shaked her arm. She didn't wake up so I went to find the bread.

I taked the bread and climbed on the chair for getting the peanut butter. There was only a little bit in. I poked with a knife but hard to catch. I getted just little scrappy bits. I wiped them on the bread but it teared in a hole. I gived up. Just eated it nothing on. I eated three pieces of floppy Hovis standing on the chair tall. I liked it standing tall.

Then I sitted on the side by the sink and runned the cold tap. Hard it came! Splash on my legs! Exciting! I drinked out of the tap whoosh! Water all across the floor to the carpet tiles. It maked dark splashes. I turned off the tap.

Then I pressed the kettle button in. It lighted up very bluey blue of space ships. I watched. It went clonk hubble. Then smoky as a swamp of the Jurassic era. Then click to off.

I waited a little while then did it again. I liked it the blue light. Then the smoky hot. It maked the doors of the high cupboards wet to dribbling. I rubbed the wetness with my finger it maked a grubby line. I did it lots lots. Then kettle wouldn't press again. I getted down.

I taked four books into our bed that was still bed. It had stayed bed for many days now. I lied under the covers for reading the books.

I was reading *Walking with Dinosaurs* book of how the skeleton of a carnivore has impressive teeth. I stopped my voice but the words went on. The words went on in my head. Like mind words! The exact words of the page not maked up. I was doing reading in my head like Meemaw!

Meemaw!

Meemaw jumped to awake.

What?!

Meemaw I can read in my head! All silent in my head look!

I did it again. Meemaw couldn't know it.

In my head Meemaw! I'm reading it all on in my head and it says the teeth and jaws of a carnivore… Oh no! Look I don't have to say it out! Look Meemaw!

Meemaw laughed a little laugh. Not a joke for laughing!

No laughing! I can read in my head! I can read in my head!

I know! I know, I understand…

Meemaw getted out of the chair came to give a cuddle. I pushed her. Not a joke for laughing.

Meemaw looked at the clock.

Bloody hell, Danny! It's nearly midnight! How long was I asleep?

She pulled down the blind went to by the sink.

What happened here?

She meaned the floor. The floor all wet of splashes

I getted a drink and spilled. I eated some bread for tea.

I didn't say anything of the kettle. The kettle is don't touch. But it was a secret. It was a secret time like the knife. Meemaw twizzled up the bread bag.

Come on, teeth!

Tale of a Tooth! Tale of a Tooth!

We brushed our teeth. Meemaw did a wee flushed away my poo. I was glad of it gone. Our pjs were still in a bag from Mick's house. Meemaw opened the bag and smoky smelly smell of Mick's house rushed out.

Yuck! I don't want smelly!

Fair enough. Bloody hell. You don't notice how bad it is when you're there, do you?

She zipped it up again the bag.

We'll just keep these on.

We were just our t-shirts. Meemaw's legs. Gone thin like poles on the climbing frame.

Meemaw went to turn off the big light. She putted her head in the cupboard of the meter.

Shit! That's gone down quick!

Meemaw looked all around.

What's eating that up then? Christ, that's all I need, bloody meter going mad.

Meemaw plugged in her phone for charging. Then she getted in next to me.

CHAPTER TWENTY-FOUR

On the bus Karen holded Meemaw's one hand in her two hands. She looked on the floor. Meemaw looked out the window only sometimes little slippy smiles at Karen. I sitted on another seat across. Even though a stranger might come. Even though that.

Meemaw had telled me Karen not coming in our flat again. Meemaw had been hitted by Karen in our flat. But still Karen was coming home on our bus. Meemaw had telled me another lie.

At our front door Meemaw letted go of Karen's hand to go in her bag for the key. Karen standed droopy. Her arms dangled down beside. A sad penguin of all alone.

I standed Spiney on the wall and he looked at her trainers. They were the pair of one gone dark. Of the Coke on the pier. I thinked of that day. I thinked we had gone on the pier but never standed in the sea. It was a other day I standed in the sea. Just me and Meemaw. I maked a wish promise to Spiney we will do it again. A promise of go in the world of sandy beaches. Just our three family.

There was no lights when we getted in.

Ah, damn it! I hoped that'd last a bit longer.

Karen flopped on our sofa. Looked at her feet.

Well, never mind. Cup of tea, K? I can boil the water on the hob.

Yeah, thanks.

Meemaw maked tea of water in the saucepan. I like to watch that. One day I watched. It maked silver bubbles in our silver saucepan. Meemaw said don't you touch sunshine but letted me watch. On a other day. A better day.

Meemaw gived tea to Karen.

Ugh.

Sorry. No milk.

Karen holded the tea of her two hands but not drinking. She looked at it the smoky tea. Blink blink. Meemaw maked a cough of not real.

I wondered if you'd like me and Danny to walk you over to your place after we've had this? Settle you down for the evening?

Karen speaked at her tea not up at Meemaw.

I'm not safe to be left.

I slided under the table into dinosaur land.

Meemaw sitted on the chair then blowed on her tea. She speaked in her very most gentle voice for it's a hard thing Danny. For sadness of a breaked thing or lost.

I didn't know if there was someone I should have called, K?

I heared upstairs man flush his toilet.

I can call anyone you'd like me to. I've got plenty of minutes.

Karen standed up very sudden her trainer bumped her tea. It runned all across the carpet tiles and sitted in a shiny puddle of one second. Then it sinked in.

You know there's no one.

The sun was in the end window. The wet carpet shined in the slanty rectangle of light. Karen's voice went sudden loud. It getted louder of every word.

I lost everyone when my bitch ex left me and told everyone lies about me! I told you this! I told you no one believed me, no one stood by me because every fucking one of them was poisoned. Every one! And I know you don't give a shit either but I've made it clear, I've told you I've got no one else. There's no one and nothing and I won't be safe on my own. I can't do it. But, you know, kick me out if you want. If it's easier for you. I'll just end up dead.

It's going to be all right, K. You know you can get through this. I'm not saying I won't be here at all. I'm not saying anything like that. It's just I think maybe we're both in a difficult place just now and...

Karen bursted into tears. She talked all through the crying. Words running on very fast each in the next one.

I know I know I'm no good for you. I know I fuck things up! I just thought you...thought you were the one, my fucking soulmate. Nat, can you really not see it? You know we're meant to be together! You do, you see it! You feel it like I do, Nat! I can't, I can't if you don't want me, I can't!

Crying and crying. Snotty and screwed up her horrible horrible face.

Meemaw still. Waiting.

Karen stopped talking. She jumped up sudden and walking to me. Fast to the table. I slided quick out from under. I runned by the bathroom door in case she was coming to get me.

But she stopped by the table still. Like a giant come over the sky of the dinosaur world she standed. She holded the table edge of her two hands. She looking down at its woody top.

I had Spiney I had Spiney but the other dinosaurs were still underneath. I thinked she was going to flip over the table bring down a disaster on their world.

But not that. Karen taked a big deep breath like going underwater. Then BAM!

Karen bammed her head down on the table. I did a big jump my shoulders leaping up. Karen reared back like a injured allosaur. But no roar at all. Another BAM her head went down. Meemaw shouted.

KAREN! STOP! STOP IT!

She runned at her. Meemaw flinged out her arms to catch around Karen. But Karen shoved Meemaw of two hands and Meemaw went falling flying across the room. She bended sideways over the chair tumbled on the floor.

BAM! Karen's head again.

Karen panting of a dog. Panting her mouth hanged open of a dog.

I taked a step to Meemaw. Meemaw sitting up on the floor by the chair. I wanted to go. Then Karen lifted her head up looked at me. Karen looked at me the last bit of the sun gone shining in her eyes and wee came. Wee runned fast hot as a hot finger of a witch down my leg in my sock. Lots. My trousers going soaked. I couldn't move my feet.

And then there was a knock on the door.

Upstairs man's voice came.

Are you okay in there?

Meemaw getted up. She was walking to the door and Karen swooped. Karen's hand over Meemaw's mouth covering. Her fingers pressed in Meemaw's cheek.

We're fine! We're fine! Sorry to disturb you. Just the kid having a tantrum.

Meemaw's eyes big round. Meemaw breathing hard. Her nostrils big to suck in the air and Karen her one hand still on Meemaw's mouth. Her other hand pulled Meemaw close. Tight. She wrapped one leg round Meemaw's legs. My Meemaw couldn't move.

Well, can you keep it down? I've got company.

Sure thing! Sorry about that.

Clump clump of upstairs man on the stairs.

Karen spitting words. Spit flied out.

You fucking dare make a sound.

She twizzled Meemaw round throwed her on the sofa. Meemaw coughed. She coughed lots.

I standed still as still. Karen walked over by the window and speaked at the glass. Her voice was gone sing song then like talking about a story of a sunny day. Happy things of a story.

It's never good enough is it? No matter what I do, people think they can just piss on me. Everyone pisses on Karen. You think you can too, don't you? After all I fucking told you. After everything. You just come swanning up to work. Spin me some shit. Some toxic shit about let's be friends. Patronising bitch.

She turned round and Meemaw jumped. Put her hand on her mouth. Hand on her mouth like Karen's hand before.

Let's be fucking friends? I told you. I told you what my ex had done to me and you were all… You were all big eyes and 'oh sweetheart…' Now you just dump me. Spin me shit about friends. I know what you are. You're some fucking benefit scum with your little freak kid living in this shithole and you think, you reckon, you can take me for a fool. You think you're too good for me! Think you can just dump me.

Karen turned round speaked quiet then. Quiet at the window.

Well fuck you. That's not happening.

Front of my trousers and one leg was sticked on me. Sticked on me. I standed still as still. Meemaw looked at me. Just one tiniest look of lifted eyes then she leaned down on the floor picked up the bag.

Karen runned. She grabbed the bag pulled it out of Meemaw's hand.

What is it you're needing, eh?

She started taking things out. Meemaw's purse the keys Meemaw's tobacco. Dropping them on the floor. Then she getted Meemaw's phone. She holded it up.

Is it this you want?

Give me the phone, Karen.

Karen holded it and looked at Meemaw. Then she taked it by the kitchen. She lifted the phone up beside her face like smiling of a selfie. CRACK! Crack the screen down on the tiles next of the cooker.

Then she throwed the phone. Meemaw ducked down it went whizzing past. Came close by my head. Then it hitted the door.

Meemaw getted up. She came to me. She pulled my head close by her leg.

Get out, Karen.

Karen laughed. Said it back.

Get out, Karen.

Meemaw picked me up. I maked a almost no because I was covered of wee. I didn't want it to go on Meemaw. But then I holded on tight. Pushed my face in Meemaw's neck.

Get out of my flat!

I heared the words inside Meemaw's body. Wobbly they came but true. I thinked my Meemaw could make her go. Make her go.

Karen whooshed past close. I feeled it the air move. SLAM!

Karen, get up.

Nah. I'm just going to sit here, I think. I'm just going to have a little sit-down on the floor here while you sort out that pissy little freak of yours, eh? You go and do that. He bloody stinks.

I didn't look up. I didn't look out from Meemaw's shoulder. I feeled her walking then we were in the bathroom. She shutted the door I heared click of the silver slidey lock. I whispered.

Meemaw!

Meemaw putted me down on the floor I opened my eyes. Very dark in the bathroom just the orangey street light shine in the pattern window. But my eyes getting used to it. Meemaw leaning on the door breathing fast. She whispered back.

It's okay, sunshine.

Meemaw bended down helped me get my wet trousers wet pants off. I keeped my whisper so quiet quiet of a mouse's voice.

Meemaw can we go?

Karen's sitting by the door. I don't think she's going to let us past right now, but we'll get out as soon as we can.

I thinked crying would come then. But I knowed it she must not hear. Meemaw finded me other trousers in a heap of some things by the toilet. But no pants no socks. She whispered close close my ear.

It's going to be okay. We'll just go when she falls asleep. Do you understand?

I nodded.

There is absolutely nothing to be scared of, Danny. There is nothing at all to be scared of. Do you understand?

I nodded again.

CHAPTER TWENTY-FIVE

It was a other early morning when I waked up. The window was in the wrong place. It was in the wrong place because me and Meemaw were in the chair. Meemaw was awake already. When I moved she whispered.

Shh…

Right in my ear. She holded her finger on her lips for no talking.

I looked on the floor by the door. There was Karen. A crocodile there and I knowed she had never moved in all the night. Still we were trapped.

Near Karen's head was Meemaw's phone. The screen was gone to diamonds and diamonds.

Meemaw whispered again such tiny words.

We're going to go, but we need to be clever. Get your shoes on right now and play on the floor. Play quietly. Don't say anything, don't ask me anything. When it's the moment, then I'll come and get you and you need to be ready to run fast, okay?

I did a nod.

Meemaw slided me gently gently off her lap. I walked slow and careful as a stalking velociraptor. I finded my shoes one and two and putted them on. No socks. I pressed the velcros.

I went to go under the table in the dinosaur world but Meemaw did a curly finger of come out. Instead I sitted on the floor by the window and the dinosaurs too.

Meemaw went to the wardrobe and taked down her box of special things. She slided it silent silent into the bag. All the moves of Meemaw were slow smooth.

Then she went to the tap and runned two glasses of water. The shoosh of the tap waked up Karen. Her blue blue eyes opened up. She blinked. Meemaw drinked one glass leaning on the kitchen side. She did a smile at Karen and then bringed the other water to me.

Morning, K.

A voice all okay and nothing wrong. But the bright the white silvery of her bursted out. No hiding of it in Meemaw this day. No hiding such brightness.

I thinked no one can see my Meemaw's colours except me. Please they can no one see. Not Karen. Please not Karen.

Karen sitted up. Her face looked wrong. It was lumped. Her forehead swelled up. Skin reddy purple of maybe to burst. No words.

I need to pop out and get some power on the key, K. And a pint of milk.

Karen sitted leaned back on the door.

Is there anything particular you fancy to eat?

Karen shaked her head. She slided away from the door. Meemaw reached out for my hand. Not looking at me just reaching. It was time. I standed up.

Why you taking him?

The white silver of Meemaw maked a shimmer. I heared shimmer in her voice.

I just thought a breath of air'd do him good. He's spent a lot of time indoors the last few days.

Karen shaked her head.

You leave him with me.

My heart jumped up in my throat and maked a squeak of noise. It wasn't me it wasn't. Karen laughed.

What's with the squeaking, Professor? You a mouse?

She putted her hand up on the side of her head.

Fuck… Can you get me some paracetamol, Nat?

Sure.

Meemaw putted the bag on her shoulder. Going. Meemaw was going and leaving me. She stopped. Meemaw crouched down and picked up poor broken phone.

I'm sorry, honey. I'll get you another one. I'll get you something better. I didn't mean it, you know?

I know.

I think I just need a few days here with you, honey. A few days for us to sort things out, yeah? Just chill together.

Sure.

Karen shutted her eyes. Meemaw looked right to me. Right to me.

Ah shit. I can't find my keys, K. I'm just gonna leave it on the latch, okay?

Sure.

Still Karen's eyes closed but talking.

I'm gonna have a quick shower.

Good plan, babe. Back in a mo.

Then Meemaw opened our flat door still looking and looking at me.

In my mind came a second splitted in panic. My legs maked me bob up ready to run but Meemaw holded up her hand. Meemaw meaned wait. Meemaw meaned be clever. I holded down my legs. I pressed my knees of my two hands. In my mind said wait legs.

Meemaw clicked the latch. Latch down means not proper shut Danny. Anyone could push it open. Then Meemaw went out. All the side of the door was a thin crack of black. Not shut.

I heared Meemaw open the front door too and I didn't hear it close. It was open. I knowed it. It was for me. But not yet. Not yet.

Karen getted up. She swayed like a tree cut of a axe and going to fall. I looked at her knees.

I'm going in the shower.

She taked one step to the bathroom. Then she stopped. I thinked of Meemaw thrown. I thinked of the fingers of Karen on her face. Such the fear in me like a giant.

On the side in the kitchen was the truck she buyed me on the Brighton day. She picked it up. I thinked she might throw. I went small small. But no. Karen came crouched down and putted it beside me. She rolled it back forward back. All of the world was her smell. Smell of mixture. Perfumey some sicky in it and under arms not Meemaw's.

You don't always have to play with the monsters, you know? You play with your truck like a good boy.

Each every word was a breeze of sicky. I nodded. She rubbed

on my head. It maked a tiny trickle of wee come. Just tiny not all my trousers. Then fast she standed up and went in the bathroom.

Click the slidey lock then whoosh of the boiler comed awake. Piiiish of shower.

Fuck!

All the water goes spray everywhere because of broken. Karen in it. All water everywhere. Karen no clothes and all wet. Now.

I grabbed up the dinosaurs. I runned. I pulled our flat door it opened and there was front door all wide open and the day outside. Meemaw there at the bottom of the steps waiting.

Danny!

We runned. All the way along the road we runned together. I was fast fast as Meemaw. At the corner Meemaw grabbed my arm. Cars by the light vrrm vrrrm. We runned across. Runned across the big busy road and all the noise of it.

A blue and white bus at the stop door closed. A winky orange side eye for going now. But Meemaw knocked. Meemaw knocked on the foldy door. Doors popped open.

Thank you! Single to Brighton.

£5.40.

I've got it in change here.

All of Meemaw's hand was money.

Just sit down. Pay me at the next stop.

We sitted down and the bus fast away!

Meemaw puffy puffy from running. She sitted back in the seat.

Danny, you're a star. You're an absolute star. You know I wouldn't have taken another step. I would never have left you. You do know that, don't you?

Yes.

A lady was watching from on a other seat. She had a anorak of purple. Hair grey in big circles on her head. She smiled.

Meemaw can I put the dinosaurs in the bag?

Of course.

It was then I looked. The borrow dinosaurs were all in my arms. But no Spiney.

CHAPTER TWENTY-SIX

I cried all the roundabouts and where the fields came. Two horses a garage a fence that goes on on I cried. I knowed we couldn't go back.

The bus was far fast from home. Meemaw and me safe of Karen but not going back. And Spiney not safe. Spiney maybe lost on the pavement. Worse in our flat and Karen.

Now she had getted out the shower and finded us gone away. Spiney would pay the price. She would get revenge of Spiney. Without me Spiney couldn't fight. Spiney couldn't do a bite with no Danny to make it. He was at her mercy the evil one.

All the world runned over of tears. I holded on the edge of the window feeled and feeled the hurt. Meemaw's arms round but too bad now. Meemaw's words too small such the bigness of hurt.

Things of imagining filled me up. Karen speaking words of hate attacking Spiney. Throwing and bangs. Such loud inside me I wanted to break all the bus window and run run back to rescue him.

Meemaw sitted on the edge of the seat. Meemaw was a bird of a fence. Small. In white silver brightness. Nothing was safe. Such was the danger. Sudden everything went to quiet inside me. Crying stopped.

The fence outside flick flick flick. The sky blue and fat white clouds. Just that that that until big houses of black and white fronts. Slow the bus then and people in cars. A lady of very yellow hair singing in her car. Her mouth wide and a smile to me. More cars. More people.

Come on, love. This is our stop.

We were near the pier of the Karen day. It smelled the same smell and it was coming a hot day. I was thirsty.

Meemaw! Drink!

All my face was nasty of snot of crying. My mouth all sticky.

I haven't got one. Just hang on, we'll get water in a bit.

Meemaw holded my hand tight crossing the road. Tight. Hot.

Are we going to Mick's house?

We stopped by a bench and Meemaw getted out her box of precious things.

Are we Meemaw? Meemaw?

No.

In the bottom is always the little brown envelope. Square envelope of a crumpley softness. Shiny flap. In it lives Meemaw's mummy bracelet. Golden. Four swirly stones of dragon eggs called opals. Darky red of dragon's blood called garnets. A ancient treasure. The most true precious thing of the box.

Meemaw taked out the envelope and squished it in her pocket of her jeans.

Thirsty Meemaw!

I know.

Meemaw was too tight holding and hurrying in the pavement of people and big shops. I pulled.

Meeeemaw! Thirsty!

No words of Meemaw just pull pull pull. A man bumped Meemaw of his arm.

But Meemaw knowed secret tiny streets. All suddenly we were in them. Red bricks little streets of no cars. Filled up of people but slow. Slow walking and more quiet. Meemaw squiggled in out of the people. But still tight of my hand and I wanted stop stop and a drink.

Meeeeeemaaaaaw!

What is it?

Drink!

I told you in a minute.

But it was a lot of minutes and no drink and I didn't know. I didn't know anything of it.

Sudden we stopped. It was a window of a shop of treasure. Meemaw looked in.

Such thirsty. Hot thirsty and people all around.

This one.

It was a doorbell. Then came buzzzzzz. I didn't know of this place. I didn't like it. And thirsty. Thirsty!

Nooooo!

DANNY!

Meemaw pulled hard we were in.

The door shut. All still. All still quiet. A lady sitted by a smoky mug. A lady of hair very long black.

Can I help you, love?

I've got a bracelet to sell, do you buy?

Let me have a look.

All in the shop was still. I went to still. The air of spickles and moving. Moving slow.

Meemaw tipped it the crunkle envelope. In the lady's hand was Meemaw's mummy bracelet. The bracelet curled up of a golden curl. The precious of dragon eggs. Dragon blood.

Oh that's unusual, isn't it? Very nice.

It's Spanish. Late nineteenth century.

Very nice. A lovely piece.

Would you be interested?

It's the sort of thing that does sell but it's not pure gold... and the stones are just opals and garnets. It's not worth much, love.

How much?

I could do you eighty.

I thought more like a hundred and fifty.

Oh no! Oh no, it's not worth anything like that, love, honestly.

A hundred and twenty?

I'll do you a hundred. As it's such an unusual piece, I could do a hundred.

Fine.

Out of the lady's drawer came purple twenties. One two three four five to a hundred:

All of the shop was sunshine and air of the spickles that are tiny spaceships. On the floor a blue blue carpet and shadows of the windows. Shadow of a teddy bear of olden days come huge. Shadow fur was fluffy. So hot. But a place of quiet. I whispered.

Meemaw I'm thirsty.

I don't suppose you could give him a glass of water by any chance?

The lady maked a huff. She getted off her chair.

This way. I can't leave you in the shop.

We went behind a curtain. Dark behind. Then a white door. Inside a kitchen.

The kitchen was of a other world. It had a window of bars of a prison. Cool green. A drip drip tap. Outside the window a wall close maked of grey stones and greenness growing.

The lady gived me water. It was a glass glass. I drinked it down cold. Good. Inside me a call of the water in my tummy. Empty inside. No breakfast. No tea time yesterday too.

All the world lifted up and went swinging. Then still again.

Meemaw was looking at the window of bars. Meemaw was still and staring. I holded the glass to Meemaw but she didn't take it. The lady taked it. The lady touched Meemaw's arm.

Okay?

Meemaw jumped.

Yes. Thanks. Thanks so much for that.

Then rush rush again. Meemaw holded my hand through the shop and clunk the door closed behind. Inside was the lady of long hair. Inside was the quiet world of it. Meemaw's mummy bracelet was gone. Like Spiney gone. I started crying again.

Are you hungry, Danny?

I couldn't say of it but inside yes yes yes.

Let's get a picnic. Come on.

Meemaw picked me up for a carry. My legs feeled heavy heavy and I putted my head on Meemaw's shoulder. Lumpy of bones.

We went back to the big road and in a Co-op that is green. Not too bad if you look for the deals. Meemaw putted me down.

Fruit, Danny. What shall we get?

I pointed of plums that I like. Purple red and zingy skins.

Meemaw getted a pot of squashy red pasta. Babybels that we have for special. I standed by sweets. Not crying now. Not asking but I standed by sweets of Haribo and pink.

No sweets. Look though, Dan. How about this?

A big a big of white chocolate! I like it best of all chocolate. Meemaw likes second best.

And water in a bought big bottle even though it's ridiculous Danny the ultimate example of human stupidity. Clean clear big bottle. Not flippy lid though.

Such a feast we buyed! Outside Meemaw gave me a straight away plum. Zing of it pop the skin. Inside sweetle and good.

We need a place that sells unlocked handsets.

'Nother plum!

Meemaw gave it.

I thinked handcuffs of the police. Meemaw maybe to get them in case of Karen.

What of handcuffs Meemaw?

No! Not handcuffs! Handsets. Phones. We need a new phone.

We came to a place called Imperial Arcade. It was a tunnel for shops. Inside a man sitted in a sleeping bag who lives there homeless. And there was a shop all phone covers on a table outside.

This'll do.

Inside was very squashed. Spinny things all crowded. I didn't like it. I pulled. Meemaw tight holded. There was a man. A very tall man of baldy head.

I need a really cheap handset. Anything that'll fit this SIM.

Meemaw showed the broken phone of diamonds. Karen had done it. Karen. Spiney.

I've got that one if you want it. A hundred and twenty.

I haven't got it.

I could do you the S3 mini for sixty.

I need something cheaper.

The man looked at me I feeled his eyes plop on my head. I standed still still.

In my mouth was the plum stone. Once was a plum stone in a library book. It was magic. It growed a great tree in a house one night. The great tree had roots they drinked up breakfast tea eated a boiled egg. I thinked if a tree popped out my mouth. A curly branch to take a phone for Meemaw.

I've got one a bit bashed up I can do for forty.

It'll work though?

Sure, sure, it's just got some chips.

Meemaw gave the man broken phone. He scooted his big thumb on and it opened up. Inside the little red card called Sim.

Sim makes it the Meemaw phone. Like a brain Danny. Like you're you because of your Danny brain.

The man putted it in the other phone. Switched on. Showed Meemaw. Meemaw did a nod.

Thanks.

Meemaw gave him two twenties and we went back out into the tunnel of shops. Out again to the street. Noise and noise. A bus close did a big rumble roar.

I thinked of the white chocolate.

Chocolate! Meemaw!

I pulled on Meemaw's sleeve but no reply. I tried to get in the bag for it the chocolate but Meemaw clutched up her hand tight. Holded tight like there was a animal in the bag for escaping. Meemaw's fingers were white of bones inside. Meemaw's skin gone a pattern of purple blue. Cold. Cold of a statue.

People came pushing us. A not good place to stand.

Meemaw!

Sudden she waked up again.

Come on!

We went in a bus stop.

This one'll do.

It was a rightaway bus! Meemaw and me getted on.

It was a strange bus. Long long. Bendy in the middle of a circle that swizzled this way that way. Squashy sides all folded. Dingle dangle handles for tall people. I thinked of holding on. I thinked of hanging down. A Danny monkey.

Meemaw was pushing me little pushes up the bus I didn't like. No time for looking. Such a horrible day of rush and push and all strangeness.

Come on, Danny. Sit down at the back there.

I wanted to know where we were going. But I wanted chocolate more.

Meeeeemaaaaaw! I waaaaaant some chocolate!

Meemaw went in the bag and getted out the chocolate. She breaked a whole big row of squares gived it to me.

Here! Here it is! Be quiet now.

Such lots! Meemaw breaked some for her too but just holded it not eating.

The chocolate was soft of the hot day. Chocolatey Play-Doh of whitey white. I loved it loved it loved it. Squish squish and stickety of my teeth.

Meemaw was fiddling the new phone. Chocolate on her knee beside. I taked it. Meemaw didn't say no.

CHAPTER TWENTY-SEVEN

Meemaw told me the tree was called a beech tree. But we were far of the beach now. All the way on the bendy bus and I thinked this was the world and we were in it.

The tree was a trunk of smoothness and wood. Very fat. I standed underneath and putted my arms all round. I looked up. Moving moving of the green. Moving up high up high high. And no one there just me and my Meemaw. We were far away.

I didn't know it that my Meemaw knowed so many of secret places. Maybe here in the forest was a house of a woodcutter or witch or bears in a story. A house for Meemaw and Danny to be hided from Karen. But no Spiney. It hurted inside me.

Come and sit down, love.

Meemaw ripped open the squishy squashy pasta. She gived me a white fork for spiking. Quite yum but floppy. It was not nice as Meemaw pasta. Meemaw maked a rolly. She speaked sudden to me not looking up.

This is called Stanmer Great Wood. It was planted hundreds of years ago. There's a tree for every letter from A to Z.

Click Meemaw's lighter.

We have to go and get Spiney now Meemaw.

Meemaw sucked her rolly. All the ground was shadows moving and moving. Shush in the air.

Here's the thing, Danny, I can't take the risk. I'm too bloody scared to take the risk. Either way. Either way, my sunshine.

Another suck of rolly then she speaked more. Smoke from her nose.

Assuming it's not too late already.

Nothing of the words meaned sense. I tried to see her colour. I tried hard hard. I sended my eyes to softness and looking. But all was the moving of shadows. Nothing still. Nothing to be known of Meemaw or this place. Mysterious forest.

Are we going home Meemaw?

Meemaw flicked. Ash went in the grass.

Meemaw?

We'll have to. We'll have to, I don't know what else… I don't know.

Make the police come Meemaw.

Meemaw didn't say.

Karen hitted your face holded you tight putted her hand on your mouth. She holded you in a kidnap of Mr Creep the Crook!

Meemaw did a smile. But it was not a funny thing.

My little chap.

She looked like proper actual Meemaw a minute.

Meemaw we have to get Spiney. Rescue Spiney then go in the world right away.

How did you get so brave?

Meemaw's eyes shined up of tears but not coming out.

I never imagined I'd have anyone in my life as brave as you.

I looked at the floppy pasta thinked shut up Meemaw but didn't say. All such strangeness. But I was hungry. I spiked three more of the pasta.

We have to go back, of course we do. And I'll make it clear this time, Dan. I'll make it clear. Whatever that takes.

We'll get Spiney! We'll find Spiney!

Of course we will. Of course. I meant it, you know, Danny, about our travelling and seeing the world. It's a real plan, but we have to go back and sort stuff. I've missed a Job Centre appointment.

Meemaw squished the rolly on the ground. I thinked about the Job Centre and the first day of Karen. I remembered she came out and sitted by Meemaw on the wall. I didn't know she was most probably a very evil witch of spells. I should have killed her of a knife. Or hitted her head. Such a evil witch and hurted my Meemaw.

The trees were shady but the sun warm coming through. Meemaw spreaded out her coat and we lied down. Meemaw putted her arm round. I lied on her booby heared her heart clump clump clump.

Meemaw's wrist on me I thinked of the bracelet gone. I putted my hand round for a bracelet. Meemaw stroked stroked my arm of her other hand.

Meemaw are you sad of your bracelet gone?

It's just a thing, Dan. It doesn't matter.

Did your mummy wear it on her?

No, not really. She used to keep it in her handbag in a little dark blue velvet box. I don't know where that went. Maybe she took it out so he wouldn't find it… Anyway, it ended up in that envelope.

Your mummy went to dead.

Her stroking hand on my arm went still.

You were a grown-up Meemaw. Then your mummy went to dead.

Stroke stroke again.

I was eight, Danny.

A pigeon bird. Very fat it flapped all the green. A little leaf falled down down.

She was runned over of a car.

No. No, she wasn't run over. She was ill.

She didn't go to the hospital for doctors. She should have went to the hospital.

I thinked of the tortoise man.

Did she have bad tummy?

No.

I squiggled. Pushed my face in Meemaw for the smell the good smell.

Danny, you know I told you how Mick was ill from the cans of drink and the long rollies and sadness?

Yes.

It was a bit like that with my mum too. But mostly it was the sadness. It was a very black sadness and she couldn't keep on living so she died.

Meemaw's heart went clump clump clump. She stroked my arm again. I flapped for get off.

Are you to black sadness Meemaw?

No. Not like that. I'm not sad like that. Not that black sadness.

I knowed it was true. It was true because Meemaw has never gone to black not ever. Not to black.

Did she go to dead in your house Meemaw? Was she sitted in her chair?

She was just in her bed, Danny, in the morning. She had taken lots and lots of pills and they had made her heart stop. It just looked like she was asleep.

There's information on the box Meemaw. You telled there is information of how many!

Yes.

She didn't read it!

She wanted to take too many. She wanted her heart to stop and to be dead.

I looked at all the tiny tiny lines of Meemaw's t-shirt. Over under over under.

Her body was dead in the bed. It had to go in a hole. In a coffin in a hole.

People came to help, Danny. The police came and a kind lady called Sue.

Sudden I sitted up.

I'm sad Meemaw! Very sad with no Spiney.

I know. I know that's worrying you but we're going to go back and find him. We'll go. We just need to re-charge our batteries, Danny. Just for a minute.

Meemaw taked off her boots. Her toes were bare in the green leafs and little sticks. I taked my trainers off. I saw the hole place of the knife at Mick's house. Nearly mended. A blue of bruise.

Meemaw lied down again and closed her eyes. I lied on my tummy close. I finded a little stick to be a person stick. He lived under the edge of Meemaw's spreaded out coat. It was a curvy soft cave. Inside was dark. Outside sunshine. He jumped high.

I diggled my toes in the leafs then in the earth. It feeled cool soft. A yawn came and I lied my head down with stick person too.

***

Danny! Come on, love, we need to make a move.

Meemaw's voice was close of my ear. The sun was gone. The leafs were loud now of sh sh sh. I was cold.

Meemaw did my shoes and putted all the food away. She picked me up. She carried me inside her coat my legs wrapped round of a monkey. Meemaw was hard of bones.

By the edge of the trees we stopped.

Do you need a wee?

Noooo.

I clinged on tight.

Have a try. Come on.

Meemaw bended down and pushed me off.

Noooo. No wee!

You can wee on the big tree, Dan!

I wanted to then. I weed all on it and maked a mark of dark. Meemaw crouched down because of no willy.

We waited by a big road for the bus to come back. The cars went neenow neenow fast. Meemaw wouldn't let me get off the seat.

She taked the new phone out looked at it. Holded it one hand other hand one hand other hand.

Can I go on it Meemaw?

I thinked of *Tale of a Tooth*. A hundred and twenty million years ago. Then I thinked of Spiney and it hurted again.

Meemaw didn't say of the phone she just all the time holded it. Holded it and staring. The cars went neenow.

When the bus came Meemaw and me sitted at the back. It was a long bendy again. People on people off.

We stopped because a red light. Phone still in Meemaw's hand I watched her thumb go on the side for switch on. Buzz. Buzz buzz buzz.

Meemaw's brown was come all over. But her finger was dancing. Meemaw was messaging. I thinked Karen. A sicky feeling came in me. Sicky of bus and nasty pasta taste.

Right. We can go back to the flat. I've messaged her and she's left.

Did you ask of Spiney Meemaw?

We'll find him when we get back.

Ask Karen of Spiney Meemaw!

I'm sure he's in the flat, love.

I thinked of him killed. I thinked of Spiney lost to me.

ASK!

A lady of Chinese was looking at me.

Ssh! He'll be in the flat.

I bursted into tears. It was worser of Meemaw not asking. Spiney the most precious of all dinosaurs and Meemaw had not asked.

I hitted Meemaw's arm. I whacked Meemaw again again. Kicked on the seat in front.

Stop it! Stop it, Danny!

Hard hard as I could then bang! Bus stopped. I falled off the seat. I falled right off. I thump banged my head and my side on the seat in front.

Danny!

Meemaw picked me up. My head thumped. My side burned of a fire. Crying again.

Shhh… Shhhh… It's all right.

Meemaw rocked me. I stopped crying. In a little while she peeled a Babybel cheese from the bag and holded it to me. I throwed it on the floor. But I taked the red soft wax. I squish squashed it and sniffed. I pressed it on the window and pulled off again. It maked pink ghosts. Inside I was sicky. My side hurted. Spiney was lost.

CHAPTER TWENTY-EIGHT

All along our road was wishes. At every car a wish of Spiney under it. But not. Kerb then black road empty. No Spiney. Ten cars one white van. No Spiney.

Not by any walls or steps. Not in a black box of recycling. Not by the Kasbah shop. The swingy sign of doner kebab and chips was there. The mens in the shop laughing. One waved to me not knowing of the crisis.

Then it was home and Spiney not found. Meemaw went up the steps and me following. Each step my feet on it and one more wish. One more wish of Spiney.

The front door was locked double for Meemaw to twizzle the key two times.

Wait!

All along had been wishes of Spiney but now I thinked of Karen.

Meemaw!

It's okay, Danny. Don't worry, love. The door's locked. All the lights are off. And I've texted her. She's not here. She told me she's gone home and we can talk tomorrow. Let's just get inside now, okay?

Our flat windows were gone to a mirror of the sky. Pretty blue. Purple at the edge and a bird in it. A seagull. But a mirror. No seeing in to be sure.

Meemaw!

I pulled Meemaw's coat for wait for stop.

Danny, if she's in there then we'll come straight back out, okay? You stand behind me and I'll look in. If she's there, then we'll go straight back out onto the pavement. We won't go in if she's there. I promise.

But if she comes in a chase! Hurts you Meemaw on the pavement!

She won't.

Meemaw pushed open our flat door and peeped her head inside. *She's not here, Danny.*

She went in and I behind her. Meemaw pushed in the key of the meter. The lights came to on. Hmmmm of fridge to alive.

I runned around looked all on the floor for Spiney.

SpineySpineySpineySpiney…

Meemaw flopped down on the sofa. Plonked the bag beside. I pushed Meemaw and lifted up the cushion under Meemaw's bot.

Take it easy, love!

Meemaw was gone to floppy again. Shaky too and rubbing her arms. I pulled. It was a emergency still and Meemaw just floppy. No good.

Help me! Help me find him!

J…just a second. Give me a second, Danny. Then I'll get the tea on and we can have a proper thorough search while it's cooking.

On the way home Meemaw had getted the electricity key charged of ten pounds and Meemaw had said potatoes gravy baked beans. But I didn't want. All I wanted was find Spiney.

NO! Meemaw look now!

God, Danny, please… I'm just going to have a wee.

Meemaw opened the bathroom door.

Scream!

One scream and Karen on Meemaw.

Shshshshshshhhh!

Flappy arms of Karen at Meemaw. Meemaw walked backwards. Arms flapping too.

Get… get… Karen, no…

My feet were sticked on the floor. Eyes sticked on Karen. On her flappy arms. One was very wrong something wrong. It was blood. All down her arm red. Karen's white shirt red. Red of blood and wet. Soaky.

Meemaw back back into the kitchen. Karen pressed her on the fridge. Pressed into Meemaw.

Babybabybaby!

Trying to kiss Meemaw. Her hand of the blood arm on Meemaw's head. Then I saw Meemaw's arm. Meemaw picked up a mug of on the side and clonk. Clonk on Karen's head.

Shit!

Hands to her head she letted Meemaw go.

Meemaw swooped to me. She grabbed my arm.

Go! Go!

We spinned around. Almost to the door and Meemaw's hand leaped out of mine.

Karen had punched on Meemaw. She flied in the air. Thud Meemaw's head on the wall. Loud. On the wall at the edge by the window Meemaw's head hitted. She falled. All in the air all was raining red. Blood drops of Karen's arm rained in the flat.

Still. All stopped. Knock knock the flat door.

Hello?

Upstairs man. Karen picked me up. She picked me up and holded her arm of blood on my back. Wet cold I feeled it.

Karen's mouth close hot and her words maked spit.

Not a word. You don't say a word.

Karen opened the door a tiny slice.

Yeah?

Hi. I just found this down the side of the front steps there as I was coming in. I guess it's yours.

Spiney. Upstairs man holding. He holded him out through the door slice for take him. I did.

Oh, cheers mate, he's been doing his nut about that monster.

Karen closing the slice but upstairs man speaked more.

Is Natalie in? I just need a word.

She's having a lie-down. Migraine.

Oh, well, if you could just tell her I'd like…

Yeah.

Door closed. Click. Karen putted me down. Push pushed in my back to the sofa.

Sit there. Shut up.

Karen went by Meemaw. Meemaw was still on the floor not getted up. Meemaw's face I couldn't see just hair spreaded out.

You silly bitch, Nat. What have you done? What have you done?

My body wouldn't move. I tried to get up. Nothing happened. I tried just move my arm but it didn't move. I was turned to stone in a statue. And Meemaw was… Meemaw on the floor. Meemaw Meemaw Meemaw and Karen saying words. Words at me. Her mouth moving.

Your mum… Stay there and don't… A little rest… Your mum…

All words turning over and round. Mouth moving on and on. But Meemaw. Meeemaw on the floor. Not moving.

Karen's arm was teared of a claw. Soft. Wet the edges. Blood. Whoosh whoosh whoosh. Blood.

I runned to the door. Jumped. My fingers slided down. My fingers slided and her arms came around me tight. No air in me. Kicking kicking. My foot thonked on her body.

Oioioi, you little shit.

Karen folded me on the floor of the kitchen. Pressed. Then pushed. Pushed to under the table.

You stay there, you understand? Stay there if you don't want a hiding! Understand?

I didn't understand. Hiding. I hided back by the wall. Karen holded up her hand of red blood. She would hurt me.

Karen standed up. She was just her legs then and wee came. Such wee I couldn't stop. And crying. Not noise. Not noise but tears running.

Tears runned all each other down my face. All wet and slidy in our flat. I looked and saw Meemaw. By the window. Meemaw still on the floor. Still like asleep. Like asleep Danny.

Karen went by Meemaw. Karen had a bottle of golden in her hand. She drinked some then flopped down on her knees. Next to Meemaw. Stroking my Meemaw's hair and words. Whisper words I couldn't hear.

Sudden Meemaw coughed. Karen jumped her hands off Meemaw's head. Meemaw coughed again and something shooted out of her mouth.

Still again. Meemaw still again. Karen stroked more and words. *Baby, baby, you have a rest…*

The cough thing had landed near. Small as a sweetcorn bit but not yellow. Pink on the greeny floor. Meemaw maked a sound a little sound. Sound is not dead. Cough is not dead.

You're all right, sweetheart, just have a rest, just have a rest, baby.

Karen poured golden out on Meemaw's face for a drink. But it runned all over. Cough again. Then still. Quiet.

Baby.

Karen lied by Meemaw rubbing. Her blood hand rubbed on Meemaw's back. She kissed on Meemaw's hair.

Spiney was in my hands. His sail. The claws of him. I tried mind words to him but it was too loud inside me.

My Spiney. Wet was on him. I looked. On the Spiney sail was red. Red of Karen blood. I wiped wiped wiped Spiney on my t-shirt. But red still. Red on him.

I looked back at the cough thing. Mysterious thing of fear. It had come flown out of my Meemaw. Sudden all sudden rushed up sicky inside me. I knowed of it. I knowed. It was a tooth. Sicky almost to my mouth. I feel smelled it come up. Burning. But it went down again.

It went to darkness in our flat. Karen still sitted up next to Meemaw. She drinked her golden. I watched. Drink. Stroke. Stroking my Meemaw.

Sometimes hanging down her head she cried. One time she looked at me. Her eyes shined in the dark.

She getted up then pushed the chair by the door. Our big chair of Meemaw reading sideways. Pushed it hard by the door.

Fuck, shit! No ideas, Professor, okay?

Then Karen lied down next to Meemaw and singed a song of a Lady in Red. Over over Lady in Red. At the end was quiet. Drip drip our tap. Hummmmm fridge. Karen's arm over Meemaw.

The golden bottle gone almost to empty. Street light in it glowed.

I heared the gzzzz gzzz of Karen. Asleep. Asleep. Long and dark. Sometimes my eyes went closed and sometimes open. Never Meemaw getted up. Long.

Light again and cars. I heared upstairs man flush his toilet. Pad pad his walking. Telly.

Still Karen was asleep. Still Meemaw was... Meemaw was still.

I looked at our chair gone by the door. Too heavy. I looked at Meemaw's bag.

Slow slow I crawled out from dinosaur land. Everything under was wet. Wet as a swamp. Inflatable trees volcanoes gone to flatness. I crawled over.

Cold wet. Sticky trousers on my legs. I crawled past Meemaw's tooth. I thinked pick it up. But too much wrong. I didn't touch.

Meemaw's bag by the sofa. I slided in my hand.

Gzzz gzzz Karen breathed. Still asleep. Asleep still.

Tried not to look at Meemaw. Not to. I was scared a sound would come. Scared of a cry. Then would be little shit and hurt me.

My fingers finded each thing in the bag. Plums, Babybels of their net, precious things box, the new phone. I taked it out.

I crawled back under. Back into dinosaur world. I hided the phone. I pushed new phone under the flatted volcano. Sticky not too wet.

Noise came of moving. Karen sitted up.

Ugh! Christ! Baby, wake up!

Karen pulled Meemaw. Rocked rocked Meemaw. But then Meemaw still again. Like asleep.

Karen heaved up. Up came the mighty beast.

Christ. Oh, Jesus Christ…

She leaned by the sink and then came a sicky. Sicky sick in the sink. Some runned down the cupboard front. Went on her sock.

She turned round. Spiked me with the blue eyes. Blue eyes in pink eyes.

Don't touch her. Stay there. I'm watching you.

Karen went in the bathroom. Leaved the door open. She pulled down had a wee. Standed up. Tug tugged her jeans. One hand.

Karen runned the tap. She putted her red blood arm under. Water runned all over it the teared arm.

Fuckshitchristfuck…

She grabbed our yellow towel fast. Pushed it on her arm. She leaned on the wall.

Then sudden her knees folded and Karen falled down. Down like a chopped tree she falled. Eyes shut. Still. Still like asleep. On the bathroom floor. Eyes closed. Not looking at me.

I pulled out the phone. It was alight of working. Charged.

I looked. There was YouTube. There was BBC news music Google. All not a help. Not for a emergency.

I touched contacts. Contacts was names. Up and down went letters of names. I didn't know.

Then library. Library. It was two greens and a orange and it said number.

I thinked a message is typing I can do. I didn't know it how though.

I touched a green of the phone. Far inside it came a brrr brrr. Brrr brr then a mouse's voice so small.

Hello?

I holded the phone next to my face. I have never done but seen Meemaw. I looked at Karen. Eyes closed. Not looking at me.

Hello.

Hello, Burgess Hill Library, can I help you?

Hello. Yes you can help me.

Do you have your borrower number please?

WSC80145672.

Danny? Is that you, Danny? This is Jane. How can I help you?

I think Meemaw is gone to dead.

CHAPTER TWENTY-NINE

The thing of here is the bed is always a bed. It smells of stinky sweet. New sheets each every night. It crunkles.

It's because of wees come in the night Ruth has it the crunkle sheet. It's under the other one. And a crunkle duvet. She said then it doesn't matter. She said we could wee for England on her beds and it doesn't matter. That was a joke wee for England. She laughed.

First night in this house I said not one word. Not even when Ruth taked off my clothes. No one has ever done except Meemaw but I was all in wee so I knowed she must. The borrow pyjamas of red blue a giraffe on the front were wet. Meemaw would take them off.

Anyway that was a lie I telled about no one else ever. That was a lie because the nurse at the hospital.

That day at the hospital was the nurse. Even then the doctor lady. Doctor lady looked right at my bot. My actual bot in a place of just a curtain. I went away. I do it lots.

All Danny goes away. I'm not there. I look at things very close and they go more real and Danny is gone.

Bathroom wall here is shiny bricks. Wall of grey shines. Overlappy overlappy overlappy. I count. They are very safe. Special.

Ruth lets me hold Spiney in the bath. Better than at hospital. Nurse tried taking Spiney.

Let's just give him a wipe over.

I screamed.

Screamed loud. She letted go. She was yellow hair and too black round her eyes.

It is today five days of no Meemaw. But she is not dead.

In the second day I told Ruth not Mummy. Ruth is slow. Ruth has brown brown eyes. Almost to black. Like inside something. I told her Meemaw. She has not forgetted.

She has my pictures safe. Comics I have done in a folder. She writed For Meemaw on the front. Then I writed too. I have writed more more words for Meemaw here. They are not all exactly but they are good.

Ruth looks at me. Sometimes I go in the bathroom and shut the door because too much. Too much looking. No slidey silver lock here but I shut the door. Ruth waits. Sometimes calls.

You okay in there, Danny? Fancy some toast?

Ruth does it right the toast. On the first time she holded the knife above. I showed her the two cuts. This way that way to make the four.

I think Ruth is not evil. Sometimes she says too much of words to me. But mostly quiet.

Sometimes I think it. I think of the ambulance came and that day.

They taked us to the hospital of the tortoise man. Meemaw on a lying down. Me a different lying down.

They splitted us apart away down the long corridor. I screamed. They holded me on it the lying down. I screamed the long corridor.

It was walls of animals. Not real animals. Animals of a cartoon. There were all bright talking. Danny Danny Danny is it?

Doctor lady had fingers of rubbery. Of tentacles of a sea creature. She touched me. I go away.

They said go to Ruth's house. I didn't know of it. But first to see Meemaw.

Pants and joggers and a t-shirt all not mine. Wrong smell and a scratchy neck.

It was big steps along. A lady holding hands. I hated hated but didn't let go. I thinked they will chase anyway. And I must go to see my Meemaw.

Meemaw was in the place of the tortoise man we were before. Tortoise man was not there. Gone hiding in his shell. He was a enemy I thinked. He looked not but he was a enemy. He maked Karen come to our flat again.

Another blue pyjamas man told me Meemaw not dead. He lifted me. A good smell of him.

Come on then. We'll go to see her. You just hold on to me, Danny. We'll see your mummy in here.

Darkly in the room he telled. Not bright talking. Slow quiet the words.

High above my Meemaw I was and her lying down.

Never before I was so high above and my Meemaw lying.

That's just the tube helping her to breathe and the machines telling us all about her body. So we can take care of her. We're looking after her now, Danny.

Meemaw's chest filled up to high. Down to low. Breathing. Breathing is not dead.

Not dead. No colour. Not a colour. But not dead.

Meemaw is not dead but now I am here. Here is Ruth's house. House of upstairs and downstairs and Max a cat who is black. Max is soft and stroke him Danny.

I like Max. His tail is a question. Green eyes.

Today came a woman Kate. It is all of people now we don't know.

All is too much of looking at me. And words. I go away.

This one Kate came. She sitted with Ruth telled me of Meemaw in the hospital. I knowed it. She telled on on and drawed of crayons.

Kate asked of Meemaw and Karen and hitting. I didn't say. I drawed a T-Rex. His two claw hands.

She asked of my bot I thinked shut up. It is private parts. It is not for saying. But here come poos knocking but never out. Not here.

After the Kate woman was gone Ruth taked me to the park. Not our park. It is a big park of flatness and too much dogs. I go in the car.

I like it better coming back. I like it the high up seat of the car and watching. Then it is the black white of Ruth's path I know. And inside is Max. Max and Lego.

But no Meemaw ever. Never she has came here. It is in a world of no Meemaw.

In all of every day now I must make spells. I thinked of this today. Sometimes I look close as close at Spiney and I see he has a live eye now. He looks his live eye in my eye. We can spell things together.

Here we must do it all of every day. Then Meemaw will wake up. We will go home maybe maybe go in the world.

I have Spiney now and never ever will I lose him again. A bad mistake. If I had not lost Spiney we would not have gone in our flat again. We would have gone away in the world and never been catched by Karen.

Meemaw not have smash hitted her head and the tooth flied out. Her head is too hurt I think. I don't know if Meemaw can wake up or be asleep a hundred years. But Meemaw is not dead.

Best of things is Karen gone away. She is in a place far Ruth said. A special hospital and locks. There are locks.

Sometimes I think here of the other dinosaurs. I think about their world. I have ruined it probably of wee. The lady of round boobies in the centre will want all back. It is a library and things must go back. They are not mine and I have ruined their world.

Meemaw told every time to understand all things must go back in a library. They live there. But one time Jane gived me *Walking with Dinosaurs* book to actual keep. Jane is in the library. Meemaw is in the hospital.

Ruth telled today this actual day of day five that they will take away the machine of breathing and Meemaw can wake up we hope. I don't hope. I am today in this house going to the bathroom wall. I am counting with Spiney. It is the best spell of good counting. It is four hundred and seventy nine without halfs. I do the halfs at the end. Two halfs make one. We are spelling Meemaw to well again.

CHAPTER THIRTY

The beach is yellow yellow. Sky is blue blue. All colours here are such brightness they shine more than the brightest of Meemaw.

Here I forget to look for the Meemaw colour. It doesn't matter. Meemaw's colours are there I know it. All colours there so it doesn't matter to look.

Orange orange juice is called naranja. I ask in the bar then Joaquin laughs.

Morning times Meemaw cleans the rooms. I am allowed at the little pool and in the garden with Spiney. I am patient. It is Meemaw's work.

I get big naranja from Joaquin. A straw in a bit of actual orange. Grey the ice cubes. All frothy.

Meemaw waves. Meemaw shouts to me from the balconies. She is high and the sky such brightness.

Hola, Danny!

I wave back.

First when we came I had to stay in our room when Meemaw was doing her work. I was not safe because I couldn't swim of no arm bands. Dangerous by the pool. Meemaw said I could learn swimming.

Every day I did it. I learned.

I do it like Meemaw no arm bands. Meemaw told it is a great achievement. It is flying in the water. I like it under best. Like the ichthyosaur discovered of Mary Anning. I am a powerful hunter in the deep.

Spiney sinks down but Meemaw gets him. Meemaw goes to the bottom. Holding her breath. She saves Spiney every time. Every time.

The water goes to little silver beans on her dark Meemaw hair. On her eyebrows. I see the place of the cut. Pinky purple now. Not so bad.

After Meemaw came out of the hospital and I had the awfullest poo in the world things getted better. Ruth telled I could go home. Meemaw taked me.

But we didn't want to be in the flat of before and Karen. That was a trouble. We went to see housing but not a help. Not a help at all Danny.

That was when Mick came. Mick getted actually up and shoes on. He walked out of his house of smelly and mess. He came to Burgess Hill on the train. He sitted in a café by the station of cheese scone. But not nice as the ones of me and Meemaw.

Mick bringed Meemaw a envelope. Not her mummy bracelet envelope but all fat of twenties. Meemaw cried. I didn't like it Meemaw crying but Mick said

It's all right, wee man.

It was.

Meemaw telled later in all whispers of going away. It was not allowed to go away because of appointments. Still to see the Kate lady and the Job Centre.

Not Karen at the Job Centre. Karen was given a sack and gone away. Far away. There are locks.

Meemaw telled me this is the first stop in the world.

Here is not appointments. Here is work for Meemaw of clean the rooms. Then money from Jorge who is the boss and Meemaw's actual cousin. I never knowed of a cousin for Meemaw. Meemaw telled she has lots of cousins. I don't have cousins but Meemaw will share.

Meemaw talks Spanish. I can of little bits too.

Spain is lots of cats. I liked Max cat I miss him but not Ruth because too much watching me.

I think of the other dinosaurs too and their lost world. We taked them back to the centre. Meemaw gived money to the round boobies lady because the ruined world was throwed away. The lady wasn't cross of us. She said

Maybe we'll get them a whole new one, eh? Or they can just run wild.

She laughed.

Every week Sunday new people come. Nearly always children from England. One week came a bigger boy Leo. He was six and nearly good at swimming like me. His trunks were T-Rexes on lots and lots. He knowed of the Cretaceous of how the meteorite came and caused a mass extinction.

We played dinosaurs and spies. We did spies on Joaquin and writed down all things. One day he was dancing in the bar. It was funny. We laughed.

Leo had two mummies. One mummy of spikey hair. I thinked of Karen. But she wasn't Karen. She was Bella. When it was time to go Bella bringed Leo to our room with a piece of paper of their address on for writing letters.

Leo cried because of missing me. I love Leo even though he is gone away now. Meemaw telled that's a great thing the loving.

Sometimes it is not sunny days. Meemaw lies sideways in the chair like our flat. She reads books of space too but maked of Spanish words. Meemaw telled she needs to brush it up. I looked but I couldn't read it. I was cross of Meemaw.

You can't read it Meemaw you can't!

Danny White! You're not the only little sparky kid there ever was, you know? I could read two languages fluently by the time I was five!

No.

Yes I could. You will too. Look…

I think Meemaw is cleverer than ever I knowed before. But not as clever as me.

One day Meemaw says we will go back to England. First I was scared. I thinked of Karen there.

You can't live your whole life running away, Dan.

Are we running away?

Only a bit.

If we went back Karen would find us.

There are locks.

She wouldn't be looking for us, love.

She would find us.

No. She'll be with someone else now.

Someone else.

Yes. She'll never stop eating people up.

There are locks. Please there are locks.

When it's getting dark me and Meemaw sit on our balcony with the smelly candle. We see Joaquin come for evening shift. Sometimes Meemaw tells stories of the mountains.

The mountains are browny velvety. In the mountains lives Small Black Bear. He is a great palaeontologist. Meemaw says he is of renown. He goes hunting in the sunny days. Hunting of fossils with friends. Grey Dog. White Rabbit. Ratty Rat.

Do they find them Meemaw? Lots of fossils this day?

Oh, they find so many, Dan. Great bones of dinosaurs.

Which?

What do you think?

They find coelophysis fossils.

They do. And, you know what, Danny? They can imagine those coelophysis come to life and running on the mountains.

They have good imaginations Meemaw.

They surely do.

Meemaw smiles then. I can see the little dark space in her mouth where her tooth used to be.

ACKNOWLEDGEMENTS

My thanks to Lauren Parsons and all the team at Legend Press. Also to my agent, Veronique Baxter, for her unstinting support.

I am grateful to friends who advised on matters as diverse as speech patterns, experiences at the Job Centre, procedures in emergency foster care and terminology in the field of domestic violence. You know who you are!

Thanks to my writing group comrades for being in it for the long haul and to all my family and friends for their encouragement.

Thanks to Pearl and Leo for showing me the great wisdom and intensity of the age of four. And thanks to Dani for seeing that with me.

COME VISIT US AT
WWW.LEGENDPRESS.CO.UK

OR FOLLOW US ON TWITTER
@LEGEND_PRESS